CU00657866

A Beautiful End

Broken Bow

Book One

Ashley A Quinn

TCA Publishing LLC

Copyright © 2020 by Ashley A Quinn

This book is a work of fiction. The names, characters, events, and places are either products of the writer's imagination or have been used fictitiously and are not to be construed as real. Any resemblance to persons, living or dead, actual events, locales, or organizations is entirely coincidental.

No parts of this book may be copied, reproduced, and/or distributed in any way without express written consent from the author.

ISBN is 9781733160049

ACKNOWLEDGMENTS

I want to thank my fellow author buddies, especially Terri, for all their help in getting me unstuck when I wrote myself into a corner. This book would not be what it is without their suggestions and prodding.

A NOTE FROM THE AUTHOR...

D o you ever look at a picture and think, "Wow. There's a story there!" That's how this book happened. One of the authors I follow on Instagram posted a picture of the ruins of an old mission in the Texas countryside. I immediately thought, "What a great place to hide a body." And A Beautiful End was born. This book started out as a small idea--that of a serial killer operating in a remote location. It blossomed into an entire world centered around a ranching family. These characters took me on a journey, that at times, I didn't even know where the boat was going. But I like the path we traveled, and I hope you do too.

If you like this book, please leave a review when you're done. It would be greatly appreciated.

You can sign up for my newsletter to get exclusive sneak peeks of this series and other goodies @ ashleyaquinn.com.

ONE

"Are you sure we're allowed to be here?" The girl's eyes tracked over the rugged terrain, bouncing from one object to the next, looking for danger. Nothing but sturdy pines swaying in the breeze, and the azure sky met her gaze. They were alone on the mountain, but trepidation still skated up her spine.

"Relax, would you? This place is in the middle of nowhere. Who's going to see us? The bears?" her boyfriend said, picking his way over the rough ground to reach the ruins of the old homestead they stumbled upon.

She gulped and looked around again. She hadn't thought about the bears. A shudder ran through her. She should have. It *was* the Colorado Rockies.

Following along behind him, she turned her attention to her footing. Rocks and small boulders littered the landscape. The last thing she needed was to trip over one and sprain an ankle. Trent would never be able to carry her back to the car. She didn't want to have to sit here in the open all alone, waiting for help.

They reached the dilapidated wooden-framed, two-room

shack. She gave it a once over, skepticism ripe on her face. It leaned so far to the right it looked as though one powerful wind gust could knock it down.

"Is it safe?"

Trent shrugged. "It's still standing, isn't it?" He took her hand and pulled her toward the structure. "Come on."

She followed him through the doorway, pulling up short as a rancid smell assaulted her. "Ugh! It smells like something died in here." She covered her nose with her sleeve and tried to take shallow breaths through her mouth as she glanced around. Her eyes watered and she fought to keep her lunch where it belonged.

The cabin was larger inside than she thought it would be. The kitchen was directly in front of her. A counter ran the length of the wall, the shelves above still holding a few tin cups. A table that looked like it would collapse if she laid even her pinky finger on it was to her right. To her left was a sitting area. An old rocker leaned drunkenly next to a woodstove, covered in decades worth of dust and cobwebs. Against the opposite wall was a desk, its surface coated in bird poop and heaven only knew what else. Beyond that, a doorway led into what she presumed was the bedroom.

She let go of Trent's hand and walked that way. The closer she got, the worse the stench became. Pressing her sleeve harder against her face, she tried not to gag.

"Oh, this is terrible. Some animal must have wandered in here and died." She stepped over the threshold and froze. A scream ripped from her chest, and she stumbled backward in horror.

"What? Abigail?" Trent ran to her, his hands grabbing her shoulders to steady her.

She pointed at the bedroom, tears streaming down her face. "There's a dead woman in there!"

Trent's eyes snapped to the doorway and went wide. "What?"

He hurried forward, while she continued her retreat toward the main door.

"Oh my God." Trent gagged as he caught sight of the image now stamped on her brain. On the bed laid a woman in a wedding gown, holding a bouquet of flowers between her breasts. Mottled and bloated, she stared sightlessly at the ceiling with opaque eyes.

Trent spun around. His boots scuffed on the worn wooden floor as he rushed toward Abigail and the exit.

"Let's go. We need to call the sheriff."

He didn't have to tell her twice. She ran from the cabin and up the embankment, fleeing into the woods the way they came. Sobs wracked her. Her breath hiccupped in and out, making her gasp for air between sobs. The image of that woman would forever be burned into her mind.

Two

"Well, this is a right mess, ain't it?"

Sheriff Sebastian Archer glanced up at Caleb Bering, his second in command, from his position crouched next to the body sprawled over the antique bed in the old homestead. He straightened his long legs and stepped back to let in the medical examiner who had poked his head around Caleb.

"Sure is." He nodded at the M.E. "Hey, Alex."

Dr. Alex Randall moved into the small room, wrinkling his nose at the smell.

"Sheriff." He pulled a mask up over his face and ran an assessing gaze over the body on the bed. "Jesus. Who found her?"

"My goddaughter and her boyfriend. They were hiking and decided to explore this place."

Alex set down the case he carried and crouched next to the woman's remains. "That's terrible. Is she all right?"

He frowned. Abigail's watery blue eyes flashed in his mind along with the tremulous smile she gave him after he enveloped her in a hug. "She's rattled, but I think she'll be okay. She's a tough kid. I sent her and Trent back to the station for formal statements. I only stuck around here because I wanted to get your initial impressions."

The M.E. huffed out a breath, turning back to the body. "Well, she looks pretty rough, but she's still mostly intact. Based on decomp and insect activity, I'd say preliminary time of death is about a week."

"Can you tell what killed her?"

"Possibly strangulation. There's some discoloration around her neck not due to lividity." He motioned to the darkened skin of the woman's neck, then looked up at Sebastian. "I'll know more after I do an autopsy."

Seb nodded. "Are you sure your office can handle this? I can call in the state if you think you need help."

Alex frowned in thought, but shook his head. "I did hundreds of autopsies when I was with the coroner's office in Salt Lake City. I might have to send some of the samples out, but the autopsy itself won't be a problem."

"Good." His county was lucky to have such an experienced medical examiner. Seb was grateful Alex Randall had tired of city life and sought a slower pace. It meant he could get an earlier jump on finding this woman's killer.

"I'm going to head back and talk to Abigail and Trent. Deputy Bering will be here if you need anything." He gestured to Caleb, who stood just outside the doorway, looking in.

Caleb gave the doctor a quick nod.

Seb's boots echoed on the plank floor as he stepped past his deputy to exit the cabin. Once outside he paused briefly and inhaled a deep breath of the clean mountain air, trying to get the odor of decay out of his nostrils. Even with the vapor rub he'd put under his nose before going in, the smell still broke through to turn his stomach. There was nothing quite as foul as the stench of decayed flesh.

Nodding to another of his deputies canvassing for evidence,

Seb started back through the trees. He was not looking forward to these interviews, and not just because he loved Abigail. He couldn't imagine coming across something like that scene at their age and hated the idea that he was going to have to make them relive it. But he needed whatever they could give him if he was going to stop this guy from killing again.

After seeing that scene, he had no doubt there would be another if his department didn't find the murderer quickly. It screamed serial killer.

Slamming the car door, London Scott rushed up the steps to the police station and yanked open the door. Her heart was still in her throat after the call she had just received.

"Hi, London. Can I help you?"

Anxiety propelled her forward to the plexiglass window and the female deputy, Alaina Wilder, manning the desk.

"Yes. I just got a phone call about my niece, Abigail? Is she all right?"

Deputy Wilder smiled reassuringly. "She's fine. A little shaken up, but unhurt."

London's shoulders sagged, and her heart settled a bit.

The woman pushed a log book toward her and a visitor's badge. "Come on through and I'll take you to her." The door to her right buzzed.

Eager to see her niece, London signed the log and snatched up the badge, then stepped through and met the deputy in the hall. Wilder led her down the corridor past several intake rooms.

She turned left at the junction and stopped in front of a room with blinds covering the windows. London saw Abigail sitting on a couch, her knees drawn up and her strawberry-blonde hair a disheveled mess.

The deputy opened the door and ushered her inside. "I'll leave you two be. If you need anything, there's an intercom on the wall. Just press the button for the main desk. The sheriff will be along soon to talk to you."

London thanked her and stepped into the room. She hurried to Abigail's side and sat down next to her, hugging the girl to her chest.

"Oh, honey. Are you all right? What happened? The deputy who called me only said you were involved in an incident. What's going on?" She stroked Abigail's hair and rocked her gently.

Abigail sniffed hard. "Trent and I found an abandoned cabin while we were out hiking," she said, her voice watery. She sat up to look London in the eye. "We went inside to check it out and it smelled terrible. I thought we would see a dead coyote or deer. But there was a—" she broke off on a choked sob, but quickly swallowed it down. "There was a woman in there, dead."

London pulled Abigail close again and held her tight. She closed her eyes and took a deep breath, trying to steady herself as she comforted her niece. What a sight to see. She hoped this didn't bring Abigail's nightmares back. The girl had worked so hard to get where she was.

The door opened and London looked up to see the sheriff step through. Sebastian Archer was a tall, dark-haired man. His broad shoulders pushed the seams on his uniform shirt, and his jeans hugged muscular thighs. His warm, dark chocolate eyes connected with hers and he smiled softly. London's belly did a little flip like it did every time he was near. He was quite the handsome man.

"Hey, London," he said, stepping into the room and closing the door. He folded himself into the chair across from the couch. Abigail turned her head from her aunt's shoulder to look at him. "Hi, Abigail. I know what you saw was trau-matic, but I need to ask you a few questions."

London clung tighter to her niece for just a moment before letting her go. Abigail sat up and swiped at the tears on her face, pulling herself together. London felt a surge of pride for the maturity her young niece was showing.

"What do you want to know?"

"Why did you and Trent go to the cabin?"

"We didn't intend to. We just went hiking and found it. Trent thought it was cool and wanted to look inside, so we did."

A slight frown marred his face. "So, he didn't know it was there before today?"

Abigail shook her head. "I don't think so, no."

"Okay. Did you see anything on your hike that seemed out of the ordinary, or hear anything strange?"

The girl's eyes shifted side-to-side as she thought back. After a moment, she shook her head once more. "No. It was quiet except for the wind and the occasional bird."

"Did you see anyone in the parking lot?"

"No, but there was another car there."

Sebastian sat a little straighter. "What did it look like?"

"It was a blue Honda sedan. Newer." Abigail shrugged. "I really didn't pay that much attention to it. It was gone when we got back to the car."

"What about the woman? I know the decay obscured her features, but did she look at all familiar to you?"

Tears welled in Abigail's eyes again. She pressed the back of her hand against her mouth and shook her head. A single tear slid free, and London pulled her close.

"Is there anything else you'd like to ask, Seb? If not, I'd like to take her home."

He shook his head. "Abigail, if you think of anything else, no matter how small, call me."

The girl nodded. London stood, along with the sheriff, and pulled Abigail to her feet.

"Where's Trent?" Abigail asked as he turned to leave.

"I just spoke with him. His parents took him home. I'm sorry I had to separate you, but it's standard procedure so you don't cloud each other's memories."

"I'm sure he'll call you later, Abs," London said, her voice soft.

Abigail nodded, and she led the way from the room.

"Hey." Sebastian touched London's shoulder as she passed by. Shivers raced down her arm. She shifted slightly so that his hand fell away. Now was not the time for her attraction to this man to rear its ugly head. She motioned Abigail to go ahead, then looked up at him.

He handed her a business card. She looked down at it and frowned.

"Dr. Michael Santori?" She looked back up at Sebastian and arched a brow.

"He's the department psychologist. Abigail might need to talk to someone in the coming days. Michael is aware of the situation and willing to listen."

London slid the card into her pocket. "I'll let her know. If she feels like she needs to talk, I'll give him a call." She shifted her feet, eager to leave before she said something stupid like she always seemed to do around this man.

He laid a gentle hand on her shoulder, sending more shock waves through her body. London clenched her teeth against the sensation.

"You can call me too, if you need anything."

"Just because Eddie's gone doesn't mean I need another big brother."

Seb's jaw twitched. "This isn't about that, London. Yes, your brother was my best friend, but I'm concerned about Abigail. What she saw out there today—" he broke off and shook his head. "I just want to make sure she's okay and that you know you have backup if you need it."

Some of the starch left London's shoulders. He was right. Abigail would need all the support she could get in the coming days.

She let out a breath. "Why don't you come by tomorrow? She'll probably be glad to have the distraction."

He smiled that little half smile that always made her heart beat faster. "I'll do that. Do you still make scones on Sunday mornings?"

She couldn't help the smile that quirked her mouth. Ever since she had known him, he'd had a soft spot for baked goods.

"I do."

His smile morphed into a full grin. "I'll see you in the morning, then."

London looked away, feeling her cheeks heat, and nodded. "I better go catch up to Abigail. I'll see you later." With a quick glance at his warm brown eyes, she scurried after her niece.

Seb watched London walk away, his eyes tracing the line of her long, graceful back and over the curve of her hips. She had morphed into a stunningly gorgeous woman over the years.

He shook his head to dispel his thoughts. He had bigger things on his plate to think about than how good London Scott's ass looked in a pair of jeans. Like, why he had a dead woman dressed in a wedding gown in an abandoned homestead.

His thoughts turned to Abigail. He hoped she would be all right. She was a tough kid and had been through some tragic stuff in her young life. More than her fair share. It didn't seem right that she had to be part of something so gruesome as a murder, too.

"Sheriff."

He turned to see his desk sergeant, Alaina Wilder, bearing down on him.

"Caleb is on the phone for you. He's got something."

With a nod of thanks, Seb headed into his office. Rounding his desk, he snatched up the phone from its cradle and hit the button next to the blinking light to connect the call.

"Hey, Caleb. What did you find?"

"A hot mess, that's what. Gentry wandered off, looking for clues, and stumbled over the leftovers of a fire. There were pieces of clothing amongst the ashes. I saw what he found. There were several fabric remnants—more than what one person would wear, I think. We might have a second victim out here somewhere."

Seb cursed long and loud. "Okay. Keep searching. I'll call the state troopers and get us some more manpower. We need to do a grid search up there now. Set up a larger perimeter and let me know if you find anything else."

"Will do, boss."

Seb resisted the urge to slam the phone down. He might only have one dead woman at the moment, but this sure felt like a serial killer. He left the FBI to get away from shit like this. The most exciting thing that ever happened around here was when Robbie Knight drank a fifth of whisky and decided to drive around town shooting his shotgun in the air.

He rubbed his forehead between his brows and sighed. Picking up the phone again, he dialed the state trooper's office. He needed more men to search those hills.

∾

"Aunt London, I'm fine. I promise." Abigail sighed tiredly. "I just really want to go to sleep."

London sat on the edge of Abigail's bed and ran a hand over the girl's silky hair. "Are you sure you don't want to sleep with me?"

Abigail rolled her eyes. "I'm sixteen. Yes, it was gross and disturbing, but it's not like—" she broke off and took a shaky breath. "It's not like when Mom and Dad died. I didn't know that woman, and I didn't watch her die. I'll be okay."

What she said was logical, but London couldn't help but remember the scared, traumatized eleven-year-old girl who had come to live with her after her parents' deaths. Abigail had looked so much like that girl again when London picked her up from the police station earlier.

But she was right. She wasn't a child anymore. And this wasn't her first brush with death.

Giving her niece's hair a last stroke, she patted her hand. "Okay. I'll leave you be." She stood. "Get some rest. If you need anything, I'm right down the hall."

Abigail smiled softly. "I know."

London pressed a soft kiss to her head. "Goodnight, Abs."

"G'night, El."

Padding softly to the door, London shut off the lights and closed the door behind her. Once in the hall, she took a moment to reset before heading downstairs to prep for tomorrow's breakfast. The work of an innkeeper was never done.

She smiled to herself as she tread lightly down the stairs, trying not to disturb her guests. Sebastian's warm brown eyes flashed in her mind. As much as he unsettled her, it would still be nice to see him in the morning. Despite how he made her heart flutter, he was a good friend. She just wished she could shake her attraction to him.

She shook her head at herself. Sebastian Archer was off-limits. He had been her brother's best friend. He was Abigail's godfather. There was no way she would ever jeopardize that relationship. It wasn't like he ever looked at her that way, anyway. She was just Eddie's kid sister. The tagalong.

Except, Eddie was gone, and she was no longer the annoying child trying to be cool and hang out with her teenage brother and his friends.

She sighed as she rounded the corner of the communal living area, heading for the kitchen. Why she continued to torture herself with thoughts of Seb was a mystery to her. That was such a dead-end street, it had flashing neon signs, proclaiming, "KEEP OUT."

The front door opened just as she reached the pocket door to the kitchen. London turned to see the middle-aged man— Doug Brown—who was in the area on business stride through the door. A frown marred his face.

"Good evening, Mr. Brown."

He stopped mid-stride and looked over at her. His frown smoothed out only slightly. "Oh, hello, Ms. Scott."

"Can I help you with something? You look a bit stressed."

He shook his head. "No. Just work. Never seems to leave me alone." He offered her a small wave. "Have a good night."

"You too."

He was up the stairs and out of view before she could even turn back around.

What an odd man.

Shaking her head, London slid open the pocket door and entered the kitchen. She still didn't know what had brought him to town other than business. Silver Gap, Colorado wasn't exactly a hotbed for executive types. They saw quite a bit of tourism, though.

She pulled several bowls from the cupboards and arranged them on the large, central island. Maybe he was here for one of the tourism industries, she mused. Or he was a developer. That sounded more likely. He was always dressed to the nines, even in casual clothes.

Frowning, she scooped flour into one of her bowls. She hoped he wasn't here to build some disgustingly modern condo or housing development on the side of the mountain. People came here because it was pristine. Wild. Not so they could catch a glimpse of someone famous. That was what the bigger cities to the north were for.

She measured sugar into another bowl. It didn't matter what she thought, though. If he wanted to build his houses, he would. She couldn't stop him, but she sincerely hoped he was here for another reason.

Finished prepping the basic ingredients for the scones she would make in the morning, London dug out the bag of mini-chocolate chips Seb liked in them. She would make his favorite as well as a batch of blueberry.

Her heart fluttered again at the thought of seeing him in the morning.

No!

She refused to go down that path again today. Clamping a tight lid on her wayward emotions, she quickly finished her breakfast prep before heading back upstairs to check on Abigail.

A quick peek in the girl's room revealed her sound asleep under her lavender comforter, her lava lamp casting a purple glow through the room. Silently, London eased the door closed and continued down the hall to her own room.

She changed quickly into a t-shirt and soft cotton shorts and burrowed under her blankets, curling on her side to face the window. It had begun to rain since they came home earlier, and droplets pelted the glass and the wind lashed through the trees.

What a dispiriting end to a dreadful evening.

Once more, Sebastian's dark eyes entered her mind. This time, she didn't chase away the image. It helped banish her depressing thoughts about the woman Abigail and Trent discovered and left her feeling comforted. Safe. She just hoped he found that woman's killer soon so her poor soul could rest in peace.

A weary yawn stretched over her face and she snuggled deeper under the blankets. Closing her eyes, she held on to the image of Sebastian's handsome face as she drifted off to sleep.

THREE

When Seb stepped through the front door of the B&B the next morning, the smell of warm bacon and fresh coffee assailed him. He smiled, instantly relaxing at the prospect of London's cooking. He and Eddie had told her for years she should open a bakery attached to the B&B. Then Eddie and Camille died, leaving her guardian to a very traumatized young girl, and London had put any dreams she had on hold to raise her niece.

"Uncle Seb!"

He turned to see Abigail running down the stairs, her strawberry-blonde hair bouncing in its high ponytail.

"Hey, munchkin." He smiled back and met her at the base of the steps. "How are you feeling today? Did you have any nightmares last night?"

She frowned up at him, her dainty features so much like her mother's, scrunching as she thought about yesterday's events. Her blue eyes, though, were all her father and aunt.

"I'm fine. I had a few, but nothing like the ones I used to have. I won't lie and say yesterday wasn't terrible, but I'm handling it all right. The shock has worn off and now, I just wonder what happened to her. Do you have any leads?"

Seb placed a reassuring hand on her shoulder. He was glad it hadn't brought back old fears and events for her. She had some horrific nightmares after her parents died.

"A few. We're working on them. I'm hopeful something will come of them."

"Good. I hope you find the person who did it. That woman deserves justice. No one should ever be treated that way. So, did you come for Aunt London's scones?"

Seb grinned. "You know I did. And the bacon."

She smiled back. "Come on. Let's go get some before it all goes cold."

Abigail led him into the large dining room off the living area where London set up the breakfast spread. She looked up as he entered. He couldn't stop the little zing that shot through him when her eyes met his.

Pasting a smile on his face and pretending he didn't like the way her t-shirt bearing the B&B's logo hugged her breasts, he walked over to where she stood, refilling the scrambled eggs.

"Good morning," she said.

He let his gaze wander over her pretty face. She hadn't bothered with makeup, and the freckles dusting her nose and cheeks were visible. Seb loved her freckles. She could be so serious and they gave her an impishness he found endearing.

Clearing his throat, he picked up a plate. "Good morning. This all looks great."

"Thanks. You want coffee? Or have you already drowned yourself in it this morning?"

"I have, but I'll always take more."

She flipped her long, strawberry-blonde braid back over her shoulder. "I'll be right back." She looked around him to her niece. "You want juice or milk, Abs?"

"Milk, please."

London spun on her heel with a nod and headed for the kitchen. Seb frowned after her, wondering if everything was all right. She seemed a little ticked.

"You piss her off or something?" Abigail asked, adding a chocolate chip scone to her plate and echoing his thoughts.

He glared down at her. "Language, young lady."

She blinked up at him, then rolled her eyes. "Whatever. So what did you do?"

Seb shrugged and began filling his own plate. "No idea. Maybe she's just tired."

Abigail scoffed. "She's always tired. The only difference today is that you're here."

That made Seb frown. He thought back to their conversation yesterday. Nothing he'd said seemed like anything that would have made her angry.

London reentered the room carrying a mug of coffee and a glass of milk. She set them down at the table, then retreated to the kitchen.

Seb's frown intensified. She *was* acting a little strange. Normally, she was smiling and talking with her guests as she worked. He finished filling his plate and set it on the table near his coffee, but instead of sitting down to eat, he followed London into the kitchen.

She was standing at the sink, a mug of coffee in her hand and staring out the window.

"Hey. You okay?"

She jumped at the sound of his voice, and coffee sloshed over the rim of her mug. Grimacing, she set the cup on the counter. "Geez, Seb. Give a girl some warning next time." She pulled a paper towel off the roll and dabbed at her hand before turning to glare at him.

He strode closer until he stood directly in front of her. Taking her hand in his, he moved the toweling out of the way to look at the red mark left by the hot coffee.

She yanked her hand back and walked around him to the stove.

"What do you want, Sebastian?"

He turned to stare at her, his hands going to his hips, a pang of hurt lancing through his chest at her obvious dismissal.

"I want to know what's wrong. You seem angry. Even Abigail noticed."

Her shoulders slumped, and she flipped a piece of bacon in the skillet.

"I'm fine. Just tired. It was a long night."

He crossed the kitchen to stand next to her. "You're not just tired." He put one finger on her jaw and turned her head to look at him. "What's wrong?"

Her blue eyes searched his before she dropped her gaze to stare at his throat. She shrugged.

"I guess yesterday just brought back some bad memories, is all. I *am* tired, so it's just a little harder to deal with. That, and I'm worried about Abigail. Why did it have to be her who found that woman?"

Seb's hand drifted to her shoulder. He toyed with her braid, the silky strands cool against his fingers. "I don't know, El. She seems like she's dealing with it well, though." He motioned to the dining area where they could hear her laughing at something one of the other guests said.

London smiled softly. "Yeah. Better than me." She sighed and turned back to her bacon.

He snatched a cooked strip from the plate next to the stove. "It's because you love her and worry about her well-being."

"I know. It's my job now that Eddie and Camille are gone."

"*Our* job," Seb corrected, stealing another slice of bacon. "I'm here if you ever need help, you know that."

Glancing up, she gave him his first genuine smile of the day. "Yes, I do." Piling the bacon from the skillet onto the plate, she picked it up and handed it to him. "Here. Make yourself useful and take that out there. I need to make another pot of coffee and then I'll join you all."

He took the plate, then dropped a kiss on top of her strawberry-blonde head. "Better hurry. Those scones were going fast." Stuffing another piece of bacon into his mouth, he turned on his heel and headed back out to the dining room.

Abigail frowned at him as he entered, clearly wondering why he disappeared. He shot her a reassuring smile as he set the plate down on the buffet, then took his seat next to her.

"Everything okay?"

He nodded and picked up his knife, cutting into his scone. "Yep. She's just worried about you."

She rolled her eyes again in typical teenage fashion. "I'm fine, Uncle Seb."

"We know. But it's our job to worry. She'll be okay." He patted her arm before sticking his knife into the butter and slathering it on his scone. Taking a bite, he closed his eyes in ecstasy as the sweet, rich flavors filled his mouth. He loved London's scones.

"I have more fresh coffee if anyone wants it," London said, entering the room. She placed the stainless-steel thermos on the table with the rest of the food, then picked up a plate of her own. She quickly filled it and took the seat next to Sebastian.

"So, introduce us to your friend," an older woman at the end of the table said. She eyed him and London with a playful smile on her face.

"Oh, yes. Of course. Everyone this is Sebastian Archer. He's a family friend. Seb, this is Mr. and Mrs. Strattman, and Mr. and Mrs. Copeland." She motioned to the older woman and the man sitting next to her, then to the younger couple across from him. "The Strattman's are here on a stop on their tour through the western states. The Copeland's are on their honeymoon."

Seb nodded a greeting to them all.

"Which, unfortunately, ends today," Mr. Copeland said. He made a face of dismay and looked over at his wife. "We've quite enjoyed our vacation here. The people are very friendly, and this town made a great central location for all the places we wanted to visit."

"I'm glad," London said.

"Yes, London's a wonderful host," Mrs. Strattman said. "She recommended the most wonderful restaurant, and we visited it yesterday—The Heartwood Grill. Have you heard of it?" she asked Sebastian.

He nodded. He knew it well. "Yes. The owner is actually my sister, and the restaurant sits on my family's ranch, The Broken Bow."

Mrs. Strattman grinned widely. "Well, aren't you lucky to have two such amazing cooks in your life?"

"How long have you two been dating?" Mrs. Copeland asked.

Seb's eyes went wide and London choked on her coffee.

"We're not together," she said, wiping her mouth with a napkin. "He's Abigail's godfather and my brother's best friend."

"Why would that stop you from dating?" the young newlywed asked.

"Yeah, why, Aunt London?" Abigail leaned back in her chair and crossed her arms, a smirk on her face. Seb narrowed his eyes at her, which only made the twinkle in hers shine brighter.

London glared at her niece before giving Mrs. Copeland a strained smile. "Seb has been a friend since we were children. He's an annoying pain in my backside."

"Hey." Indignation colored Seb's voice.

She arched an eyebrow at him, and he grinned at her. She shook her head, a rueful smile breaking free and dispelling the tension.

"So, you two grew up together?" Mr. Strattman asked.

Seb nodded around a mouthful of scone.

"I was my brother's tagalong," London said. "Eddie was seven years older than me. In the summer, my mom would leave me home with him. He, of course, wanted to go out with his friends. I'd promise not to tell Mom and Dad if he took me along."

"We did a lot of hiking, didn't we?" Seb said, smiling over at her.

She nodded. "Among other things." She waggled her eyebrows, and he laughed.

"You're thinking about the mine—"

London's hand shot out to cover his mouth. She angled a glance over at Abigail, her face expressing that he should not continue that train of thought.

Eyes dancing in mirth above her hand, he nodded in understanding.

"What?" Abigail asked. "What did you do at the mine?"

London removed her hand and gave the girl an admonishing look. "Things that will get you in trouble if you dare try them with Trent and your friends."

Abigail gave the still smirking Sebastian a sly look. "You and I need to talk later, Uncle Seb."

He laughed again and tapped her nose. "Nice try, munchkin, but I value my skin."

"Yes, not to mention that place is condemned," London added.

Seb arched a brow. "It was when we were kids too."

She glared at him. "You're really not helping, Sebastian."

He shoved a piece of bacon in his mouth, deciding that silence was probably his best bet right now.

The others laughed.

"You two are so cute," Mrs. Strattman said.

London blushed bright red, but kept her mouth shut. Abigail giggled. Seb just grinned, enjoying watching London squirm. Even twenty-some years later, it was fun to tease her.

He sat back in his chair and sipped his coffee, enjoying a welcome break with his two favorite people in the world, wishing he could stay right here. All too soon, though, the real world would intrude. He had a date with the M.E.

With a sigh, London hung her dish rag over the divider in the sink, finally finished with the breakfast dishes. She picked up the plate next to the sink she made up for Mr. Brown and turned to put it in the fridge.

Abigail walked in as she closed the door.

"Hey, kiddo. You about ready for church?" London still needed to run up and change. She looked at her watch. They would be cutting it close. Seb lingered longer than she thought he would, and now she was behind.

"Yep." She hopped up on a stool at the island. "Can I ask you something?"

Minutes ticked away in London's head, but she leaned against the counter. She would always make time for Abigail. God would understand.

"Sure."

"Why haven't you and Uncle Seb ever dated?"

London's eyes widened and Abigail rushed on.

"I mean, he's a handsome guy and you're just beautiful. You get along great and have known each other forever, so why haven't you ever been more than friends?"

"Honey, I don't feel that way about Sebastian. I never have."

"Oh, that is such crap. I see the way you look at him when he's not looking. I see the way he looks at you too. There's obviously a spark there, so why not act on it?"

Sebastian looked at her like he liked her?

No. London immediately tossed that thought away. Seb was affectionate, but all his attention was brotherly. He had never once exhibited any sort of attraction to her. Abigail was just hoping for more than what was really there.

She fiddled with the end of her braid as she considered her niece's question. "It's more complicated than that. I admit I find Seb attractive—what woman wouldn't? But he really is just a friend. That's all he can ever be. He's a fixture in our lives. I know how much you love him and I wouldn't want to jeopardize that by starting something with him that may not work out."

Abigail frowned thoughtfully. "What if it did, though? He could make you really, really happy, El."

"Honey, I am happy."

"Really? Because you're always tired and you spend no time on yourself. For yourself."

"That's because I have a business to run and a teenager to raise."

Abigail sighed. "First off, I'm pretty much raised. I'm sixteen and I spend most of my free time with my friends. Instead of using that extra time for yourself, you've taken on more work. I mean, how many volunteer projects does one woman need?"

"Abigail—" London tried to break in, but her niece just kept talking.

"And second, you have running the B&B down to an art. Most of your evenings are free—which you've filled with your endless projects. You need to go out and have some fun.

Relieve a little stress. Seb would be good for that. And if not him, then why not some other guy? Ryan Marsters thinks you hung the moon."

London frowned. "The hardware store owner?" Dear lord, he was close to fifty.

Abigail nodded. "And so does Mr. Carroll."

Now, London's eyebrows shot to her hairline. "Your math teacher?" She couldn't believe she was having this conversation with her teenage niece.

She straightened away from the counter. "Abs, I love that you're concerned about me, but I'm fine. Really. I don't need a man to be happy. I have you and this place—both of which I love. I have a good life and I'm not looking for more, honey."

Abigail shrugged. "I'm just saying—maybe it's time for you to do something for you." She waggled her eyebrows and grinned. "Even if that something is Uncle Seb."

London knew she was blushing to her roots, but she couldn't stop it. The man had that effect on her even when he was nowhere around.

"One last thing and then I swear I'll shut up. I know you don't need a man to be happy, but wouldn't it be nice to have one anyway?" She stood and headed for the door. "You should go get changed so we aren't late." Her smile was wicked as she strode from the room.

London groaned and scrubbed her hands over her face. Teenagers.

She followed Abigail, but ran up the stairs instead of turning into the living room. Was Abigail right? Was she only existing and not really living? She hadn't been lying when she said she was happy. She was. They had a good life here. London had tried her damnedest after Eddie and Camille's car accident to make a stable home for their daughter. She had worked her tail off to bring in more business so Abigail would have a steady, secure home. But she had neglected her own life in the process, she knew that.

Maybe it was time she tried dating again. It would be nice to have a man around. Someone to go on dates with. To snuggle with by the fire on cold nights and to eventually share her bed.

Unbidden, Seb's face crossed her mind. His dark eyes looking down at her, the laugh lines crinkling as he grinned, black stubble dusting his strong jaw.

She shook her head to dispel the image as she unlocked the door to the family quarters and hurried to her bedroom. Crossing to her closet, she stripped off her jeans and t-shirt and yanked a sundress off the hanger. She stepped into it, angry at herself that she could not get Sebastian Archer out of her mind. The man just spoke to her. Call it hormones or pheromones—or both—her brain refused to let him go, no matter how much she told herself he was off-limits.

Maybe she would talk to her friend Rayna. She was always trying to set London up. The next time she tried, London was going to let her, because she could not continue like this—she was tired of pretending he didn't wind her up every time he quirked that beautiful mouth of his. And Sebastian deserved a friend who didn't give him the attitude she had given him that morning.

She shook her head at herself as she pulled a cardigan on over her dress. She had been looking forward to seeing him, but the moment she spotted him, looking fresh from the shower in his jeans and snug, stone-washed, green t-shirt, lust had kicked her in the gut and her mood had taken a nose-dive.

Finding a pair of sandals that went with her dress, she slid her feet into them. The man hadn't helped matters any by touching her in the kitchen. She'd been so distracted by the feel of his hands, it had been all she could do to form a coherent sentence. She was just thankful she'd had Abigail on her mind as well, so she didn't have to lie to him about why she was upset. She *had* been concerned about her niece—still was—but primarily, in that moment, she had been angry at herself for being so attracted to him. Why did he have to be so damn sexy?

FOUR

Seb pushed through the doors to the morgue at the local hospital. The smell of death hit him as soon as he stepped over the threshold. London's scone did a roll in his stomach. He opened his mouth, trying not to breathe through his nose.

Alex Randall looked up from prepping their victim's remains for autopsy to greet him.

"Perfect timing. I just finished examining her for trace evidence."

"Yeah? You find anything?" He wandered over to the cabinet on the side wall, searching for a mask and the peppermint essential oil they used to cover up the smell of decay.

"Maybe. I took some scrapings from under her nails. I'm hoping she managed to scratch her attacker. If she didn't, I probably won't have any usable DNA on her from her killer. I found evidence of sexual assault, but no semen. The guy must have used a condom."

"Did you get any particulate evidence?"

Alex shook his head. "Not of her killer, no. I found dirt, though, in some scratches on her back. I don't think she was killed in the homestead. Or, if she was, part of her assault took place in the forest. It looks like she was lying on a rough, dirty surface while she struggled. There are abrasions all over her back. Her dress is clean, so he dressed her post-mortem. I sent it to Katie to see if she can run it down. It's vintage and cheap from the looks of it, so I'm not sure she'll have much luck," he said, mentioning their head crime scene investigator and forensic scientist, Katie Mitchum.

Finally finding what he was searching for, Seb put a couple drops of the oil in a mask and slipped it on over his face. He walked closer to the exam table to get a better look. Now that she had been cleaned up a bit, the bruises on her neck were much more pronounced. He could see individual finger impressions marring her flesh.

"Was she strangled to death?"

Alex nodded. "Possibly." He motioned to the bruising. "I measured the span from the tip of the fingers to the tip of the thumb, giving us an approximate hand size. I should be able to ballpark a height from that. Whether that was the actual cause of death, though, well—" he held up a scalpel, "we'll see."

Seb took a couple steps back as Alex made the first incision, knowing from experience that bodies this decayed were often liquified on the inside. He really did not want that on his shoes.

The body hissed as the built-up gases escaped, sputtering bodily fluids. Alex made quick work of opening the chest and abdomen and clipping the ribs to expose her internal organs.

"I swear, I don't know how you get anything out of that," Seb said, watching Alex examine her organs in situ before inserting a tube into her aorta to drain the blood from her body.

Alex shrugged. "It's just a matter of knowing what healthy anatomy and normal decay look like and finding the abnormalities." He made a cut and lifted the heart from the chest. "Like these." He pointed to the surface of the heart.

"See the little dots all over the pericardium—the membrane around the heart?"

Seb nodded.

"Those are petechial hemorrhages, which happen either when the body's platelet count is extremely low, or with asphyxiation. In the latter case, it's caused by increased pressure in the veins, forcing small vessels to bleed."

"So, she was strangled to death."

"I'd say it's likely, yes. There were no gunshot or stab wounds. I also didn't find any puncture marks on my exam. I'll run a tox screen, though."

"Can you tell me anything about her?"

"She's in her mid- to late-twenties. Good physical condition, so most likely from a middle-class background. She's tall too. About five-nine."

Seb nodded. As soon as Alex finished the autopsy, he planned to go back to his office with the new information and try to narrow down their victim pool. It wasn't much, but it was a start.

Seb rubbed the bridge of his nose, a headache beginning to pound between his eyes from staring at reports all day. He would love to focus all his attention on the murder case, but as sheriff, he was responsible for much more. Mondays meant catching up from the weekend.

His door opened and Caleb Bering poked his head through. "Hey. I just got off the phone with the M.E. The forensic artist in Denver emailed him the composite sketch of our victim. He forwarded it to you."

Shoving aside the pile of paperwork, he pulled his keyboard forward and logged into his email. Caleb came around to stand behind him. In moments, Seb had the image open.

He tipped his head, staring at the sketch. There was something familiar about her.

"Ever seen her before?" he asked Caleb.

"No, can't say as I have. She looks familiar, though."

"Agreed." He hit the print button, and the printer sputtered to life, quickly spitting out the image. "Take the sketch and go through the list of women we compiled yesterday from Dr. Randall's preliminary results. Maybe we've seen her there."

"You got it, boss." Caleb's utility belt creaked as he walked out of the room.

Seb only glanced at his deputy as he left, his attention on the image on his computer screen. She really looked very familiar.

Strawberry-blonde hair, caught up in a French braid, and blue eyes glaring daggers at him flashed through his mind.

London.

That was why this woman looked so familiar. She reminded him of London. And Abigail.

Agitation made his stomach churn. This case had all the hallmarks of a serial killer. It hadn't been a crime of passion. The crime scene was clean, her body moved and staged. Whoever killed her was a sophisticated, methodical man.

The voice in the back of his head niggled at him. There had been no evidence of contamination at the crime scene, which meant it probably wasn't the guy's first kill.

Switching screens as the thought hit him, Seb opened the NCIC database and quickly filled out the search form with the victim's parameters, looking for any other similar, unsolved homicides.

Six open cases popped up, four of them in the western United States. He quickly scanned through the two east of the

Mississippi and ruled them both out. One woman had been found at home, and in the other case, the prime suspect was the husband, and he was on the run.

Turning his attention to the other four, he read through the files, his concern growing as he looked through each report. All but one of them appeared to match his case.

Seb swiped a hand down his face, the churning in his gut worse. If he was right, the Jane Doe in the morgue made victim number four.

His eyes strayed to the photograph on his desk.

Four women who looked a hell of a lot like London and Abigail.

He pulled out his phone and shot off a quick text to his goddaughter, asking her how she was doing.

Almost immediately, he got an eye roll emoji back followed by, "I'm fine. Thanks for checking on me," and a heart.

Stifling a laugh at her teenage impertinence, he dialed London. He didn't know what he would say when she picked up, but he would think of something.

As the phone continued to ring and then rolled over to voice-mail, he frowned. It wasn't like her to not answer. She carried her cell everywhere because it was also the primary line for the B&B.

Trepidation soured the acid in his stomach. He was going to need heartburn medication before this was all over.

Needing to reassure himself London was all right, he shut down his computer and left his office. He would just take a quick drive over there and check on her. When he found her, he would just tell her he was there to check on Abigail. She couldn't be mad at him for that.

He climbed into his truck and quickly pulled out of the parking lot, headed east. London's B&B, The Lilac Inn, was just outside of town on two acres of land. It offered a quiet respite for her guests, but right now it was making him nervous. The property butted up to the national forest—the same forest where Abigail and Trent found the body.

Once he reached the edge of town, he sped up. The two miles to the B&B flew by and soon he saw the lilac bushes, from which the inn got its name, framing the drive. His truck rumbled up the stone driveway, and he parked in the guest lot on the side of the garage.

Shutting off the engine, he climbed from the vehicle and made his way to the front door. He took the porch steps in one long stride and threw open the door.

"London?"

The living room in front of him was empty, so he wandered to the kitchen. It was spotless but it, too, was void of life.

Reversing course, he headed back into the living room and ran up the stairs.

"London, are you up here?"

None of the guest room doors were open. In fact, it felt like no one was home at all. He continued down the hallway and knocked on the always locked door of the family quarters, calling her name again. When she still didn't answer, worry settled heavy on his shoulders. He turned on his heel and ran back downstairs, through the kitchen into the mudroom where he yanked open the door to the garage. London's SUV sat in its bay.

"Where the hell is she?"

He spied the door leading to the backyard. It was the only place he hadn't looked yet. In three long strides, he crossed the garage floor and pulled open the door.

Relief made his shoulders sag as he spotted her out near the large oak in the middle of the yard, elbow-deep in a bag of potting soil. He jogged across the grass and called her name.

When she looked up, he couldn't help but smile. She had a streak of dirt across her cheek.

"That looks nice." He motioned to the row of flowers she'd planted around the tree and came to a halt a few feet away.

"Thanks. I got tired of looking at bare ground. What's up?"

He took in her sweaty appearance. Tendrils of her light red hair escaped her braid and fluttered around her face in the breeze. His heart clenched, and the air left his lungs in a rush. He felt like he'd been sucker punched. She was so damn beautiful, even sweaty and dirty.

He swallowed hard and shrugged, forcing his gaze on the flowers she planted. "I just came to see how our girl is. She still doing okay?"

London nodded. "She's fine. She's not even here right now. Trent came and got her about an hour ago. They were going to go out to eat and hang with friends."

"No more hiking, I hope."

Her mouth quirked. "Probably not for a while, no. She said they planned to stick close."

He gave a quick nod. "Good."

She dug another hole and plopped a plant in it. "So, did you really come here just to check on Abigail, or was there another reason?"

Yeah, he knew he should have come up with a better excuse. He texted Abigail all the time, and London knew that. His mind whirled as he tried to think of another plausible excuse for driving out here. He didn't want to alarm her by telling her the truth—that he was worried about her safety. The killer may have fled the area by now. All the other murders had been spaced out by hundreds of miles.

He surveyed her property, thinking, before he looked back down at her, an idea coming to him.

"Have you had dinner yet?"

"It's just now five o'clock, Seb. I've been out here planting."

His head bobbed. "Right. So, you want to go grab a burger or something?"

Her gaze narrowed as she looked up at him. The sun glinted off her hair, turning it to a burnished gold. "Why?"

"Can't a friend ask a friend to eat dinner?"

She wagged a finger between them. "You and I don't go out to eat together unless Abigail is with us. You were primarily Eddie's friend, not mine."

Seb sighed. Her reticence to be his friend—a real friend—was getting old. Eddie had been gone five years now, and he had been back in town for two years. When was she going to accept he wasn't just her brother's friend anymore?

"Come on, El. You know that's not true. Eddie might have been my best friend, but you're my friend too. I have always been there for you, and I always will be. So what do you say?"

Her eyes drifted past him as she contemplated his offer.

"My treat," he said, with an arch of his brow, hoping to tempt her.

She rolled her eyes and huffed. "Fine. Let me finish planting these flowers and get cleaned up. I can meet you at Boone's in about half an hour."

Seb shrugged. "I'll wait." Hunkering down next to her, he picked up the flat of plants and worked one out of the tray to hand to her. She loosened the root ball and set it in the hole, covering it with the rich soil.

They made quick work of planting the last of the flowers. Seb helped her gather up her gardening supplies, carrying them to the shed.

"You go get changed. I'll put all this away."

"You're sure?"

"Yep."

With a quick nod, she turned and headed for the house.

Seb tried hard not to watch her walk away, but failed. Lust stirred in his gut at the gentle sway of her hips and the sight of her long, silky legs exposed by her shorts. And at five-ten, there was a lot of leg to look at.

Whirling around, he yanked open the shed door and walked inside, putting a firm lid on his emotions. Lusting after London would do nothing but leave him aroused and frustrated. He couldn't even get her to admit they were good friends. What chance in hell did he have of convincing her they should be more? None, that's what. Besides, it probably wasn't wise for them to start something. If it went sour, it could harm his relationship with Abigail, and that was something he would never do. That girl meant more to him than anyone. He had been the favorite "uncle" since she was born, but since Eddie died, he'd become much more than that. He imagined the love he felt for her was much like what he would feel for his own child.

Seb stored London's gardening tools and the remaining potting soil before closing and locking the shed. Shoving his thoughts about his relationship with London to the back of his mind, he pulled out his phone and brought up his notepad app, jotting down a few notes about the cold cases he found on the NCIC database. He needed to contact the detectives in charge of the cases and have their files sent to him. If they could find something to link the four victims, they might find a suspect.

The backdoor off the kitchen opened, and London stuck her head through. "I'm ready."

Seb's breath caught in his throat. She had changed into a light blue, floral-patterned dress. Its loose skirt fluttered around her legs. Her toes, painted a coral pink, peeked out of a pair of strappy, heeled mahogany sandals. Already a tall woman, the heels brought her closer to his six-foot-five height.

She had pulled her hair out of its usual braid and brushed it smooth. It fell in coppery waves around her shoulders. His hands twitched, and he shoved them into his pockets, phone and all, to keep from reaching for the silky tresses as he walked closer.

He cleared his throat. "You look nice."

She smiled softly. "Thanks."

Hands still buried in his pockets, he tipped his head, motioning for her to follow him around the house to his truck. Once they reached the vehicle, he risked removing a hand to open her door for her.

She smiled her thanks as she climbed inside and he clutched the door frame until his knuckles were white. Her milky skin with its dusting of freckles looked silky soft.

Once she was seated, he closed the door and walked around the front of the vehicle to get in beside her. Her floral scent enveloped him in the confines of the cab, and he fought back a groan. It was going to be a long drive.

With a flick of his wrist, he started the truck, then immediately rolled down his window. It was a warm day, but not so hot they needed the air conditioning. He hoped she didn't mind the breeze, because he needed the flowing air to dispel her scent or they wouldn't make it to the restaurant without him pulling over to bury his face in the crook of her neck and drink his fill.

At the end of her drive, he turned right, away from town.

She sat forward immediately, a frown on her face. "Where are we going?"

"The ranch. I figured we could eat at Heartwood."

"But you said burgers."

"You can get a burger there."

"A fancy burger. The Heartwood Grill isn't exactly a burger joint. That's like a date place."

He rolled his eyes. "It's also a get-a-burger place. And a steak place. After the day I've had, steak sounds fantastic."

Her eyes traced over his shirt and gun belt before settling back on his face. "You should have said something before we left. I could have followed you. Now you have to bring me back home before driving the exact same route to get home yourself."

He shrugged. He was still a little jarred by her resemblance to their victim—to all the victims he had uncovered—and didn't want her out alone. There was no way he would tell her that, though. London was as independent as they came. She would ream him a new one if he suggested she couldn't take care of herself. He knew she could defend herself if someone broke into the inn. The woman was a crack shot and owned several weapons. But she didn't carry concealed, so if someone ran her off the road and tried to abduct her, she had to rely on her own two hands to fight back. She was a strong woman, but he doubted she would be able to fight off a man intent on harming her.

"I don't mind. It's not that far."

She hummed a non-answer and rolled down her own window a bit, staring out at the countryside as it flew past.

"I'll probably go back into town after we eat, anyway. I have some things I want to check out for my murder case."

She glanced at him. "You need to rest too, Sebastian. I know you were in the office bright and early this morning. And that's after you spent the weekend there too."

"I know, but Bering is my only actual detective and on a case like this, he needs an extra set of seasoned hands. Be happy I'm taking an actual dinner break."

"I am, but you better make sure you rest or I'll sick Abigail on you," she said with a wicked grin.

He laughed. His goddaughter would indeed hound him to death until he agreed to take a break, and he loved her for it. It was nice being around people who cared about him. It was a big part of the reason he'd left the FBI and moved back home, and it was definitely why he stayed now.

Seb looked at London out of the corner of his eye while he drove. Regardless of whether she wanted to admit it, she was a part of that group that cared. No matter what the status of their relationship, he was extraordinarily happy to have her in his life and he would do anything to keep her safe. Even if it meant lying to her about why he was hanging around. Until they caught this killer, he was going to stick to her like glue whenever he could. She would hate it, but he didn't care. Keeping her safe was all that mattered.

London's eyes adjusted to the dim lighting of The Heartwood Grill as Sebastian ushered her inside. As they waited on the hostess to seat them, she surveyed the room. It had been a while since she was in here. The restaurant was a large log cabin. Sebastian's oldest sister, and the restaurant's proprietor, Tara, had left the walls natural. Giant support beams stood throughout the room, stretching from the floor to the twenty-foot ceilings. Fairy lights wrapped the rafters and enormous wrought-iron chandeliers hung throughout the space, providing a low, warm light for the diners.

What London loved most about the décor, though, were the pictures. Tara went with a nature theme, but instead of animal heads hanging from the walls, she decorated with haunting, beautiful photographs of both the animal life and the people of Silver Gap. London's favorite was of a herd of horses, thundering over the grassy plains of the valley. Easily five-feet long, it was sepia-toned and hung prominently over the fireplace that dominated one wall. Tara told her once that she wanted to capture the essence of what made Silver Gap such a wonderful place, so she'd taken a series of photos that did just that and used them to line the walls. The restaurant's name—The Heartwood Grill—showcased the hard, beautiful core that had shaped the history of the valley.

The hostess's arrival pulled London from her thoughts.

"Hi, Mr. Archer." The girl's eyes flicked to London. "I see you won't be eating alone tonight."

A blush stole over London's face. Good lord, the girl thought they were on a date! She was glad the lighting was dim so no one could see the fire in her cheeks.

Grabbing two menus and two sets of silverware, the young woman motioned for them to follow her. She led them to a table near the windows, overlooking the deck that jutted out into the trees.

"Is this all right or would you rather sit outside?"

Seb looked at her and arched a brow in question.

"Why don't we sit outside? The bugs aren't bad yet, and it's a warm evening."

He nodded and the girl quickly changed course for the French doors set into the wall of windows.

London sat in the chair Sebastian pulled out for her and looked out over the lush foliage that had sprung up in the last few weeks. The light scent of geraniums from the planters scattered around the deck wafted around her on the soft breeze. She loved spring. The biggest reason she bought the B&B was because of the lilac bushes. She had always admired them every time she drove past. When the property went on the market, it had been spring and the lilacs were in full bloom. Their sweet scent had washed over her when she toured the grounds and she was sold. Her father gave her the down payment and co-signed the loan. She had thrown herself into making the inn a success and never looked back.

She glanced at Seb from the corner of her eye. He was looking at the menu, even though she was sure he knew it by heart. Maybe she should have looked back a little more. Maybe she would have a husband and a child or two by now if she had. Instead, she was sitting in a fancy restaurant, contemplating how sexy her brother's best friend looked in his uniform shirt and a day's worth of stubble dusting his firm jaw.

"So, is Abigail really doing okay?"

London turned her attention back to Sebastian. She nodded and picked up her menu. "She's fine. Much better than I thought she would be. She's been a little quieter, but she's not letting it get her down. The girl is resilient, I'll give her that."

Seb quirked a brow. "She's had to be."

She couldn't argue with him there. Abigail was a passenger in the car accident that killed her parents. They had been coming back from a ski trip in poor weather and slid off the road into a ravine. Eddie died instantly, but Camille held on for several hours until she finally passed out and died from blood loss. Abigail had been asleep when they went off the road. Her position, sprawled over the backseat, saved her. She still broke several bones, but none of her injuries had been life-threatening. Her worst injury was the psychological one. It took eighteen hours for someone to find them. By that point, Abigail had been sitting in the car, in freezing temperatures, with her deceased parents for twelve hours. She'd been one very traumatized girl when London arrived at the hospital.

She glanced at Seb over the top of her menu. He had been there that night, too. It was his sturdy presence that got her through the hours Abigail was in surgery to set her leg and arm. He hadn't left her side other than to shower and eat the entire time Abigail was in the hospital. Even then, he had become a fixture at the B&B while she healed. He also helped her plan Eddie and Camille's funerals. Her parents had been out of the country at the time of the accident, and when they returned, they'd both been too distraught to do more than float along.

"Hi, Sheriff. Ms. Scott. What can I get for you guys tonight?"

London looked up at the waitress's bubbly voice and recognized one of Abigail's friends. She smiled at the girl. "Hi, Kaylee. I didn't know you were working out here."

Kaylee nodded. "I've been here about a month. So, are you guys ready to order?"

Seb arched a brow at London, and she tipped her head, telling him to go ahead. She quickly glanced through the menu while he ordered and found something that sounded decent.

Orders placed, London sat back and stared out at the trees, her mind still on how Seb had been there for her and Abigail. She didn't think she ever thanked him for being there. For helping her when her parents couldn't. She wasn't sure she would have made it through those months without him.

Looking at him from the corner of her eye, she took a deep breath. "Sebastian, I want to say thank you."

He frowned. "For what?"

"For something I should have a long time ago. All this has brought back memories from when Eddie and Camille died, and I realized I never thanked you for being there for me and Abigail. So, thank you."

He smiled that smile that made her heart flip-flop in her chest, and leaned forward, elbows propped on the table, his chin resting on his hands. Those gorgeous brown eyes twinkled brightly in the low lights.

London resisted the urge to fan herself as lust smacked her square in the gut as she looked into his dark eyes.

"I knew you were grateful. I also knew you were overwhelmed. I wish you had let me help more. You always were stubborn."

She tipped her head. "True. But I still should have said thank you. I don't think I would have kept it together as well as I did without you there."

Her heart skipped several beats when he reached out and took one of her hands in his.

"You're welcome, El. I will always be here for you."

London got lost in the intensity of his eyes. As she sat there, locked in his gaze, the merriment faded from his eyes. Fire sparked in their depths and she felt an answering heat low in her belly. His fingers tightened around hers, sending sparks shooting up her arm.

"So, when did I miss this happening?"

She and Seb both jerked at the voice intruding on their moment. They looked up to see his sister standing over their table.

London did her best to put a welcoming smile on her face, but she knew it was strained. She was still reeling from what just passed between them.

"Hi, Tara."

Tara flashed her brother an impish grin. "Hi. So, when did this happen?" She waved a finger between the two of them.

Seb's face turned red and he let go of her hand to sit back in his chair. "Nothing is happening. We just decided to get something to eat."

Tara hummed. "Sure. And London's in a pretty dress and you two are staring at each other like you're the only people in the room because you're just getting dinner. Okay." She rolled her eyes.

London felt her face flame. She *had* put on a dress that made her feel pretty instead of a clean pair of shorts and a t-shirt.

"Tara—"

She waved a hand, cutting her brother off. "I didn't come over here to give you grief. When Kaylee said you were here with London, I just wanted to say hello. It's been a while."

London smiled, more genuinely this time. "It has. This place has really taken off."

"Right?" Her smile was brilliant. "I didn't think the popularity would last, but I still have people driving from Denver and other big cities to eat here. I have to pinch myself some days."

"Well, the food is fantastic, so why wouldn't people want to come from miles around?"

Seb's phone rang, and he fished it out of his pocket, glancing at the screen. "Sorry. It's Bering. I need to take this." He rose from the table, answering it, and walked toward the deck railing.

Tara plopped down in his empty seat and propped her chin in her hand. A mischievous grin quirked one side of her mouth. "So. I know I said I didn't come to give Seb any grief, but I still want to know how long this has been going on between you two. He hasn't said anything about dating anyone."

London bit back a groan. She loved Tara, but the woman could be like a dog with a bone.

"Nothing is going on. We really did just come to get dinner."

"Uh-huh. I saw that look. That was not a friends-getting-dinner look."

She shifted in her chair, her face still hot. It hadn't felt like a friends-getting-dinner look, but she wasn't sure how to label it. "I don't know what to tell you, Tara. We aren't dating. He came to the B&B to check on Abigail, then asked if I'd had dinner. I hadn't, it was five o'clock, and I was hungry, so here we are." She shrugged, hoping she looked nonchalant. To be honest, the invitation had surprised her. What she said to him was true—they didn't do dinner without Abigail. Unsure of his reasons, and knowing how much his mere presence sent her hormones into overdrive, she had fallen back on the argument that he wasn't really her friend. That he just tolerated her because of Eddie. She'd seen the flash of hurt in his eyes and felt terrible about it. The truth was, she knew they were friends, but didn't know how to handle her attraction to him without pushing him away. She enjoyed his company, but it was becoming increasingly difficult to be around him without wondering what it would be like to be in his arms. To have his hands running over her body as he kissed her senseless.

Tara's delighted laugh brought her out of her thoughts.

"Oh, this is fantastic. I wondered how long it would take before you two realized you were meant for each other."

London's eyes widened.

"I've been waiting for this day for years. He's always had a soft spot for you, but it sure has taken him long enough to realize there's more there."

She frowned. Was Tara right? Did Seb feel more for her than just friendship? That look he'd laid on her a minute ago felt like more, but they had been friends since they were children. Why would that suddenly change now?

Seb returned to the table before she could contemplate it further, and Tara stood to give her brother back his seat.

"Everything okay?" London asked him.

He nodded. "Just an update on the murder case."

"How's that going?" Tara asked. "Any suspects yet? Or a name for the victim?"

Seb shook his head, a pensive frown forming between his eyebrows. "No. Caleb found a few possibilities for her identity. But we need to wait on DNA to confirm if one of them is the woman from the homestead."

Tara shivered and crossed her arms. "This whole business gives me the willies. Stuff like that doesn't happen around here. I, for one, hope you catch this guy soon."

"Believe me, I'm trying." He leaned on his elbows and rubbed at his temples. The lines around his mouth and eyes deepened, and suddenly, he looked much older than his thirty-nine years.

Without thinking, London reached across the table and laid her hand over his. She tried to ignore the electric jolt zipping up her arm. "We know you're doing your best. You'll find the man responsible."

He turned his hand over in hers and squeezed, offering her a ghost of a smile.

London looked away before she got sucked into Sebastian's hypnotic gaze again. She turned to Tara and quickly wished she hadn't. The woman stared down at them, grinning from ear to ear.

"This is so great."

London slid her hand back, blushing bright red.

"Seriously, Tara. Would you quit? We're not dating."

Tara rolled her eyes and waved her hand again at her brother's words. "Whatever. London, were you planning on coming to book club Wednesday evening?"

London nodded. "So long as all my day's guests arrive before then, yes."

"Good. I will see you then. I need to get back to the kitchen. *But*, I'll send over some wine for you two to celebrate your new relationship. I'd drink with you, but duty calls." She whirled on her heel. "So great!" she said as she walked away.

Seb groaned. London stared out at the trees, unable to look him in the eye without turning ten shades of red. She darted a glance at him. He was still rubbing his temples.

"I'm sorry about my sister."

She cleared her throat and mustered the courage to look at him, willing her blush to stay away. "It's okay. No matter what she thinks, I know we're just friends."

His head bobbed, and he picked up his water glass. "Right. Friends."

As she watched him take a drink, London couldn't help but wish Tara was right.

"Come in and I'll make you some coffee before you head back to the station. I have a feeling you're going to need it." Seb's boots echoed on the stairs of the B&B's front porch as he climbed up behind London.

She inserted the key in the lock and turned to look at him as she pushed the door open.

Her golden red hair fell over her shoulder, the shiny tendrils brushing over her soft skin. Seb clenched his fists to keep from reaching out.

"I really should just get going."

She rolled her eyes. "Coffee only takes a few minutes." Not waiting for an answer, she stepped inside, expecting him to follow.

Muttering under his breath about keeping his hands to himself and stubborn women, he followed her into the house and through the living area to the kitchen. He leaned against the counter and crossed his arms, watching her work.

"You don't have to do this, you know. The station has coffee. Hell, so does Boone's."

She smiled up at him, her eyes twinkling. "Yes, but mine's better."

He wouldn't argue with her there. She had found the perfect ratio of grounds to water for her machine. He had never had a bad cup of coffee at the B&B. She also kept a bottle of the creamer he liked in the fridge.

While the coffee brewed, she dug into the large pantry for the paper to go cups, quickly producing one. Seb got the creamer from the refrigerator and plunked it down on the counter next to the sputtering coffee machine.

An awkward silence descended over them. Usually, they didn't have any problem finding something to talk about, but tonight, that intense stare-down they had at the restaurant stymied Seb's tongue, and the easy-going relationship he had with her was missing. Sexual tension had taken its place. It wasn't like he'd never noticed her beauty before. But tonight, it was taking everything he had not to grab her and kiss her until they both forgot it was a bad idea.

Giving in to the urge to at least touch her, he reached out and skimmed a hand over her shoulder and the silky tresses of strawberry-blonde hair resting there. Goosebumps erupted over her skin and her pupils dilated as she looked up at him, startled.

Seb's gut clenched and his blood heated in response to her reaction. He moved away from the counter to stand in front of her, curling his hand lightly around her bicep. Her chest skimmed his as she took an unsteady breath. Seb cupped her face with his free hand and stared down at her. Uncertainty shone in her eyes alongside a hum of desire.

His own body vibrating from the need coursing through him, he lowered his head until his lips were only millimeters from hers. Her warm breath puffed against his mouth and he bit back a groan.

The coffeemaker beeped at the same time the door to the garage opened and Abigail walked in.

Seb jumped back and looked over his shoulder at the girl who stopped just inside the door. An enormous smile spread over her face as she took in the deer-in-headlights look on their faces and the flush on London's cheeks.

"I'm not here." She walked into the room and headed for the door to the living area. "I just need to grab a sweatshirt and I'm leaving again." She made a shooing motion.

"Continue what you were doing." In a flash, she was through the kitchen door, leaving Seb and London alone again.

He looked back down at her, the awkwardness growing now that the moment had been interrupted. She had her arms crossed over her chest, effectively shutting him out. The desire he glimpsed before was banked, but the uncertainty was still there.

He pushed a hand through his hair. "I should probably go."

She nodded and spun around to fill his cup. With an efficiency born of running an inn, she poured the coffee and added a dollop of creamer before snapping a lid on the cup and handing it to him.

His fingers brushed hers as he took it, and he had to clench his teeth to rein in the fresh wave of need that threatened to buckle his knees. The longing that sprang to life in her eyes didn't help matters any.

Hurried steps on the stairs and the bang of the front door as Abigail left, snapped him out of his thoughts before he threw rationality to the wind again. He took several steps back and turned toward the door. "Come lock the door behind me?"

She frowned. "I don't normally lock it until nine if I'm home."

"El, there's a killer on the loose and Abigail found the body. Humor me, please?"

Understanding lightened her eyes, and she nodded. Together, they walked to the main part of the house. As they reached the entry, motion on the stairs drew Seb's attention. He glanced over to see a man dressed in casual but expensive clothes descending the stairs.

"Hello, Mr. Brown," London said.

"Ms. Scott." The man barely cracked a smile as he reached

the main floor. His eyes flicked to Seb and over the badge on his shirt before he continued to the door.

"Make sure you have your key with you. I'll be keeping the front door locked for the foreseeable future."

The man paused and frowned, then nodded. "Understandable. You are here most of the day alone." His gaze shifted to Seb once more, before his eyes darted away.

Seb narrowed his own and studied the man as he exited the house. Something about him set off his internal radar.

London held the door open and looked up at Seb. He peered down at her, frowning.

"What do you know about that guy?"

"Mr. Brown?" She shrugged. "Not much. He said he's here on business. He didn't elaborate, and I didn't ask."

"What's his first name?"

"Doug. Why?"

"He seems a little sketchy. Wouldn't really look me in the eye."

"Some people just don't like cops, Seb. And you are rather intimidating."

The corners of his mouth turned down, and he stared out at the drive as Brown drove away in a late-model Mercedes. "Maybe. But with everything that's happened, anything that feels a little off is going to get my attention." And that man definitely felt off. He would get Seb's full attention as soon as he got back to his office.

"I'll see you later. Lock up behind me and don't open the door when you're alone for anyone you don't know."

She nodded. "I'll be careful."

His eyes locked on hers and that urge to kiss her reared its head again. He was in such deep trouble.

Forcing himself to break eye contact, he nodded once and walked out the door. It took everything he had not to turn around and run right back in.

FIVE

L ondon closed the rear gate on her SUV with a thud, ready to head home and unload all the groceries she just bought. Climbing into the driver's seat, she exited the store's parking lot. Two blocks down the road, the sign for the hardware store caught her eye, and she groaned. She forgot she ordered some specialty sconces to put up in the living room to enhance the farmhouse décor. Mr. Marsters had called over a week ago to tell her they were in.

For just a moment, she entertained the idea of driving on and sending Abigail to get them later, but quickly dismissed the idea. Just because her niece said the man had a crush on her didn't make it true. And she couldn't avoid him forever. It was a small town.

She slowed down and turned into one of the angled parking spaces lining the street. Shutting off the engine, she inhaled a deep breath.

"You can do this. Abigail was probably just imagining things."

With a quick shake of her head, she got out of the vehicle

and headed inside. Mr. Marsters was at the counter and smiled when she entered.

She offered him a small wave and walked up to him.

"Hi, Mr. Marsters. I'm here to pick up my sconces."

"Oh, right. They're in the back. Let me go get them."

London leaned against the counter and surveyed the store after he walked away. She should get some spray paint while she was here for the outdoor table she picked up last week.

Straightening, she wandered down the paint aisle and stopped in front of the spray paint display. Now, to decide on a color.

"London. I thought that was you."

She looked up from the can of speckled eggshell paint in her hand and smiled at her friend and local coffee shop owner, Macy Briggs.

"Hi, Macy."

Macy walked closer, her eyes on the paint in London's hand.

"What are you painting?"

"A table. I found it at a flea market last week. It'll add some much-needed seating to my outdoor patio."

"Well, that sounds more fun than why I'm here. My extra-fancy, over-priced espresso machine took a crap on me and I'm hoping I can fix it."

"Oh, no! What's wrong with it?"

"The steamer nozzle broke off. I found a couple pieces I think will work until the actual part comes in." She held up two different nozzles. "Neither of them is as long as the one that broke, but they'll do for now. I just hope the threading lines up or I'm screwed. Even with the rush I put on the part, it will still be Thursday before it's here." She motioned to the paint. "Enough about my troubles. I'd rather not think about them. Is that the color you're going with?"

"Maybe. Do you think it'll get too dirty sitting outside?"

Macy nodded. "I know you like your light colors, but I'd go with this one." She grabbed a can off the shelf in a much darker shade. It was speckled like the other one, but a chocolate color.

London pictured the chairs she'd bought to go with the table. They would look nice with that color. She put the eggshell paint back and took the other can from Macy and grabbed a second one. "Sounds good to me."

The women turned and headed back to the front counter.

Mr. Marsters had returned with her lights, but London motioned Macy ahead of her, knowing that the other woman needed to get back to her café and fix the machine.

"So," Macy said, a spirited glint in her eyes. "I saw you and a certain drop-dead gorgeous sheriff together last night at Heartwood. When did this start?"

London rolled her eyes and sighed. "Nothing is going on. We had dinner. As friends."

"Sure, you did. Friends don't hold hands and stare deeply into each other's eyes."

"You sound like Tara."

"Wise woman." Macy giggled. "If a man looked at me like that, the 'friends' label would be gone by morning." She handed Mr. Marsters her credit card.

London flushed and Macy's eyes widened.

"Oh my God, did you?"

Turning redder by the second, London shook her head. "No. Nothing happened. We ate, and he took me home." *And he almost kissed me in my kitchen.*

"You rode together?" She tossed her hands up. "Totally a date."

"It was not a date!"

Macy took her bag from Mr. Marsters and grinned at London. "If you say so. I gotta run, but I'll see you Wednesday and you can tell me and the others all about your non-date."

London held back a groan. Barely.

Macy waggled her fingers and scampered out of the store to go fix her coffeemaker.

She looked up as Mr. Marsters cleared his throat.

"So, you saw the sheriff yesterday?"

She nodded and stiffened, hoping he wasn't about to ask her about her relationship with him too.

"How's his investigation coming? Any leads?"

"Not that I know of." She sagged against the counter, grateful he wasn't going to grill her about her non-date with Seb. "He's working every angle he can, though. He went back to work last night after we got back from the ranch."

"He's a good cop," he said as he rang her up.

She nodded. "Yes. If anyone can solve this case, it's Sebastian."

"I heard your niece and her boyfriend found the woman. She doing okay?"

"She was a little shocked, but has come to grips with it. Mostly, she just wants Seb to find the person who did it, so that woman can rest in peace."

"I understand that. My sister was murdered years ago. The cops never caught her killer."

"Oh, Mr. Marsters. I'm so sorry. I didn't know that. That's terrible."

He looked down, not meeting her eyes, pain etched on his face. "It was. She was young—only twenty-one. But after thirty years, I don't think they'll ever find who killed her."

She laid her hand over his. "You never know. Maybe you should ask Seb to look at the case after this one ends. He's a very good investigator and might be able to bring you some closure."

He nodded and sniffed. "I might do that." He held out her receipt. "Here you go. I'll carry these lights out for you."

London followed him outside and opened the back-passenger door, so he could set the light boxes on the seat.

"Have you heard when my faucet will be in?" Besides the sconces, she had also ordered a new kitchen faucet. One with a big pull-down spigot she could turn on and off with a touch. She couldn't wait for that to come in, but it was on back order.

"No. But I'll call the wholesaler and see if they can give me an estimate."

"That'd be great. Thank you."

"Not a problem. And listen, you be careful out there. The sheriff can't be around all the time to keep you safe. If you need anything, I'm only a phone call away."

London fought the blush threatening to break free. Abigail had been right. "That's very nice of you, Mr. Marsters. Thank you."

He nodded and shut the door. She walked around to the driver's side and climbed in, giving him a wave as she started the engine. Ryan was a handsome man, but much too old for her. It was a shame, though. He was nice.

London sank onto her mattress and sighed. After returning from town, she'd tackled her never-ending chore list, and checked in two more couples who were staying the week. With the summer season starting, she had people coming and going nearly every day now. She was tired and ready to welcome the peaceful oblivion of sleep before she had to be up to make breakfast.

Just as she relaxed and closed her eyes, there was a knock on the door to the family quarters down the hall.

Groaning, she sat up, vowing to roast whichever guest

dared disturb her if they didn't have a good reason for knocking so late.

She tossed a robe over her pajamas and padded barefoot down the hall, flicking open the lock. She pulled the door open to see Doug Brown standing there.

"I'm sorry to bother you so late, Ms. Scott, but I found this on the doorstep outside when I came in just now."

London pushed the door open wider and took the small box from him with a frown. "Thank you, Mr. Brown."

His head bobbed once. "You're welcome. Goodnight."

She muttered goodbye and closed the door, locking it once again, her attention on the package in her hand. It wasn't large. Six inches square, maybe. It was wrapped in brown paper and had her name written over the top in neat block letters.

She carried it back to her room and set it down on her dresser. Sliding one finger under the seam, she tore the paper to reveal a white box. She lifted the flap on the lid. A notecard sat on top of a bundle of six bath bombs.

More curious now than before, she opened the card and gasped as she read it.

So you smell as sweet as your pretty flowers.

– XO

She frowned down at the gift. Who would send her something like this? The only man she had any kind of romantic relationship with was Seb, and that was stretching the definition. She highly doubted he would send her a gift anonymously. No, if he gave her a present, he would give it to her himself and not leave it at the door.

But who did that leave?

Ryan Marsters's face flashed in her head.

Would he? She really didn't know him all that well. If he was nursing a secret crush on her, maybe he would leave a gift on her doorstep.

A glance at the clock revealed it was much too late for her to call him and ask. She also didn't want to embarrass the man if he hadn't sent it.

With a huff, she pushed the box away and crawled back into bed. Answers would have to wait until morning. As she snapped off the bedside lamp, her earlier feeling of relaxation was gone. So much for a restful night's sleep.

~

"You okay, El?"

London blinked at her niece, taking a moment to register that the girl had asked a question. "Yes. Sorry. I'm just super tired today." It had taken her quite a while to fall asleep after receiving that gift, and then she'd tossed and turned the rest of the night.

"You can go up and go back to bed if you want. I can handle breakfast and the cleanup."

"Oh, honey, that's so nice of you, but I'll be all right. I just need to get another cup of coffee in me."

Abigail giggled. "You sound like Seb."

"Someone mention my name?"

London looked past Abigail to see Seb standing in the doorway in a clean uniform shirt and jeans, his hair still damp from the shower. She ached to run her fingers through it and over his freshly shaven jaw. She picked up her coffee mug instead and took a big gulp of the burning liquid.

"What are you doing here?" Abigail asked.

Seb stepped into the kitchen and ruffled the girl's hair. London shot him a look, pleading with him not to mention that she had called him early that morning and asked him to come over.

He shot her an imperceptible nod. "Your aunt's cooking is just so good, I decided I needed another dose."

Abigail's smile was blinding as she looked between the two of them, not fooled for a minute that there wasn't something brewing between her aunt and godfather. "Well, you're in luck. She made breakfast burritos this morning."

"She mentioned that yesterday. That's why I'm here."

London motioned to the stove. "Help yourself." She turned to Abigail. "Abs, would you take all the toppings out and arrange them on the buffet and then check to make sure there's enough napkins in the dispenser?"

Abigail nodded and gathered the bowls onto a tray, leaving her aunt alone with Seb. London poured him a cup of coffee, then took another swig of her own.

He sat down at the small table in the kitchen and lifted the burrito he just made to his mouth. "So, what did you want to talk to me about?" He took a big bite and waited for her to start talking.

She turned and pulled the box she received last night out of one of the cabinets. She laid it on the table in front of him.

"That was left on the front porch last night. Doug Brown found it when he came in late and brought it to me."

Seb frowned and put down his food. "What's in it?"

"Bath bombs. And a note."

He flicked open the lid and took out the card, holding it by the corner with his napkin.

"You don't know who it's from?" he asked after glancing at the unsigned card.

She shook her head. "No." She scuffed the toe of her shoe on the floor and looked down.

"What?"

She looked back up at him. "What?"

"You're not telling me something. What is it? Do you suspect someone?"

With a sigh, she looked up at the ceiling before turning back to him. "At first, I thought they might be from you. After the other day—" she broke off and glanced away, the muscles in her jaw working overtime as she clenched her teeth, trying not to remember the way her body responded to their near-kiss. "Anyway, I figured if you wanted to give me something you wouldn't leave it on my porch unsigned. The only other person I can think of is Ryan Marsters."

Seb's eyebrows shot up. "The hardware store owner? He's in his fifties."

"I know, but Abigail said she thinks he likes me, and when I was there yesterday, some things he said seemed to support that."

"I can stop in and ask him—"

"No!" Hands outstretched, she cut him off. "I don't want to embarrass him. He's a nice guy. Can you just run the box for prints? If he sent it, I don't care, but I would like to know for sure. I mean, what if it wasn't him? What if there's someone out there watching me I don't know about?"

Seb's jaw flexed as he considered that idea. "Yeah. All right. I'll run it. What do you want me to do with it once I get some results?"

"Just hang on to it. I'll figure that out once I know who it's from."

He nodded and set the note back in the box. "Has anything else unusual happened that you can think of?"

She bit her lip as she thought and stared over the rim of

her cup at a point on the wall behind his head. "No. But if there *is* anything else, you can bet I'll call you."

"Maybe—" he broke off and sat back in his chair, running a hand through his hair. "Maybe I should stay here for a while."

London's heart skipped and then beat a staccato in her chest. "What?"

Hesitation pinched his features. He squeezed his eyes closed for a moment. When he opened them again, a tired resignation shone from their dark depths.

"El, I think it would be a good idea if I moved in for a bit. I didn't want to worry you, but now that you're getting anonymous gifts, you should know that you bear a bit of a resemblance to my murder victim."

All the blood drained from her face. She sagged into the counter behind her as her knees turned to jelly.

She what?

Seb was in front of her in an instant, easing the coffee mug from her hand and setting it behind her. He took her hands in his and bent at the knee so he could look her in the eye.

"Honey, I'm not going to let anything happen to you, I swear."

She stared into his chocolate eyes and some of the shock began to fade. "Why are you just now telling me this?"

He straightened and sighed, but didn't release her hands. "Because there was no evidence this guy kills more than one woman in a city at a time. It didn't—doesn't—feel likely that there will be another murder in the area."

London frowned. "Wait. There have been other women murdered like the one Abigail and Trent found?"

Seb nodded. "I've found three other cases in surrounding states similar to this one."

"Jesus, Sebastian." She pulled her hands from his and

moved away, needing room to think. She rubbed her forehead, staring at the floor before turning back to him.

"So, if you aren't concerned there will be another murder, why do you want to move in?"

"Because the timing of your gift bothers me. I don't like coincidences—not in a murder case, and certainly not when it involves you."

Attraction reared its head again at his words. Why did the man have to be so sweet?

"If you stay here, I don't know where you're going to sleep. All my guest rooms are booked and the extra bedrooms in the family section don't have beds. One is my office and the other I've been using for storage."

"I can bunk down on the couch in the sitting area of your apartment upstairs."

Her eyes widened. "That couch is a two-seater. You're six-foot-five."

He shrugged. "Then I'll bring over a sleeping bag and camp on the floor. The point is that I don't feel comfortable leaving you and Abigail here alone at night. I can sleep anywhere."

"We aren't alone. I have a houseful of guests. No one would dare try to get in here."

"Maybe, but we don't know that for sure. What if he concocts some lure to get you outside? I know you. You'd tell your guests and Abigail to wait inside while you check things out."

She frowned. He made a good point. "What if I promise to call you first?"

He just stared at her, and she sighed. He knew her too well to think calling him would stop her from going out before he arrived to investigate, especially if she thought there was a threat to her guests. She had several firearms and wouldn't hesitate to use one of them to defend her home.

"Fine. But I don't want to hear you complain about your back because you slept on the floor."

"I'll bring an air mattress."

She couldn't stop the giggle that escaped at the boyish smile on his handsome face.

"Where are you going that you need an air mattress?" Abigail asked, coming back through the door from the dining room.

"Your sitting room floor."

"Huh?" The girl's gaze bounced between the two adults.

London heaved a sigh. "Seb thinks he needs to stay here for a bit. Apparently, I look like the woman you and Trent found, and he wants to err on the side of caution."

The girl's eyes grew wide as she stared at her aunt. "Uh, yeah. I think that's a good idea too." She turned to Seb. "How much danger is she in?"

"She may not be in any, but I'm not taking any chances with safety for either of you. This murder was well-executed. Which means he's patient and will wait for the right opening. Until I catch him or we get an indication that he's moved on, I'm going to be a fixture around here."

Abigail nodded. "You don't need the air mattress, you know." She picked up a bowl of sliced fruit and turned toward the door. "Aunt London's bed is plenty big for both of you."

"Abigail!" London's face turned bright red.

The girl tossed them both a saucy smile and strolled out of the kitchen.

Face flaming, London refused to look at Seb. Instead, she moved in front of the stove and started cracking eggs into the skillet. She already had enough for everyone, but if she didn't do *something*, she was going to run crying from the room. It was getting harder every day to ignore how he made her feel. Why couldn't she have a crush on a man who wasn't off-limits?

The hair on the back of her neck rose and goosebumps erupted down her arms when Seb came up behind her and curled his hands over her shoulders. Leaning in, his breath washed over her ear, making the fine hairs around her face flutter. She bit back a moan and gripped the spatula in one hand and the skillet handle in the other.

"One day, you and I are going to have to address this." His voice was low and rumbled along her nerve-endings.

She steeled herself against the desire to turn in his arms and press her mouth to his. Instead, she took a shaky breath and scooted the eggs around in the pan. "No, we won't, because there's no point. It can't go anywhere." How she wished it could, but for Abigail's sake they had to stay just friends.

His hands tightened for a moment before he let her go and stepped back. "I need to get to work." His voice held a note of resignation.

She gave him a quick nod and continued to stare down at the skillet, moving eggs around. He opened the drawer next to the fridge and grabbed the foil to wrap his burrito. When he brought his plate to the sink, she cast a glance at him from the corner of her eye, unable to let him leave without one last look. His jaw was set and his expression strained. She hated what this was doing to them, but they simply couldn't jeopardize his relationship with Abigail.

He looked over at her and caught her staring at him. Electricity zinged between them and he swallowed hard. "I'll be back by dark. Make sure you lock up if you're here alone."

Without waiting for an answer, he let himself out through the garage door.

London expelled the breath she hadn't realized she was holding. Looking down at the skillet, she made a face of disgust. The eggs were burned. She picked up the pan and dumped its contents into the garbage disposal. Seb made her brain as addled and fried as the eggs.

Squinting against the bright sunlight, Seb stepped out of his truck and walked toward the employee entrance at the station, his hands full of his briefcase and his breakfast. He hadn't lied to London when he told her he needed to get to work. But he had used it as an excuse to leave. He could have stayed and finished his food, but her dismissal stung and he needed to get out of there before he did something that would forever change everything.

Juggling the items in his hands, he swiped his ID over the card reader and let himself into the building.

"Boss!"

Seb looked across the bullpen to see his desk sergeant waving at him from the other side of the room. Changing direction, he headed her way.

"Bering said he needs to talk to you," she said when he got close. "He's in his office."

"Thanks, Alaina." He gave her a quick nod and spun on his heel, altering his course once more.

He walked past his door to poke his head inside Caleb's office.

"What's up, Bering?"

Caleb looked up from hunting and pecking at his keyboard.

"I heard from the lab. They found at least two sets of clothes and they were burned months apart."

Seb frowned. "So, he's using the same place to burn the victims' clothing, even though he's abducting them from different states. We need to go back over that burn site. There might be more evidence there, if he frequents it."

Caleb nodded. "I was thinking the same thing. I have Gentry gathering field equipment and I called Randall's office about getting a couple forensic techs to come with us."

"Good. I'd come with you, but the mayor called before I even left my house this morning demanding an update in person as soon as possible. Where are you on identifying our victim?"

Caleb sighed. "Nowhere. She doesn't match any missing person in the state. Randall ran her DNA against theirs and none of them matched."

"Have you tried neighboring states?"

"Not yet. That was on my to-do list for today, but then I got the call from the lab about the clothes."

"After my meeting with the mayor, I'll run a search. See what I can come up with."

Commotion behind him made Seb turn to see Aaron Gentry coming down the hall.

He turned back to Bering. "Here comes your help. Let me know what you guys find." He pushed off the wall and went to his office. Juggling his briefcase over his wrist, he inserted the key in the lock and opened it. When he walked around his desk, he noticed the message light blinking on his phone and hit the playback button so he could listen to his messages while he finished his burrito.

The first message was from the mayor's assistant, reminding him of their meeting. He rolled his eyes and hit the button to skip it. The mayor wasn't bad, but Seb hated playing politics. Thank God it wasn't an election year. The next several were from reporters, asking for an update. The last one, though, had him sitting up and paying attention.

"Sheriff, this is Detective Jace Travers from the Haskell PD in Nebraska. I got your email about your murder case and I think we need to talk. Give me a call." He listed his phone number.

Seb stuffed the rest of his burrito in his mouth and dialed as he swallowed. He had emailed the police departments handling the three murders he found on the NCIC database. Haskell was one of them.

Travers picked up on the second ring.

"Hi, detective. This is Sheriff Archer, returning your call. You have some information for me?"

"Maybe. From your email, I think you might be right that the cases are connected. Tell me, when you found the woman, was she posed in a wedding dress?"

Seb's burrito settled like lead. "Holding a bouquet of flowers?"

"Fuck. I knew that scene was too sophisticated for a run-of-the-mill murder."

"In my NCIC search I found two others that match. I haven't heard back from those departments yet."

"Do you mind some company? I'll bring all my files, but I'd like to see yours too. If we put our heads together, maybe we can stop this guy."

"Sure. When do you think you can get here?"

Travers sighed. "Let me talk to my lieutenant to get the approval, but I should be able to be on the road in a couple hours. It's a six-hour drive there, then."

"Okay. Let me give you my cell number and when you get close, call me and I'll tell you where to meet me. And don't make hotel reservations. I have a place you can stay." He rattled off his number.

"Sounds good. Appreciate it. I'll let you know when I head out so you know about when to expect me."

"See you soon."

Seb set the phone back in its cradle, a surge of anticipation coursing through him. Maybe this would be the break they needed to find this killer.

Six

Laughter greeted London when she walked through the back door of Macy's coffee shop, Peppy Brewster, that evening after dinner. Once a month, they met here for a girls' night, masquerading as a book club. They talked about the book, but spent far more time sipping wine, snacking, and gossiping.

She pushed through the kitchen door to the main dining area where Tara and Macy already sat with the other member of their group, Rayna Nydert.

"Hi guys." London smiled at her friends and set the box of macarons she made that afternoon on the table beside them where all the other goodies were spread out.

"Oh, what did you make?" Macy asked, standing to see what was in the box.

"Macarons. Brownie, strawberry lemonade, and cookies n' cream."

Macy groaned and took one of each. "I both love and hate our monthly get-togethers." She stuffed the strawberry lemonade cookie in her mouth and moaned in delight. "When are you going to let me convince you to sell these in the café? You could make a killing on these things."

London grinned and grabbed a wine glass, filling it with a deep red pinot noir. "I don't have time to bake the amount you'd need to sell. It took me all afternoon just to make these three batches."

Macy pouted. "How about as a special now and then?"

She tipped her head. "That might work."

The other woman squealed. "Awesome!"

"So, London," Rayna said. "I hear you went on a date with Sebastian."

London groaned. "It was not a date. It was dinner. Between friends."

"Didn't look like just dinner," Tara said, stuffing a cookies n' cream macaron in her mouth.

London glared at her. "You all better watch it, or I'll take away the cookies."

In unison, all three women hugged the macarons to their chests.

"There's no need for such drastic measures. Drink your wine and tell us what really happened," Rayna said.

Doing as she suggested, London took a hearty gulp. It was too bad she couldn't get drunk, but she had to drive home. Some liquid courage might help her deal with Seb sleeping in her house tonight.

She sat down in one of the chairs. Eyes downcast, she toyed with the stem of her glass. "Nothing happened. Like I told Macy, he came to check on Abigail and it was around dinnertime. He asked if I'd eaten and when I said no, suggested we go get something. I only had a few guests at the inn and wasn't planning on cooking much for myself, so I said yes."

"So, why were you holding hands then?" Tara asked. "I saw the way you two were looking at each other."

London sighed. "This whole business with the dead woman brought back some memories from when Eddie and Camille died. We were talking about that."

The other three women shared a look. Rayna leaned forward and laid a hand on London's arm. "I'm sorry. We didn't even think about how this must affect you and Abigail."

She blew out a breath. "It's okay. We're doing all right. Abigail's a strong girl. She's handling it well."

"And you?" Tara asked, her voice soft.

London shrugged. "I'm doing okay. Although, this morning made me a little more uneasy."

"Why?" Macy asked.

"I got a present last night left on my doorstep. Bath bombs and a note that said, 'so you smell as sweet as your pretty flowers.'"

"What the hell?" Tara said. "Did you tell Seb?"

She nodded. "First thing this morning. That's when he told me I look like the murder victim."

"What?" Macy's exclamation was ear-piercing. "Please tell me you're being extra cautious."

"I am. And Seb's—" she broke off and inhaled a deep breath, eyeing each of her friends. "He's moving in."

Sly grins spread over all three women's faces. London rolled her eyes. "Get your minds out of the gutter. He's sleeping on the living room floor of the family quarters."

Macy's grin only grew. "Anyone want to take bets he's off that floor by the end of the weekend?"

London groaned and covered her eyes. "I hate you all."

They all laughed.

"Why are you so against a relationship with him? You two get along great and it's not like he's hard to look at," Rayna said.

"I don't want to risk his relationship with Abigail. She has to come first."

"Hon, the girl is sixteen. Things going south between you and Sebastian will not hinder her relationship with him. In two years, she may not even be living under your roof," Macy said. "I think you're just running scared."

London frowned. "No, I'm not."

"You totally are," Tara said, joining the conversation. "And so is Seb. You both have feelings for each other. Just admit them and move on."

"You're one to talk, Miss-I-haven't-had-a-date-in-years."

Tara held up a finger. "But I *was* married at one point. Since then, I've opened a business, and it has sucked up all my time. Your business is well-established. You don't have an excuse. I don't think you're scared about jeopardizing Abigail's relationship with Seb. I think you're scared of risking your own. If things go bad, you've not only lost a boyfriend, but a friend."

"She's right," Rayna said. "But if you don't risk it, you could lose out on the greatest thing to ever happen to you. He could be your forever."

London took another gulp of her wine and cast skeptical glances over the rim at the others. Was that really why she avoided starting something more with Seb? Was she hiding behind Abigail to save her own feelings? It would take more wine and a lot of soul-searching before she would have that answer, she was afraid.

"So, not to change the subject, but do you have any idea who sent the box?" Macy asked.

Grateful for the reprieve, London seized it. "Not really. No one has asked me out lately, and I haven't noticed anyone paying me any extra-special attention." She didn't mention Ryan Marsters. On the off-chance he was the one who sent it, she didn't want to embarrass him. He was sweet, and she didn't want him to think she was laughing at him by sharing his feelings with her friends.

"What's my brother doing about it?"

"He took the box and note to see if he can get any usable prints. I'm not really all that worried about it, to be honest. It's probably just from some local man who's too shy to say anything to me yet. If there hadn't been a murder, it wouldn't even be registering on the creepy-meter. Strange, yes, but not creepy."

"Well, I am glad he's moving in with you, even if it isn't for the reason we all want," Macy said. "It's too coincidental, and in this case, you can't be too cautious."

The others murmured their agreement.

Secretly, London was glad too. The gift was ill-timed if it was from someone who simply had a crush, and it gave her the creeps.

Cold seeped through Seb's clothing as he leaned on the bed of his truck, awaiting Jace Travers's arrival. He turned the collar up on his jacket and wished he hadn't taken his heavier coat out of the vehicle. Tonight was a huge contrast to the warm weather they'd been experiencing over the last week.

Headlights pierced the darkness, and he straightened. It had to be Travers. This far out of town, there wasn't much traffic.

The vehicle—a late-model pickup—slowed as it approached the turnoff for The Broken Bow's drive. It turned onto the gravel path and came to a stop behind his truck. Seb walked forward as the driver shut off the engine and stepped from the vehicle.

He took stock of the man who emerged. An inch or two shorter than his own six-foot-five, Jace Travers was a large man.

Dressed casually in jeans, a polo shirt, and a jacket, muscles strained the fabric. Honey-colored hair, cut short on the sides and longer on top, waved in the slight breeze.

"Detective Travers?"

The man nodded and held out a hand. "Jace, please. It's nice to meet you, Sheriff. Sorry it's so late. I got held up in Haskell."

Seb shook his hand. "That's all right. I'm just glad you made the drive. And call me Seb. If you'll follow me, I'll show you to where you'll be staying and we can go over what we both know."

They climbed back into their vehicles and Seb led him through the gate and up the lane, past his sister's restaurant and to a cluster of buildings that made up the family compound. It consisted of the main house and several smaller homes for him and each of his siblings, and a bunkhouse for their ranch hands who wanted to live on the property.

He led Jace to a one-story, white clapboard house in the middle of the complex. Parking out front, he grabbed his briefcase from the passenger seat and got out of the truck, meeting Jace at the edge of the walkway leading to the front porch.

Jace looked around, interest shining in his blue eyes. "Where are we?"

"This is my family's ranch. This," he motioned to the house in front of them, "is my house. The other smaller ones belong to my siblings. My parents live in the main house over there." He gestured to the larger two-story house with its gray siding and full front porch. Lights shone in the windows on the lower level and Seb knew his mom and dad were probably in the living room watching some weekly crime drama.

"Come inside and I'll explain why we're here."

The men clomped up the porch steps and Seb opened the door, leading Jace into the modest living room. Rich leather furniture dominated the room, set around an area rug in shades of red and gold. Pictures of his family lined the beige walls, and a TV sat mounted over the fireplace.

Seb tossed his keys into the dish on the table by the door. "You want a beer?"

"Wouldn't turn one down."

They wandered into the kitchen. Seb set his satchel on the table and pulled two local craft brews from his refrigerator. Popping off their tops, he handed one to Jace, then took a swig from his own.

"Have a seat." He motioned to the small table tucked into the corner of the room.

Seb took the chair by the window and set his beer down, opening his briefcase. Jace laid his file folder down and flipped it open.

"This is everything I've got so far," Seb said, pushing a folder across the table at the detective.

Jace handed over his own folder and both men started reading.

The similarities were alarming. Both women were discovered in abandoned buildings on a bed, wearing a vintage wedding dress, with their hands placed on their chest and holding a bouquet of flowers. He pulled out the picture of the woman Haskell PD identified and his gut clenched. Charity Bledell. She bore a resemblance to London as well.

"I'd say we're definitely looking for the same man," Jace said, looking up from the file.

Seb nodded. "Yeah. I see you didn't have any more luck finding a lead on the killer than I have."

Jace shook his head. "Nope. Other than the flowers, which were picked from the wild, and the dress, which we couldn't trace, there wasn't anything else left on her body or under her nails. Our tox screen didn't show any drugs in her system. The M.E. said she'd been dead about a month when we found her. She disappeared a few weeks before that."

"So, he held onto her for a bit?"

Jace nodded. "Yeah. The coroner also found evidence of rape, but couldn't get any DNA."

"Was she a local?"

"Not really. She was in the area for seasonal work at the state park. Our M.E. got a partial print from her, and it was in the law enforcement database. She had to be fingerprinted for her job. We never found her clothing or her ID."

"I think I might have a lead on that. We found a small bonfire site when canvassing the mountainside for clues, and it contained remnants of clothing from more than one person. Our lab identified at least two sets and said it's possible there were more, but they had turned to total ash. Do you know what Ms. Bledell was wearing when she disappeared?"

"Jeans and a pink sleeveless blouse. Her roommate reported her missing after she didn't come home from a date. And before you ask, we checked out the man she went out with and he came back clean. He said they drove separately, and he said goodnight to her at the bar, then went home. He bought gas on the way to his house. We have a receipt for that and the neighbor's doorbell camera across the street verified him arriving home ten minutes later. He didn't leave again until the next morning."

Seb sat back, thinking. "I got phone calls from the other two departments today. They said pretty much the same thing you did about how she was found. They also never found her clothes or ID. I think the killer might be local to this area since we found the clothing remnants here."

"That, or he's afraid someone might find the clothes, possibly because he's moving or someone moved in with him, so he needed to dispose of them all. He might be mobile too and needed to ditch them."

He could see the argument there. It was possible something about this last victim could link him to her—blood or other trace evidence—and out of fear, he had burned all the clothes, not just hers. But it didn't explain the difference in when the clothes were burned.

"If that was the case, then all the clothes would have been burned at once and not at separate times."

"Okay, let's go with your theory, then. The guy's a local. Who do you think it could be?"

That was the million-dollar question. He had his fair share of drunks and rabble-rousers, but someone capable of such a cold-blooded killing? No one came to mind.

"To be honest, I'm not sure. No one is leaping out at me. I have one guy I want to look into, but I doubt it's him."

A curious frown dipped Jace's brow. "How so?"

"My—friend, London Scott, had a present left at her door last night. It was a box of bath bombs with an unsigned note. She gave me a name of who she thought it might be from, but wasn't certain. One of the local store owners may have a bit of a crush, but he's a lot older than she is. I also can't see him doing something so heinous. He's a nice guy. A little lonely, maybe, but not a killer." Seb's mouth tightened at the thought of someone stalking London. Innocent or not, he didn't like it.

"What makes you think her gift is connected to the murders?"

Seb took out his phone and pulled up a picture he took recently of London. She had been elbow-deep in flour, baking, and looked adorable. He hadn't been able to resist, despite her pleas for him to put the phone away.

He showed the picture to Jace. "This is London."

His eyes widened.

Seb clicked the phone off and stuffed it back in his pocket. "I know. She could be a dead ringer for either of our victims. I told her I'm moving in for the foreseeable future."

Jace studied him, and Seb could tell he was trying to figure him out.

"What's your relationship with that woman? You said friend, but you hesitated."

Seb sighed and took another pull of his beer. "It's complicated. My best friend was her brother and I'm godfather to his daughter, Abigail. Eddie died about five years ago along with his wife in a car accident. London took over raising her niece. She doesn't want to start anything because it could risk my relationship with her, but Abigail is sixteen now. I'm starting to wonder if things went sour between us, if it would really affect what I have with Abigail. She's like a daughter to me. I don't see anything ever changing that."

Jace took a sip of his beer. "Take it from someone who knows, don't wait. If you have feelings for this woman—real, could be forever-type of feelings—act on them. Life's too short."

He studied the younger man over his beer bottle, but said nothing. The set to Jace's jaw said it all.

"Well, regardless of the status of our non-relationship, I'm staying with her starting tonight." He pushed back his chair and stood. "Come on. I'll show you the guest room and you can get settled in while I pack a bag."

Seb led him down the hall to a tidy room. A maple frame, queen-size bed sat in the center of one wall, covered by a light blue quilt and flanked by matching end tables. A dresser hugged another wall, completing the bedroom suite. More photographs like those in his sister's restaurant graced the walls.

Jace walked up to the one hanging over the dresser of an old cowboy, knees crooked from years on a horse, standing in the middle of a herd of cattle. The sunset cast golden rays through the dust and put deep shadows on the hollows of his face.

"Wow." He looked back as Seb. "Do you know who took this?"

"My sister, Tara."

Jace peered at the photo again. "I think I'd like to meet her sometime. See what else she's taken."

"I imagine you will while you're here. She owns the restaurant we passed on the way to the family complex. She was a photojournalist before she moved back home and decided to open a restaurant."

"Why did she give up her career?"

"It's complicated." It wasn't Seb's story to tell, so he stopped there.

Jace gave him a quizzical look but didn't ask any further questions.

"Did you eat?" Seb asked.

"I had a burger from a fast-food joint a couple hours ago. I figured I'd find a grocery store and get some snacks to tide me over."

"I'll take you down to The Heartwood before I head to London's. Right now, though, why don't you go get your bag while I pack, then I'll take you over to the main house to meet my parents. I told them you were coming, but I want them to meet you. So they're not wondering if you're the detective I talked about or some random stranger."

Jace nodded. "Sounds good. And thanks for letting me stay here. This is a lot nicer than any hotel room."

Seb smiled. "You haven't seen London's B&B. If she had room, I'd have recommended you stay there."

"Still, it's nice to have some privacy. I'm not much for crowds."

"You will definitely have solitude out here," he said as he turned on his heel to exit the room. Jace followed, and they went their separate ways.

In his bedroom, Seb grabbed a duffel from his closet and

quickly stuffed it full of clothing. He wasn't sure how long he would need to stay, but he didn't plan on coming back until he knew for sure London was safe.

As he packed, he couldn't help but think about what Jace said. Maybe it was time he asked London on a date. He was tired of denying he didn't have feelings for her. Tired of pretending he didn't want to wrap his arms around her and just hold her. He'd been attracted to her for years—even before he returned permanently to Silver Gap. The last two years had only made that attraction stronger. He couldn't imagine life without her and wanted her to be a bigger part of it.

Frustrated and still unsure of what his next move should be, he tugged the zipper closed on his bag with a little more force than necessary. He wished he had time to go for a long run, but he needed to get over to the B&B. It would be dark soon.

Back in the living room, Jace stood near the fireplace, looking at the pictures on the wall.

"You've got a big family. How many of you are there?"

"I have two brothers and two sisters. You?"

"Only child."

One corner of Seb's mouth rose. "Bummer."

Jace grinned. "It wasn't all bad. I didn't have to argue with anyone over who got the Nintendo."

Seb laughed. "Brady and Thomas were terrible about that. There were several times they both wished they were an only child."

"I'll bet." He pointed to another picture. "Is this your friend Eddie?"

Seb stepped closer. He peered at the picture and smiled. Eddie, Camille, and Abigail grinned back at him, silly party hats on their heads. "Yeah. That was taken about a year before the accident at Abigail's tenth birthday party." He pointed to another picture of Abigail and London sitting on the mantle next to the TV. "I took that one at Christmas this past year."

"She looks happy."

"She is. London's had a lot to do with that. I was an FBI agent when Eddie and Camille died, so I can't take the credit for a lot of the healing she's done. I did what I could, but it was hard to be there consistently when I lived in Denver and was frequently away on assignment. Two years ago, the sheriff here retired, so I returned home and ran for election. It's been nice being in her life full-time."

"And you didn't step on any toes by just throwing your hat in the ring after being away from the area?"

He shook his head. "Not really. My family is well known around here, and my chief deputy didn't want the job. Said he liked not having his head on the chopping block with the city mayors and the county commissioners. I spent years dealing with bureaucrats, so the politics were something I was used to. None of the other deputies on the force had the qualifications to take on the job, and none of the other candidates from other local agencies had as much experience as me."

Jace nodded and glanced over the family pictures once more, his eyes pausing on London. "Cherish them, man. You never know what life will throw at you."

Again, Seb got the feeling there was a story behind that comment, but didn't ask. It wasn't his business. Instead, he hooked a thumb toward the door. "You ready to meet my folks and grab some food?"

Jace turned away from the pictures and nodded. "Lead the way."

"We'll take the cars. Normally, I'd walk over to Mom and Dad's, but I need to get to town." He led Jace outside where they made their way over to the main house a quarter mile away. When they reached the house, Seb took the steps two at a time and rapped his knuckles on the door and paused a moment before twisting the knob and letting himself in.

As he had predicted, his parents were in the living room, watching television.

"Hi, honey," his mother said with a smile. She had her silver-streaked brown hair pulled back by a headband, revealing her pretty face.

His dad echoed her greeting and muted the TV.

Seb smiled back. "Mom, Dad, this is the detective I told you about earlier, Jace Travers. Jace, these are my parents, Lee and Jenny."

"Sir, ma'am. It's nice to meet you." Jace tipped his head and offered the couple a warm smile.

Lee unfolded his long frame from his seat to come over and shake Jace's hand. A smile brightened his normally serious face, laugh lines creasing around his dark eyes.

"You too, young man. Seb said you've come to help him solve this murder."

"Hopefully, yes."

"Good. If you need anything, don't hesitate to stop by."

"I will. Thank you, sir."

"Call me Lee."

Jace nodded.

"Did you boys eat?" Jenny asked, coming to stand next to her husband.

"I was going to take him down to The Heartwood."

"Oh, that's much better than the ham sandwiches I was going to offer you," she said with a chuckle.

Seb grinned down at his mother. "I don't know about better, but I think we're both hungry for more than just a sandwich."

Jenny affected an affronted air, but spoiled it with a smile. "Fine. Go. Let Tara feed you."

Seb laughed and kissed his mom on her cheek. "I still love you."

The screen door at the back of the house banged and Seb straightened, turning toward the hall. Boots thumped on the wood floor and his brother Brady appeared. He paused in the doorway when his eyes landed on Jace. He cast a small frown at Seb.

Recognizing it for the question it was, he introduced them.

"I'm glad you got some help," Brady said to Seb as he shook Jace's hand. "Bering is a good cop, but I think he's out of his depth on this."

Seb agreed. Caleb had lived his entire life where the crime rate was low and murders were few and far between. There was a reason the department didn't have a full-time detective.

"Jace will be staying at my house. I'm staying with London and Abigail until this blows over."

Brady grinned. "It's about damn time you did something about that woman."

Seb looked at the ceiling, biting back a groan. "Why does everyone keep saying that?"

Jenny giggled. "Because we all know you're meant for each other. Your father and I have known it since London was a teenager."

He rubbed his forehead and sighed, tired of explaining his relationship with London to everyone. He glanced at Jace. "I'm beginning to see the benefits of being an only child."

Jace laughed.

Seb just shook his head and looked at Brady. "Would you let Thomas and Maggie know about Jace? I'll tell Tara when we see her. We're going to her restaurant for dinner."

"She's not there."

Seb frowned. "Where is she?"

"It's the first Wednesday of the month."

His frown only deepened. "So?"

"Book club? With your girl, Rayna, and Macy?"

"Shit, I forgot about that." He leaned forward and pressed another quick kiss to his mother's cheek. "We need to go. I don't want London driving home alone in the dark."

"Why the hell not?" Brady asked. "She's been doing it for years."

"I'll explain later." He headed for the door. "Come on, Travers."

Jace waved a quick goodbye to the others and followed Seb back to the cars.

"You can go on ahead into town. I can find my way to the restaurant."

Seb hesitated. He knew he was probably overreacting. There was nothing indicating that London was in any imminent danger. "You're sure?"

"Hell, yes. Go find your woman and make sure she's okay."

He only stood there another moment before he pulled on the door handle and hopped up into his truck. "Come to the station in the morning. I'll find you a desk and you can dive in with the rest of us."

Jace gave him a thumbs up and moved toward his own car. Seb didn't wait for him to follow.

The four women exited the back of the café, giggling like schoolgirls. None of them had more than a glass of wine the entire evening, but the girl time allowed them to let loose. London always left feeling lighter.

A black truck rumbled into the parking lot as they said their goodbyes. She recognized Seb behind the wheel. He came to a stop beside her car and some of her lightness fled as she automatically tensed, steeling herself against the onslaught of feelings he always provoked.

"Seb, do you not know what 'girls' night' means?" Tara said in a droll voice.

He flashed a grin at his sister. "Hey. I waited till it was over. I'm just here to make sure London gets home safe."

"And what about the rest of us? Are we chopped liver?" Rayna said.

London stifled a laugh at the look on his face. He immediately backpedaled.

"It's just that London matches the victimology of the killer and I—"

Macy's laughter cut him off. London couldn't hold back her own giggles. He looked so flummoxed by Rayna's question.

"Relax, copper," Macy said. "We know why you're here for El and not the rest of us."

He visibly relaxed, then speared London with his dark eyes. "I take it they know about your present?"

"Yes. And my resemblance to your victim."

"Good. Then they can keep an eye out for anything weird. Are you ready to go home?"

She nodded, noting the weariness in his voice and the slight droop around his eyes. Seb was tired.

"I'll see you guys later," she said to her friends. They murmured their goodbyes again and climbed into their cars. London started the engine to hers and followed Sebastian out of the parking lot and onto the road leading to the B&B. In minutes, they were turning into the drive.

She pulled into the garage and shut off the car. Abigail's car sat silently next to hers, but she knew the girl wasn't home yet. Trent had picked her up and wouldn't bring her back until her curfew at midnight.

Exiting her vehicle, she rounded the car and took out the

box with the leftover macarons. She shut the passenger door just as Seb walked into the garage. He took her keys from her and unlocked the interior door.

She set her things down on the counter and looked up at him. "I need to prep for breakfast tomorrow, but if you want to go on up and get settled, you can."

"Actually, do you mind if I make a sandwich? I haven't had any dinner."

"What?" She pointed at the small table tucked against the wall. "Sit. I'll make you something. What do you want?"

"You don't need to go to any trouble. A sandwich is fine. Mom offered me one, but I wanted to get back to town before you headed home."

She crossed her arms and cocked an eyebrow at him, refusing to budge.

He huffed and sagged into a chair. "Fine. I don't care what it is. Something quick. It's been a long time since lunch."

She immediately spun around and went to the fridge and took out ingredients for a gourmet grilled cheese. She had planned to make some brie and cranberry tarts for breakfast later in the week, but she figured she could spare some of it to make him dinner.

"So, why did you skip dinner? Did something break on your case?" she asked as she cut the rind off the cheese.

He let out a long sigh. "Sort of. I got a call this morning from a detective in Nebraska. They had a murder there last year that matches the one here. He drove in today and I met him out at the ranch this evening. I was going to eat at The Heartwood, but then Brady mentioned your book club and I wanted to be here to make sure you made it home all right."

The thought she might not have made her pause for a moment as she prepped his food. "I would have been fine. You could have taken the time to eat."

He shrugged. "I'd rather make sure you're okay. It's not like I can't eat later."

She tossed a mock glare over her shoulder at him. "If you want your brain to function properly, you need to eat."

He laughed. "If that's the case, I must be a genius, because I skip meals all the time and do just fine."

She rolled her eyes. Picking up the pieces of brie she sliced off the wheel, she layered them onto some bread she'd baked that morning and put them on a baking tray. Pushing the button for the broiler on the oven, she slid the tray inside and set the timer before moving back to the fridge.

"Do you want some pasta salad with this?"

"Sure."

Spying the container on the bottom shelf, she picked it up and set it on the counter, then grabbed a plate from the cupboard and spooned a healthy portion onto it.

"What do you want to drink?"

He yawned and ran a hand over his face. "Coffee."

She glared at him for real this time. "It's almost nine o'clock, Sebastian."

"Fine. Water."

Her movements efficient, London poured his water, then put two slices of cooked bacon into the microwave to warm them up. While they warmed, she sliced an apple. As she finished, the timer beeped, and she pulled his sandwich from the oven. Layering the warm bacon and apple slices over the melted brie, she drizzled the whole thing with honey and set it on the plate with the pasta salad, then sliced it in half.

Tearing off a couple sheets of toweling and taking a fork from the drawer, she carried the plate and water glass over to the table, then sat down across from him.

"So, tell me about this detective. What's his name? Did he share anything useful? And why did you meet him out at The Broken Bow?"

"His name is Jace Travers. He confirmed we're dealing with a serial killer. The M.O. of the murder in Haskell matches the one here. And I'm letting him stay at my house. You're the only lodging around here other than that rundown place out off the highway. I figured since I would be staying with you, he could have my house." He took another huge bite of his sandwich. "This is good," he said after swallowing.

She eyed a point over his shoulder and tried not to imagine the way he would look sleeping, especially as that image was of him naked and in her bed. "About that. Are you sure it's a good idea? I think I'll be fine with all the guests here."

He dropped the sandwich back on his plate, an intense frown marring his handsome face. "I'm not budging on this, London. Either I stay here or you can kick everyone out and you and Abigail come stay at the ranch."

Her eyes narrowed and her hackles rose at his ultimatum. She had never done well being told what to do. Eddie always thought he was the boss of her when they were children because he was so much older. It had never ended well for him and it wasn't going to for Seb, either.

"Sebastian Archer, if I want you out of here, you will leave, do you understand? I only agreed to this arrangement because I think it'll help Abigail feel better about what's happening, but if you don't stop acting like my big brother, you can go home."

He leaned forward, his mouth tight. "Let's get one thing straight. Brotherly concern has nothing to do with why I'm here."

Before she could react to that statement, he rose halfway out of his chair to lean the rest of the way over the table and seal his mouth to hers.

Too stunned to do more than squawk in surprise, she reveled in the feel of his lips against her own. That lush mouth she had admired for years was unyielding, but soft. As the surprise faded, sensation took over, and she responded to the kiss.

He cupped the side of her head in one hand to steady her and then deepened the kiss. London eagerly let him in. He tasted like honey. The kitchen faded away until it was just them, existing in a plane of pure heat. By the time he broke their lip lock, she was nothing but a quivering ball of nerve-endings.

London sat stunned in her seat. Her gaze connected with his. The fire, while banked slightly, was still there in his eyes.

"Why did you do that?" she asked, her voice just above a whisper.

He took an unsteady breath and raked a hand through his hair. "Because I'm tired of pretending I don't have feelings for you. Of sidestepping this insane attraction. I like you. I have for a long time."

Her eyes widened in shock. "What?" she squeaked.

The pocket door to the kitchen slid open and London about fell out of her chair. She turned her head to see Doug Brown standing in the doorway, wearing nothing but a silk bathrobe and slippers.

Seb growled in frustration and stood, walking to the sink to lean against the counter and stare out the window.

London cleared her throat and rose. "Mr. Brown, hello. It's late, and the kitchen is closed to guests. There are snacks and drinks in the dining room if you're hungry."

"I know, but it's not that. My shower isn't working," he said. "All I get is cold water."

The desire fled only to be replaced by confusion. "What?" She looked back at Seb. He turned on the hot water tap on the sink and stuck his hand under it.

"It's not getting warm."

London groaned. "Great."

He pushed away from the counter. "You stay here and

work on breakfast prep. I'll go check it out. Maybe the pilot light went out."

"I hope that's all it is." She turned back to Mr. Brown. "I'm sorry. We'll get it straightened out as quickly as possible. Thank you for letting me know."

He nodded and backed out of the kitchen.

"Where's your flashlight?"

She pointed to the cabinet under the sink. "Down there. You'll need my keys too. But I can go look at the heater. Finish your food."

He just frowned at her for a moment before opening the cupboard door and grabbing the flashlight. Walking toward the door, he snagged her keys from her purse, then stopped to stand in front of her.

That now familiar heat ratcheted back up in London's belly at his proximity.

"It'll keep."

From the fire in his eyes, she could tell he meant more than just the food.

With one last lingering look, he brushed past her to exit the kitchen.

London covered her face with her hands. What the hell just happened?

Seven

Seb twisted the key in the lock and yanked open the door to the utility room with a little more force than necessary. The world seemed to be conspiring against him in his attempt to convince London they should be more than friends. Her guest had terrible timing.

He did his best to push the best kiss of his life from his mind and reached for the light switch. Millimeters from flipping it on, he stopped. Was that gas he smelled?

He sniffed again and lowered his hand. It was.

He backed out of the room, then turned and ran back to the kitchen. London stood at the counter, preparing to chop fruit for tomorrow morning.

"There's a gas leak in the utility room. I don't know how bad, but we need to evacuate the inn and call the fire department."

She blinked at him for a moment before her eyes widened. "What?"

"I smelled gas when I went in there. Go get all your guests to the evac point. I'll call the fire department."

As she raced from the room to do as he asked, he took out

his phone to dial 911. After reporting the problem, he ran outside to help guide the guests to safety under the large maple on the front lawn.

He walked up to London. "Is this everyone?" He ran an assessing look over the group. Three couples stood huddled together in conversation while Doug Brown stood off to the side, back against the tree, looking annoyed. Seb narrowed his eyes and studied the man. The background check he ran on the guy came back clean, but something about him still felt off. Maybe he needed to dig a little deeper.

London nodded. "The Strattman's aren't back yet and neither is one of the couples who checked in earlier today. Everyone else is here."

Sirens sounded in the distance, and flashing lights soon flickered through the growing darkness.

Seb turned to London. "Keep your guests calm. I'll let the lieutenant know what's going on."

She nodded, and he jogged forward to meet the firetruck as it blared up the drive and came to a stop in front of the garage.

Several men clambered from the truck, garbed in their turnout gear. One man spotted Seb and headed toward him.

Seb waved, recognizing fire lieutenant Declan Briggs.

"Seb. What's the situation? We got a call that someone smelled gas."

"Yeah. From me. London and I were in the kitchen when one of her guests came down to say there wasn't any hot water. I went to check the water heater and didn't even get the light in the utility room turned on. The smell of gas hit me as soon as I stepped in the room."

Declan nodded. "We'll check it out. Where in the house is the room?"

"Toward the back. When you go in the front door, there's a short hallway to the right that goes past the stairs. It leads to a game room. It's off the back of that, next to the bathroom."

"Do you know where the gas meter is?"

"Back of the house."

Declan turned to his men and let out a sharp whistle. "Stickley, go shut off the gas around back."

One man peeled off from the group. He grabbed a wrench and flashlight from the truck and took off for the back of the house.

"The rest of you, get the fans out." He turned back to Seb. "Once the gas is off, we'll check out the heater and the pipes. Is everyone accounted for?" He cast a glance at the group standing by the tree.

Seb nodded.

"Good." Declan's radio crackled to life as the fireman who went to shut off the gas gave the all clear.

"Hang tight. We'll get this cleared and hopefully everyone back in soon." Not waiting for a response, he turned to jog back to the truck and helped his men carry equipment into the house.

Seb walked back to London.

"What did he say?" she asked.

"They turned off the gas at the meter and are going in now to check the heater and the pipes."

While they waited, Seb stood there, arms crossed and legs spread in a wide stance, doing his best not to throw an arm over London's shoulders and tuck her into his side. He wasn't sure she would be receptive to such a gesture.

She had been to his kiss, though. A low hum started in his gut just thinking about it. That kiss had twisted him up and made him realize that all his other relationships—even the ones he thought had been great—were mediocre compared to what London made him feel.

He glanced at her from the corner of his eye. She stared at

the house, arms crossed over her chest and her face pinched in worry. Unable to stand there and watch her like that without comforting her, he curled a hand over her shoulder. She reached up and covered his hand with hers, giving it a squeeze. Seb moved a little closer and covered her other shoulder.

"It'll be okay," he whispered in her ear. He knew how much the inn meant to her and hated to see her so worried about it. This place had been her dream for a long time; it would devastate her if anything happened to it.

Minutes ticked by with only an occasional thump or shout from inside as the firefighters worked. Just when he thought London might run in there herself to help, Declan came back out. He spotted them and headed their way, removing his helmet and tucking it under his arm as he walked.

"London, who has access to your house besides your guests?" he asked when he reached them. He brushed at a lock of auburn hair that had fallen over his forehead, leaving it more disheveled than it was before.

Seb's mouth turned down. That was a rather ominous question.

"Until this weekend, I've left the doors unlocked during the day so the guests can come and go. With the murder, Seb asked me to start locking up, so I have been the last couple days. Why?"

Declan's deep blue eyes bounced back and forth between them before his mouth settled in a grim line. "Your pilot light was out. Now, your heater is fairly new, and they all have a valve that automatically shuts off when the light goes out to stop gas from leaking into the house. The valve on yours didn't close."

"So, there was some sort of mechanical malfunction?" she asked.

"Not exactly. Someone deliberately damaged the valve."

London gasped and covered her mouth.

"You're sure?" Seb asked.

Declan nodded. "There are saw marks from probably a file on part of the mechanism. When the light went out, it closed and the valve flap snapped off and it wasn't able to block the flow of gas." Declan looked at Seb. "I left everything untouched so you can have a CSU take pictures and run it for prints."

Seb muttered an oath under his breath. "Okay. Thanks."

"Why would someone do that?" London looked up at him, her pretty blue eyes watery. "It doesn't make any sense."

He agreed. It seemed unlikely that the same person who sent her the bath bombs would also try to blow up her house. But was it possible she had a stalker and an admirer? He scrubbed his hands over his face and sighed. Why couldn't anything be simple?

"Can you guys check the rest of the gas lines in the house to make sure there aren't any more problems?"

Declan gave a quick nod. "Already have my men on it. As soon as I get the all clear, everyone can go back inside. The fans make quick work of venting the gas and should have gotten it all by then."

"Thanks, Deck," London said. "I appreciate it."

"Not a problem. I wouldn't recommend relighting the heater, though, until you can get it fixed. If you can't get a plumber out here tomorrow, let me know and I can come by and fix it."

"I will keep that in mind," London said. "Thanks."

"Sure thing. I'll see you guys later. Holler if you need something." He walked away to go help his men, leaving them standing there to process what he said.

"What do we do, Seb?"

Rage filled Seb's chest as he looked down at her. She was hugging herself again, and tears threatened to spill down her cheeks. Whoever was behind this better hope there were witnesses when Seb found him.

"I'm going to call in a crime unit, *discretely*, so we don't alarm the guests. Then, you and I are going to have a very serious talk about installing some security cameras around the property."

"I don't have the budget for that."

"We'll figure something out, but I can't be here twenty-four-seven and there isn't enough of a connection between you and my murder case to justify posting an officer on the property. I can probably get some volunteers, but there may be holes in the schedule. I told you yesterday, I won't take chances with your safety or Abigail's and I meant it."

She swallowed hard and nodded. Seb felt a surge of pride when she took a deep, steadying breath and straightened her shoulders. "Right. I will go tell everyone what's going on without alarming them and offer them a complimentary night for the trouble. When you find the person responsible for this, I want reimbursement to be part of their punishment."

Seb's mouth quirked. "Duly noted."

When she walked off, he took out his phone and called dispatch to request a crime scene unit, resigning himself to the fact that sleep was going to be put off a little longer.

Bleary-eyed and only partially awake, London stumbled into the living room on her way to the bathroom the next morning. As she walked past the couch, her foot kicked Sebastian's ankle and sent her crashing into the wall. The clothing in her arms went flying.

She hit with a loud thud and pain radiated up her forearm. Holding the bruised appendage, she turned around to glare at

Seb in the dark. "For heaven's sake. Why are you *behind* the couch?"

Anything else she was going to say died in her throat when he sat up and reached one long arm over the back of the end table to snap on the lamp. Her bra had landed on his chest. His one hundred percent naked chest.

A teasing gleam entered his eyes as he held up the lacy garment. "This is not how I imagined waking up, but I'm not complaining."

Oh my God! She knew her face was as red as the firetruck that had been there last night, but she couldn't help it. Stepping forward, she snatched it out of his hands and quickly gathered up the rest of her clothes.

A massive yawn cracked his jaw, and he stretched. His naked chest glowed bronze in the soft light, a dusting of fine, black hair covering his pecs and trailing down his rock-hard abdomen to disappear beneath the afghan.

London gripped the clothing in her hands and locked her knees as she watched his muscles flex with the movement.

"I tried to stretch out on the other side, but unless I wanted to move the furniture, there wasn't enough room for me without blocking the door. It was just easier to lie down back here."

She swallowed hard and looked at a point over his shoulder. If she made eye contact with him now, she would melt into a pile of goo at his feet. "Maybe for future reference, scoot up a little more." Without waiting for a reply, she spun on her heel and high-tailed it down the hall to the bathroom, fleeing from the temptation he presented. No matter what he said last night, she still didn't think a relationship between them was a good idea.

Crossing the bathroom threshold, she stopped herself from slamming the door at the last second. She didn't want to wake Abigail, though, she probably already had with her header into the wall.

Inhaling a deep breath to steady herself, she turned on the shower tap and stripped out of her pajamas. She stuck her hand in the water to test the temperature; it was still ice cold.

"Crap." Last night's events came rushing back, and she hung her head. A cold shower was not how she envisioned starting her day. She heaved a sigh. Steeling herself for the icy spray, she stepped into the tub, stifling a yelp as the freezing water hit her skin. It was like taking a dip in the river at the start of the spring thaw.

She hurried through washing her hair and skipped the conditioner. A quick lather and rinse of her body and she turned off the water, shivering so hard her teeth chattered. Irritated now, she tore back the curtain and grabbed a fluffy towel from the linen closet and wrapped herself in its warmth. Taking a smaller towel out, she dried her hair. At least now she wasn't all hot and bothered by the sight of Sebastian's chiseled muscles.

Dressing quickly, she exited the bathroom and prayed he had put on a shirt. She didn't think the cold shower would help her with a second sighting.

He sat on the couch—still shirtless—watching the morning news. She did her very best not to look directly at him as she walked toward the door.

"I'm going to head down and make breakfast. Stop in the kitchen before you leave for work and I'll feed you." She bent down to slide on her shoes and sent a glance at him from under her arm.

He stood up, clothes in his hands, and London jerked.

He wasn't wearing any pants.

Thrown by the sight of his snug gray boxer-briefs, clinging to hair-roughened, muscular thighs—not to mention the very male part of him outlined in stark relief by the tight fabric—she crashed into the door.

"Are you all right?" he asked, stepping toward her.

She held out a hand and scurried back to her feet. If he touched her, she would not be responsible for wrapping her legs around his waist and kissing that delectable mouth of his.

Hair now a complete mess, she blew at the strands covering her face, swiping at them when that failed. "I'm fine. Totally fine. Go take a shower. I'll see you downstairs." Deciding it was best to just beat a quick retreat, she grabbed her shoes and flung the door open, hurrying out and closing it behind her. As it snicked shut, her eyes widened in horror. She had left her phone and keys inside.

Biting her lip, she stared at the doorknob.

"Dammit!" Her harsh whisper filled the hallway.

She took a deep, steadying breath and lifted her fist, hesitating a moment before tapping lightly on the door. Hopefully, he hadn't retreated to the bathroom yet, so she wouldn't have to knock louder and wake Abigail.

The door opened and she came face-to-face with Seb's glorious chest. Her eyes darted up, away from temptation, to his face. He stared at her with a curious look.

"I forgot my phone and my keys."

"Oh." He stepped back and let her in. She hurried past him and into her bedroom where she scooped them off her dresser. When she turned around, he leaned against the doorjamb, arms crossed, biceps bulging.

All the blood left her brain and headed south to pool low in her belly. She couldn't have formed a coherent sentence if her life depended on it.

"You okay?" he asked. "You seem a little scattered."

She shook her head to try to make her brain work again. "I'm fine. Just tired."

Move! Why did he continue to block the door? Did he not know how he looked standing there?

London straightened and took a step toward him, hoping he'd get out of her way.

He remained where he was, though, and London stopped in front of him, clutching her phone, keys, and shoes so she didn't reach out and touch that perfect chest.

"I thought you needed to take a shower," she said, doing her damnedest not to look down.

His eyes blazed as he stared at her. "I do. It's too bad you already took one."

Fire raced through her to light up her face. Her breath came in shallow bursts.

She clutched her things tighter until her knuckles turned white.

He swayed closer. She could feel the heat radiating off of him. Her fingers tingled, wanting to touch. She clenched her teeth and willed herself to keep her distance.

He had no such desire, however, and shuffled closer. She had to tip her head to look up at him. His dark eyes stared down at her, need blazing.

She wilted a bit under the intensity and let her hands— still full—rest against his chest. He brought a hand up to cup her face and stroked her cheekbone with his thumb.

"Seb." The word came out on a sigh. Her eyes fluttered at his touch.

He leaned down and pressed the lightest of kisses on the corner of her mouth, then stepped back.

"Go. Before I decide I want to see what that bra looks like on you." His voice was rough, and his muscles rigid as he stood to the side to let her pass.

At least she wasn't the only one feeling this insanity.

She forced her feet to move and crossed to the door, fumbling with the things in her hands to turn the knob.

Wrenching the door open, she stepped through. As she pulled it closed, she couldn't resist one last look at all that masculinity on display. He stood where she left him, but now he had both hands on his hips and his eyes locked on her.

Their eyes connected again. She bit her lip as another surge of desire hit her and closed the door.

A soft groan passed her lips as she leaned against the wall. She closed her eyes and hung her head, trying to get herself under control. Every nerve-ending she possessed was on high-alert after that encounter.

Pulling in a deep breath, she bent and tugged on her shoes, then headed for the stairs. She knew having Seb stay with them would lead to disaster. It was only six o'clock in the morning and she had not only made a fool of herself in front of him twice with her clumsiness, but he had also left her a trembling mess. Thank God he had to go to work. She could only imagine what state she would be in by the end of the day if he stuck around.

She descended the main staircase at a light jog, then moved through the dim living room and pushed open the pocket door to the kitchen. Today's breakfast was crepes with fresh fruit and homemade whipped cream. She also had bacon and some amazing blueberry pork sausage links she had picked up at the farmer's market when she ran her errands the other day.

She opened the fridge and began taking out items. Soon, she had settled into a rhythm that helped her push her libido and her complicated feelings for Seb to the back of her mind. By the time he came downstairs, she had pulled herself together.

He walked up behind her to look over her shoulder at what she was cooking on the stove.

"Is that Henry Dickinson's blueberry pork sausage?"

She nodded.

"You bought another pack for everyone else, right?" he teased.

She smiled up at him. "I bought three."

He groaned. "Good girl."

Rolling her eyes, she motioned to the coffeemaker. "There's coffee ready. And some crepes on that plate there." She used her tongs to point at the dish covered with a paper towel.

Seb took a plate from the cabinet and began to fill it. Once he had his crepes full, London put three of the sausage links on his plate. He pouted, asking for more, but she just shook her head. "I have a full house. That's all you get."

His mock glare was cute, but she wasn't about to fold. "Eat some bacon. You'll live."

He huffed a laugh and snagged several pieces off the platter before retreating to the kitchen table.

"You're going to call a plumber this morning, right?" he asked after devouring his sausage.

"Yes. I hope I can get one to come out on such short notice. I hate to impose on Declan on his day off."

Seb waved a piece of bacon. "He won't mind. He doesn't like to sleep during the day after a shift, so he'll be up."

She hummed a non-answer. Just because he was awake didn't mean he wouldn't be busy. Macy's brother was nothing if not active. He hated to just sit around. She knew he spent most of his days off hiking, or skiing in the colder months.

The scrape of the chair leg on the floor drew her attention back to Seb, who had finished his breakfast. He put his plate in the sink, then came to stand beside her at the stove.

All that desire from earlier came flooding back at his nearness and the intensity in his dark eyes. She focused on the crepe in her pan, trying not to let her hormones get the better of her again.

He laid a finger on her jaw and turned her head so she had

to look at him. All the moisture left her mouth as she met his gaze.

"Remember to keep the doors locked. I'll be back this evening sometime."

She nodded, her throat too dry to speak.

He grazed her bottom lip with his thumb, holding her chin in his fingers. His eyes followed the movement. London swallowed hard, her own eyes going to his mouth. She wanted to feel it against hers again. Last night hadn't been nearly enough to quench the fire he lit inside her.

Her eyelids fluttered closed as he leaned in and pressed his lips against hers in a featherlight touch. Need surged and she swayed closer. The pressure increased only slightly before he pulled back much too soon.

He cleared his throat. "Please be careful." His voice was low and rolled over her. "I'll see you later." He released her and stepped around her to head for the door.

"You too," she pushed out through her tight throat.

He paused at the doorway. Giving her one last, intense look, he nodded and then he was gone.

She leaned against the counter, and as she came back to reality, she smelled something burning.

"Dammit!" The crepe was burned. She tipped it out of the pan onto Seb's plate in the sink.

Yep, having him around was a total disaster.

Seb wrinkled his nose in distaste and rolled his eyes, glad the mayor couldn't see him over the phone. The man called at least once a day for an update, and it was wearing on his nerves. The conversations always started innocuous enough, but by the end the man would inevitably insinuate that they should call in the state to handle the investigation. Seb had run point on cases like this one—and much worse—as an FBI agent. If he thought he needed help, he would ask for it.

Caleb peeked his head around the door, a big smile on his face as he waved some papers.

Seb sat a little straighter and frowned in curiosity. He held up a finger.

"Bryan, I'll have to call you back. Something's come up that I need to deal with." Not waiting for a reply, he hung up over the mayor's protests.

Caleb walked into the office. "The mayor again?"

Seb nodded and sighed. "Yep. Like clockwork. What do you have?" He gestured to the papers Caleb carried.

The deputy handed them over. "I think I found our murder victim. Still waiting on DNA to confirm, but she matches the facial rec as well as stature and age."

Seb took the papers—a missing person's report—and perused them. "Amy Beckett, twenty-seven. A temp worker at a ski resort in Aspen."

Caleb sat down across the desk.

"Her brother in Dodge City reported her missing in—get this—January."

Surprise made Seb's head shoot up. "What?"

"Yeah. It blew me away too. It's why I had so much trouble finding her. I was only looking back a couple months because Dr. Randall didn't find any signs she had been held for very long."

"Wherever he kept her, she must not have been tied up."

"Or it was with something that wouldn't cause any injury. Like a padded cuff or something."

"So, our guy holds his victims for a while before he kills them."

"Yep."

Seb hated to think what happened to these women in the time they were captive. He already knew they were raped, but he could only imagine what else this psycho did to them or made them do.

"Have you talked to her brother yet?"

"No. I think we should make the notification in person. Only problem is that I have to be in court this afternoon on a different case. Can you go?"

"To Kansas?" He wasn't too keen on leaving the area with the trouble at the inn. "What about Wilder? She's handled death notifications before."

Caleb shook his head. "It's her day off and she went to Denver. Come on, Sheriff. It'll get you out of your afternoon phone call with the mayor." A wide grin split his face.

Seb laughed. "True. If I go, though, you need to keep an eye on London and Abigail until I get back tonight. There's something going on out there, and I have a feeling it's tied up with this case. I hope I'm wrong and it's just someone with an overzealous infatuation."

"What happened?"

Seb quickly filled him in on last night's drama.

"I just wish we had enough to warrant posting an officer."

"Doesn't mean some of us won't volunteer on our off-time. In fact, while you're gone, I'll put together a roster and come up with a schedule."

"That would be great. I appreciate it."

Caleb stood. "Not a problem. We all like London and would hate if anything happened to her. You better get a move on if you don't want to be rolling back into town at midnight."

He shooed him out. "Yeah, yeah. I need to wrap up a couple things first, but it won't be long. Is Travers still in the conference room going over our evidence files?"

He nodded.

"Ask him if he wants to go with me. I hate doing these alone and he might have some pertinent questions."

Caleb gave him a quick salute and left.

Seb swiped his hands over his face and groaned. Driving to Kansas to give a death notification was not what he wanted to do today, but it was necessary. He picked up his phone and called London.

The phone rang several times, and Seb's concern grew. Just before it rolled over to voicemail, she picked up, breathless.

"Hello?"

"Hey. It's me. Everything okay?"

"Fine. I was just in the middle of chores. What's up?"

"I need to go out of town for the day. We ID'd our victim and I have to go to Kansas to talk to her brother."

"Kansas? Will you be back tonight?"

"Yes, but it'll be late. Caleb's going to hang out at the inn this evening until I get back. You might have another deputy there this afternoon. He's putting together a rotation until we catch this killer."

Her sigh came over the line loud and clear. "I really don't think that's necessary. There are people in and out of here all day long."

"And someone still managed to slip in and sabotage your hot water heater."

She sighed again. "Fine."

He resisted the urge to say good girl. "Good. I'll call you a few times today to check in, so keep your phone on you. You should anyway."

"You know I do."

"Just make sure you have it."

"Yes, Dad."

He huffed a laugh. "Be careful."

"I will." He could hear the smile in her voice.

He hung up just as Jace walked in the door.

"Bering said you want me to go with you to Kansas to talk to Amy Beckett's brother."

"Yep." He grabbed a file off the stack on his desk and flipped it open. "I need to finish reviewing these reports and sign off on them and we can go. About an hour sound good?"

"Sure. You think we'll get anything useful from him?"

He shrugged. "I hope so. A place of employment and a home address would be a good place to start."

"Agreed. All right. I'll be in the conference room. Come get me when you're ready."

"Will do."

As Jace's boot steps faded, Seb shuffled papers and signed the first report and moved on to the next one, ready to get on the road and hopefully get some answers.

"Thanks for coming," London said as she opened the door for Declan Briggs. "I tried every plumber in the area and the soonest any of them could get to me was Monday."

Declan stepped inside, carrying a toolbox, a sack from the hardware store, and a set of work gloves. "Not a problem."

She led him through the house to the utility room and unlocked the door. He stepped inside and set his things down near the heater. "This shouldn't take too long. I just need to replace the valve."

"Great. Can I do anything to help?"

"You can put me together a plate of those macarons Macy raved about. My mouth was watering while she told me about them."

London laughed. "You and your sister have almost as big a sweet tooth as Seb. I'll go put some in a bag for you and you can take them home."

"Don't tell Macy or she'll beat me up and take them from me." The lines on his face crinkled with his bright smile and his deep blue eyes sparkled in merriment.

He wasn't wrong. She mimed zipping her lips. "What macarons?" She smiled and left to put his treats together.

Footsteps on the stairs had her looking over as she crossed the living room. Abigail stepped off the last runner, looking disheveled and grumpy.

"You okay, honey?"

Abigail nodded. "I forgot there wasn't any hot water and stepped into a cold shower. I'm awake now."

London giggled. "Come on in the kitchen and I'll fix you some breakfast."

"Did you make Grandma's cinnamon rolls?"

"No, that's tomorrow's breakfast this week. I made crepes. Do you want that?"

"Is there bacon?"

She rolled her eyes. "Is the sky blue?"

Abigail snorted. "Okay, yeah. That was a stupid question."

They walked into the kitchen and Abigail sat at the table while London took the crepe batter out of the fridge and heated the pan on the stove.

"What was all that noise I heard this morning? The banging on the walls."

London fought the blush that wanted to steal over her skin. "I, uh, tripped and hit the wall."

"Oh. What did you trip on?"

"Seb's feet."

She laughed. "How did you trip over his feet?"

London added a ladleful of the crepe batter to the pan. "He decided to sleep behind the couch because he didn't want to block the door. When I came out of my bedroom, I didn't know he was back there and I kicked his ankle on my way to the bathroom." She tipped the pan, swirling the batter.

"Ouch. You know, all that could have been avoided if you'd let him sleep in your bed."

The crepe pan clattered on the stove. "Abigail!"

The girl gave her a cheeky grin. "I'm just saying, you two really need to stop fighting this attraction. Life's short. Don't be a dumbass."

"Language."

She rolled her eyes. "Stop avoiding the issue, Aunt London. Just admit you want to jump his bones and move on."

London groaned and swirled the crepe again. This was not an appropriate topic of discussion to have with her niece. "My love life—or lack thereof—is none of your business."

"Ooo, we're getting touchy." She leaned an elbow on the table and put her chin in her hand. "Did something happen?"

This time, London couldn't stop the blush. She flipped the crepe. "Again, none of your business."

"Something happened. You're blushing. Did you kiss? Did you get past first base? Do I need to buy earplugs?"

The last question caught London off-guard, and she barked out a laugh before she could stop it. She smothered her smile and aimed a glare at her niece as she slid the crepe out of the pan onto a plate and then spooned in another ladleful. "I am not having this conversation. Get the fruit and whipped cream out and fill this crepe."

Abigail sighed and got up to do as she was asked. "Fine. But if I come in one night and it sounds like a brothel, I'm sleeping at Macy's."

"Oh my God! Just stop, please. There will be no brothel sounds or any other—*sounds*." She knew her face was now as red as the strawberries Abigail put in her crepe, but she couldn't help it.

She laughed. "Fine. I'll give you a break. But in all seriousness, I know *something* happened—don't throw it away because you're worried about me. You two dating will never change my relationship with him. None of us will let that happen."

London cast a glance at her, but said nothing. She really didn't want to talk about Seb or her relationship with him. She was still reeling from the sight of him in his near-naked glory this morning. All she really wanted was to push all thoughts of him from her brain so she could function like a grown woman.

She finished Abigail's second crepe and tipped it onto her plate. Wiping out the skillet, she set it back on the stove before taking the box with the macarons out of the fridge.

"Are you eating macarons at nine in the morning? Geez, he really did mess you up."

London rolled her eyes. "These are not for me. Declan's in the utility room fixing the water heater. I told him I'd send some of these home with him."

"Oh. Better make sure Macy doesn't know that. She'll steal them."

London laughed. "That's what he said."

"When are you going to make them for her to sell at the café?"

"Soon. I think I might have time to make a batch after this weekend. All my time tomorrow and Saturday will be sucked up making Lee and Jenny's anniversary cake for their party Saturday evening."

"What time do I need to be out to the ranch to help set up?"

"Tara said two."

Abigail nodded and stuffed the last of her first crepe in her mouth.

Declan walked in just as London put the last macaron in the bag.

"Hi, Declan," Abigail said.

He waved at her.

"Done already?" London asked.

"It was a quick fix."

"That caused a lot of trouble."

"It could have been worse. I'm not sure whoever did it intended to cause the inn harm."

London frowned. "What do you mean?"

Declan leaned on the counter. "This place is active. You almost always have guests, especially this time of year. That means water is in use frequently. There wouldn't be time for the gas to build up to the point it would cause a catastrophic explosion because someone would notice the lack of hot water."

"Like Mr. Brown did."

"Exactly."

"Then what was the point?"

He shrugged. "Not sure. But I doubt it was to kill you or to destroy the inn. To gain attention, maybe? Gauge our response time? In any case, I hope the lab can get some prints off the pieces they removed last night so nothing else happens."

"Me too."

"Uncle Seb is staying again tonight, right?" Abigail directed the question at her aunt.

London nodded. "He'll be here every night until they catch this guy. Although, he may be late tonight. He called a little while ago to tell me he has to go to Kansas for an interview. They identified the woman you and Trent found."

"Really? That's great. I hope they can get some answers now. What was her name?"

"I don't know. He didn't tell me and I didn't think to ask." She looked at Declan. "Have you had breakfast? I still have crepe batter left."

"And fresh whipped cream." Abigail poked the bowl in front of her.

"Hell, yeah." He sat down next to Abigail at the table.

London smiled and turned back to the stove. This was what filled her soul; cooking for the people she loved.

"So, are you going to be at Mr. and Mrs. Archer's anniversary party?" Abigail asked.

"Maybe. I have to work Saturday. The guys and I might try to stop by if things are slow."

"I hope you can. Brady hired Trent's band to play. Jaxon just wrote a new song. It's a slow one. If you come, you should dance with Aunt London. Make Uncle Seb jealous."

"Abigail. Don't start that again." London warned.

The girl gave her a wicked grin, but said no more.

Declan arched an eyebrow and looked at London. "Did I miss something?"

"Uncle Seb and Aunt London kissed."

"I never told you that," London said.

"Oh, but you did. Your face told me."

"It's about damn time," Declan said. "I swear, the two of you have been dancing around each other for years."

London resisted the urge to growl. Why was her love life the topic of conversation with *everyone* lately? She flipped the crepe in her pan and ignored him.

"She doesn't like to talk about it," Abigail said in a stage whisper. "Thinks the whole thing is a bad idea."

"Even after she kissed him?"

"Oh, for Pete's sake," London said. "Yes, we kissed. Yes, it was amazing. No, I don't know where it's going or even where I want it to go. Now, can we pick a different topic, please? And I swear on all that's holy, Declan Briggs, if you breathe a word of this to Macy, I will never make another macaron for you in my life. Got it?"

Eyes wide, he nodded.

London thrust the bag of cookies at him and glared, eyes conveying that she was dead-serious. When he took the bag, she turned back to the stove to finish his breakfast, her anger simmering as hot as the crepe in the pan. Why couldn't everyone just butt out? If she wanted to date Sebastian Archer, she would. If she wanted to ignore this crazy attraction and go on pretending she was nothing more than his best friend's kid sister, she'd do that too. Hell, if she wanted to run off with her reclusive and weird guest, Doug Brown, no one would have any say in it. All she wanted was space to come to her own decision, but everyone kept poking their nose into it. Instead of helping, they were just causing friction.

She tipped Declan's second crepe out of the pan onto a plate, then handed it to him.

"Abigail, are you going to be around for a while?"

The girl nodded, mouth full of the last of her food.

"Good. I'm going to run to town to get the rest of what I need to make Lee and Jenny's anniversary cake. Hold down the fort." She looked at Declan. "Remember what I said."

He held up his hands. "Not a word."

"Good. You two enjoy your breakfast. I'll be back later." She beat a hasty retreat out of the kitchen to fetch her purse. Hopefully, she could get in and out of the hardware store and the grocery without having to discuss her love life with anyone else.

EIGHT

I t was five-thirty when Seb parked his truck behind the Dodge City police cruiser at Jack Beckett's house. The two-story, craftsman-style home was well-tended and welcoming with its sage green siding and the bright red flowers filling the beds around the front of the house. He climbed out and met Jace and the local officer around front.

"I sure am glad it's you two who get to break this news. I hate doing death notifications," the officer said.

"All of us do," Jace replied.

The officer gave a solemn nod and walked through the grass to the front door. Seb and Jace followed, hanging back as he knocked on the door. Footsteps—both big and small—sounded inside. Seb heard the soft murmur of a woman and the higher pitch of a young child. The door swung inward, revealing a slender woman in her early thirties. Her long, mousy brown hair was piled into a messy bun on top of her head. She had a baby girl on her hip, who looked at them with wide blue eyes, and a little boy who was about two with equally wide eyes peeking out from behind her leg.

She frowned at the three of them. "May I help you?"

"Is Jack Beckett home?" the officer asked.

The woman went a little pale and nodded. She turned her head inside. "Jack!" She looked back at them. "This is about Amy, isn't it?"

"Let's just wait for your husband," Seb said. He only wanted to have to say this once. It was hard enough without having to repeat it.

A tall, slim man came around the corner of the living room and moved toward the door. His strawberry blonde hair caught Seb's attention. It was a match to his sister's as well as their other victims.

He stepped into the doorway next to his wife. "I'm Jack Beckett. Is this about my sister?"

"Yes, sir. I'm Officer Seacourt with Dodge City PD. This is Sheriff Sebastian Archer from Boone County, Colorado, and Detective Jace Travers from the Haskell police department in Nebraska. They'd like to talk to you."

Blue eyes serious, Jack waved them inside.

"I'll be in the kitchen with the kids," his wife murmured. She squeezed his hand, then took the little boy's hand and led him down a hallway to the right of the stairs.

Seb nodded in thanks to the officer who was already retreating to his police car, and followed Jack inside. They stepped to the left of the stairs into a large living room. Jack waved them onto a tan couch and sat in the matching chair.

"Can I get either of you something to drink?"

"No, thank you, Mr. Beckett," Seb said. "As you've surmised, we're here about your sister."

"She's dead, isn't she?"

Seb nodded. "I'm afraid so. Two teenagers in my jurisdiction came across her body in an abandoned homestead last Saturday."

Jack stood and paced to the window, looking at the quiet street. "I knew when she didn't call for our weekly check-in that something bad had happened." He turned back to them. "How did she die?"

"She was murdered. Strangled."

Jack's face crumpled, and he blinked back tears. He pressed the fingers of one hand to his eyes and took a deep breath, collecting himself. "Do you know who did it?"

"Not yet," Jace said. "That's where we're hoping you can help us out."

Jack came back over and sat down. "Anything."

Seb and Jace shared a glance, then Seb dove right in. "Mr. Beckett, we think your sister is the victim of a serial killer operating in the western United States. When she was found, the crime scene set off some alarm bells for me and I did some digging. So far, we have four victims, including Amy, who share the same physical description and the same manner of death."

"Oh my God," Jack breathed. "That's why you're here." He motioned to Jace.

Jace nodded. "The victim in my jurisdiction was found last November."

Jack's Adam's apple bobbed as he swallowed, eyes wide. "What can I do to help?"

"The missing person's flyer said she was in Colorado as a seasonal worker in Aspen. Can you tell us where she worked and lived?"

"Um, yeah. She worked for one of the Ski Resorts—Aspen Trails—and she lived in an RV with another one of the lodge employees."

The mention of a roommate made Seb's gut sink. Jack Beckett shouldn't have been the only one filing a missing person's report. Unless she called Jack to tell him his sister was missing and he filed the report for the both of them. "What's the roommate's name?"

"Rebecca Carson. She's from Idaho, Amy said."

"Have you heard from her since Amy went missing?"

Jack shook his head. "I tried calling Amy when she missed our weekly call, but never got an answer, and I don't have Rebecca's number."

"Did the police in Aspen search for your sister?" Jace asked.

Jack nodded. "Yes. They went to her RV, but no one was home and there weren't any cars around. When they inquired at the lodge where she worked, the manager said he hadn't seen her."

"Did they ask about Rebecca?"

"I don't know. They didn't seem too concerned about either of them, honestly. They said the seasonal workers were fickle and moved on without notice a lot. I think they just thought Amy—and probably Rebecca too—took off and didn't bother to tell anyone. But Amy wouldn't do that to me. We're close. Our parents aren't the greatest and we had to rely on each other a lot when we were young. Yes, Amy is—was—more of a free spirit than me, but she was still a good person. Responsible. She enjoyed living in the tiny RVs and apartments. Said it was freeing to not be tied down to anyone or anything."

"What was the name of the RV park?"

"It didn't have one. It's on the resort grounds for employee use."

"Did Amy ever mention anyone? A boyfriend? A guest who was overly friendly? A local?"

Jack scoffed. "Amy was beautiful. Men fell at her feet. As a barista and bartender during the busy season, she had all kinds of people who paid her attention. Every week, there was at least one person she'd tell me about. A lot of times it was just frat boys looking for a good time who hit on her. Sometimes it was men who were out for a weekend without their wives. But she never mentioned anyone who gave her the creeps."

"Do you know if she ever had relationships with any of those men?" Jace asked.

Jack shook his head. "We didn't really talk about her love life much, but I know she dated. Never seriously, though. Like I said, she liked not being beholden to anyone."

"Can you think of anyone who would want to hurt your sister?"

"No. As much as I've been hoping she just decided she wanted to be completely free of everyone, I've also been thinking the worst. I wracked my brain trying to come up with anyone who might have had a reason to harm her. No one sticks out."

Seb looked at Jace, silently asking if he had any other questions. The detective gave a small shake of his head. Seb flipped his notebook closed and stuffed it back in his breast pocket before standing.

He held out a hand. "Thank you for your time, Mr. Beckett. I'm sorry about your sister, but we will do everything we can to find who did this."

Jack took his hand and shook it. "I appreciate that. Amy was a nice woman. She didn't deserve to have this happen to her."

"No one does," Seb said.

Jack nodded, then shook Jace's hand.

Seb handed him a business card. "If you think of anything else that might be pertinent to the investigation, call me. My cell number is on the back."

Jack turned the card over, glancing at it, and nodded. "I will. Thank you."

"We'll show ourselves out. Good night." Seb turned and led the way out of the living room. The wood door closed heavily behind them.

"He seemed pretty upset," Jace said as they climbed into Seb's truck. The Dodge City officer was long gone.

"Yeah. We still need to check out his whereabouts when the other women went missing, but I don't think he was involved in any of this. His grief seemed genuine."

"I think we need to go to Aspen tomorrow."

"Yep." Seb sighed and rubbed the back of his neck, exhausted. "You know, I left the FBI in part to get away from cases like this." He scrubbed his hands over his face and growled in frustration.

"You could always call in the FBI. The killer's crossed state lines, so technically it could be a federal case."

"No." He twisted the key in the ignition. "I would never hear the end of it if I called in my buddies from the Denver office. I can handle this case even if I don't want to." He put the truck in gear. "Come on. Let's go get some food and go home." London's face wandered through his mind.

Yeah. Home.

NINE

L ondon looked around her kitchen at the mess she and Tara made baking the Archer's anniversary cake. Pans littered the counters; flour and powdered sugar dusted everything, including them. With the back of her hand, she swiped at a bead of sweat rolling down her temple.

"How about we take a break and have some lemonade out on the back patio while the cake finishes baking?"

"I like that idea." Tara turned to take two glasses out of the cupboard.

London took the pitcher of lemonade from the fridge and poured it into the glasses. The two women each grabbed a glass and stepped out the back door.

"Thanks for coming over to help me bake," London said as she settled into one of the deck chairs.

Tara took a sip of her lemonade. "Anytime. As much as I love my restaurant, every once in a while I need a break. Hanging out with you is just a bonus."

She concurred. Girl-time was a precious commodity in London's life. They were all so busy, any chance they had to do something together, they did. She glanced out over the yard and felt herself begin to relax. Baking always helped her clear her mind. So did spending time with good friends.

When she'd gotten up this morning, she had been eager to start the day even though she was exhausted. She'd gone to bed around ten last night, but hadn't drifted off until she heard Seb let himself into the apartment about midnight. Then, sleep had been fitful. She kept imagining him out there, sprawled over the floor in nothing but his underwear and that afghan. It had made for some rather vivid dreams and an uncomfortable arousal that lasted most of the night.

Abigail was right—she should just invite the man into her bed. At this point, London had a feeling it was inevitable, and didn't know why she still fought it.

"So, my brother went to Aspen today, right? With that detective from Nebraska?"

London looked over at her and nodded. "They left first thing this morning so they can hopefully be back by supper."

Tara shifted in her seat, frowning.

"What?"

"Nothing."

Now London frowned. Tara was fidgeting worse than a dog with fleas. "Not nothing. What?"

She heaved a sigh. "I met that man the other night. Jace. He was outside Seb's house when I went home."

"Okay." London drew out the word. "Was it bad?"

Tara swirled the lemonade in her glass, staring at the pale liquid. "No. Yes." She sighed and looked up. "I don't know. Have you met him yet?"

London shook her head.

"Wait until you do. He's hot. Like, beautiful and buff and —hot." She heaved another sigh. "I haven't been so attracted to a man since my husband."

She frowned again, failing to see how that was a problem. "Why is that a bad thing?"

"Because we got to talking, and he complimented my pictures, saying how he'd seen some amazing sights while riding his motorcycle up the Oregon Coast last year and wished he had the talent to capture the beauty of the landscape."

London's frown deepened. "How is that bad? That sounds pretty sweet, actually."

"It was, but he *rides a motorcycle.* I am not interested in another adrenaline junkie."

Understanding dawned on her. Tara's husband had loved anything dangerous. Sought it out, in fact. Tara had too at one time.

"Maybe he just likes motorcycles."

"No. He's got that alpha look to him, just like Sean did. And he drives a truck so red it's almost neon, it's so bright. No one who doesn't enjoy an intense thrill drives a truck like that." She sat back in her chair and glared out at the yard. "He probably skydives on his days off and climbs mountains without a safety rope."

"He lives in Nebraska. Where would he find a mountain?"

Tara turned the glare on her. "You get my point. Danger is probably his middle name."

London sighed and decided not to argue with her. Tara was determined she was right, and it would take a freight train to convince her otherwise.

"Fine. But I don't want to hear about how you're sexually frustrated."

Tara giggled. "How about we talk about your frustrations instead?"

London groaned and let her head fall back against the chair.

"When are you going to put my brother out of his misery?"

"*His* misery? I'm the one who has to walk through my

living room in the mornings with blinders on because he only sleeps in his underwear."

"Oh, honey, you should just look."

"I can't, because then I can't think straight. His boxers leave very little to the imagination."

"Ew! No. I do not want that visual in my head." She waved a hand, her face souring.

"Sorry, but it's true."

"Okay. Let's talk about something else."

"Hey, if it takes talking about Sebastian's man-goods to get people to stop asking me about our relationship, I will go into full detail."

Tara set down her drink and waved both arms, laughing. "No. No. I get it. I'll stop. No more questions about you and Seb."

The oven timer beeped from inside. London squinted at her friend. "Saved by the bell." She pointed a finger at her. "I will hold you to that," she said, rising from her chair.

Tara stood beside her. "Don't worry. I will behave." She shuddered. "Thinking about any of my brothers in the nude is just—yuck!"

London laughed. She wished she felt the same. Maybe then she would get some peace.

"Wow. This place is busy," Jace said as he and Seb pulled into the parking lot at Aspen Trails Resort and Lodge. Cars filled the parking spaces and people filled the outdoor terraces.

"Yeah. There's a music festival this weekend. I guess people are starting to arrive for that. We've also had a pretty warm start to June, so there are probably a good deal of hikers and campers here too."

"I haven't been to this area to hike before."

"You should come sometime. There are some pretty vistas, especially when it snows," Seb said, climbing from the truck. "We're actually lucky we haven't had any snow in the lower elevations in the last couple of weeks. Have you hiked anywhere in Colorado before?"

"Yeah. More in the Pikes Peak area. I've done some mountain biking too. And camping, although I prefer Montana to camp. Fewer people."

"So, are you a native Nebraskan?"

He nodded. "I'm a Husker, born and bred. I did a stint in the Army out of high school, but came right back after I spent four years in and out of the sandbox. Don't know as if I'd recommend it, but it paid for my college."

"Is that how you got into police work?" They wove their way through the parked cars, reaching the massive wooden portico on the front of the lodge.

Jace nodded. "I was military police. I liked the work, but wanted to do more on the investigative side of things, so I enrolled in a criminal justice program at the University of Nebraska. I knew I'd need the degree if I ever wanted to be a detective. How did you decide on the FBI?"

"I was one of those kids who grew up knowing what I wanted to be. I thought the feds were the coolest thing, and I never wavered in my desire to be one. And I wanted to be the best, so I actually went to law school and got a law degree."

Jace's eyebrows shot up. "Seriously?"

Seb nodded.

"But you still gave it all up."

"I don't really see it that way. My degree, my time as a federal agent—it all gave me the experience I needed to land this job and to be near my family. I love what I do. More so now than before because I'm home. I didn't realize the importance of that until I couldn't be there when London and Abigail needed me."

"She really means something to you, doesn't she? London."

Seb nodded. "More and more all the time." He pulled open the glass doors to the building and stepped inside, pausing a moment to let his eyes adjust to the dim interior. Built log cabin-style, natural wood beam walls glowed gold in the morning sun streaming through the floor-to-ceiling windows on the back of the lodge. Giant pine supports held up the roof over the great room and slate tile floors shone from years of wear.

They turned right and headed for the restaurant in search of Amy Beckett's boss. A smiling hostess greeted them.

"Good morning. Sit wherever you'd like and I'll bring out some fresh coffee in just a moment."

Seb flashed his badge. "Actually, we're here to speak to your boss, Tyler Petrosky."

"Oh." She glanced around the room, then pointed to a man behind the bar. "That's him."

"Thank you." With a nod, he and Jace made their way through the diners to the bar where a short man with a balding head stood, slicing limes.

"Tyler Petrosky?"

The man nodded. "You must be Sheriff Archer."

"I am. Thank you for taking the time to meet with us."

"Sure. On the phone, you said this had something to do with Amy Beckett. Not sure what I can tell you. She wasn't here long. Couple of months."

"You're aware she was missing?"

Tyler nodded. "Was?"

"Her body was found a few hours southeast of here last weekend. She was murdered." He watched the other man as he shared that news. Tyler's eyes widened, and he seemed genuinely shocked.

"Oh my goodness. I thought she'd just up and left. I get a

lot of those. They get a taste of how busy we get and can't handle it, then one day decide to move on and don't give me any notice. I thought that's what she'd done until the Aspen police showed up, asking when I'd seen her last."

"And that was?"

"New Year's Eve. The lodge had a big party, and she tended bar that night."

"And you're sure you didn't see her after that?"

He nodded. "Her next shift was on the second and she never showed up."

"Did you see anyone that night who paid more attention to her than usual? Someone who flirted more or wanted her and only her to fill his drinks?"

Tyler shrugged. "Honestly, I couldn't tell you. We were slammed, and I was waiting tables with the staff when I wasn't breaking up scuffles between guests who'd had too much to drink. If there was someone here who wanted to harm her, I didn't see them."

"What can you tell us about her roommate, Rebecca Carson?" Jace asked.

"Rebecca?" He frowned and arched an eyebrow. "She's missing too?"

Jace nodded. "The police here tried to contact her when they were looking for Amy. They concluded that the women took off together."

"No, that's not right."

Seb and Jace shared a look.

"Why do you say that?" Seb asked.

"Those girls got along great, but Rebecca wasn't a wanderer. Amy I could see doing that. She was a real free spirit. But Rebecca was saving to get an apartment in town. She wanted to get hired on full-time here and work her way up. She had potential too. Smart girl."

"Okay, Mr. Petrosky. Thank you for your time." Seb slid a

business card across the bar. "Please call if you think of anything that might be useful."

The man nodded. "I sure hope you find who killed her and that you find Rebecca. They were good girls."

Seb and Jace walked back toward the main lodge.

"How the hell did Aspen PD get this so wrong? All they had to do was talk to that guy to know something wasn't right," Jace said.

"That time of year, they probably had their hands full. And Petrosky's not wrong—a lot of the seasonal workers do skip town without giving notice. They tire of the long hours or the cold and they just leave. Amy and Rebecca likely weren't the only women to vanish suddenly last winter. That they disappeared together adds credence to them leaving voluntarily. It takes skill—and brawn—to abduct two women at once."

"But that doesn't mean it didn't happen."

"No, I agree. But this place, at that time, is the perfect way to abduct someone and have no one realize it for a while." Seb squinted as they walked back out into the sunshine. Instead of getting back into the truck, though, they followed the signs for the employees' quarters, and meandered down a dirt path through the woods. It soon opened up to a clearing where a small wood cabin with an "Office" sign over the door sat at the edge of a large, stone parking lot. A driveway cut through the woods to the left of the building and disappeared into the forest. Scattered in the trees, Seb could see RVs and even some tents where the seasonal employees stayed.

Boots crunching on the gravel, they walked across the lot to the cabin and knocked on the door. It quickly opened to reveal a middle-aged woman in a tank top and shorts, her dark hair pulled back in a ponytail. She ran an assessing gaze over both of them, her eyes lighting up as she took in their appearance. Seb steeled himself for the flirting he could see coming from the gleam in her eyes.

"Hello there, officers. You the ones who called?"

Seb nodded. "Yes, ma'am. You're Emily Young?"

The woman nodded and continued to stare.

"We're here about Amy Beckett and Rebecca Carson," he continued.

She gave him a last once over, then motioned them inside. The interior was a miniature version of the main lodge only not as elegant. It had the same natural walls and slate floor, but the furniture was homier and worn. It was also very warm even with the windows open.

Seb ran a finger around his collar as sweat dripped down his temple. "Your AC broken?"

She nodded. "Maintenance is supposed to come fix it today. It's just super warm right now because I ran the oven this morning. I made muffins. Want one?" She eyed him up and down like she would rather eat him than a muffin.

He cleared his throat. "No, thank you."

She turned her eyes on Jace. "How about you, handsome?"

Jace offered her a tight smile and shook his head.

"What can you tell us about Amy and Rebecca?"

"They were quiet. Social, but quiet. No raucous parties like some of these yahoos." She stared at Seb again. "I could use a man like you around to help me tame this lot. Tall and buff with a badge."

"I'm sure if you call your local police, they'll send someone out."

She rolled her eyes. "Yeah, and blame me for the party. I'm just glad management understands the quality of the workers they hire, so I don't get fired when they have their drunken orgies back there."

Jace coughed and covered his mouth with his hand. Seb

glanced at him and could see the smile twinkling in his eyes. He bit back one of his own. Flirt or not, she was a character.

"Would you happen to still have any of their stuff from the RV they shared?"

Emily shook her head. "It was cleaned out."

Seb frowned. That was the first he was hearing of that. "By whom?"

She shrugged. "It was like that when the police searched it after Amy's brother reported her missing."

"There was nothing? Not even a knickknack?" Jace asked.

"Nope. I didn't even find any spare pens. Whoever it was took everything."

"And no one saw anything?"

She braced her hands on the long counter that served as a check-in desk and leaned back. "Not that I know of. But the RV they shared was toward the back, and they didn't have any close neighbors."

"Can you show us, please?"

She pushed off the counter. "Sure. I can't let you go inside because it's occupied, but I can show you the lot."

They followed her outside and into the woods. Seb was impressed by the set-up they had here. There had to be a hundred or more RVs situated in the trees, and a handful of tents. In the middle of it all was a grassy area with picnic tables and a long cinderblock building that housed showers and bathrooms for those in the tents.

The campground was mostly deserted, but there were a few people milling around. They all eyed Seb and Jace with interest. Even though they were in civilian clothes, their guns and badges were on display.

"This is it," Emily said, stopping in front of a newer white RV with gray and black accents. An AC unit whirred on top and two plastic chairs sat on the deck attached to the side. A wind chime hanging from the awning frame clinked in the light breeze.

Seb walked around back and was met with nothing but wilderness.

"Hey, Jace."

The other man wandered around to the rear of the RV.

Seb pointed. "There's nothing past the campground. It wouldn't be that difficult to get an ATV with a sled back here and load all their belongings on it."

"But why?" Jace frowned. "I mean, it doesn't make any sense. Why take all their stuff too? Amy was what he wanted. And where's Rebecca?"

"My guess? Out there somewhere." He tipped his head toward the trees.

"We need to call Aspen PD and find out who was in charge of this case."

Seb nodded and turned around, heading back out. "Yep. Hopefully, they thought to dust for prints."

He paused when he reached the campground manager. "Did you notice anyone hanging around the campground who shouldn't have been before Amy and Rebecca went missing?"

"This area is off-limits to guests and they usually respect that. I can't recall seeing anyone, though."

"Was there anyone out of the ordinary?" Jace asked. "A contract worker, a hiker, a local person?"

She started to shake her head, but stopped. "Wait. We had some plumbing work done right after Christmas. One of the pipes to the bathhouse froze and busted. There was a guest here who was a plumber and offered to fix it."

"Do you remember what he looked like?"

"Oh, forty or so. Fit. Blonde."

"You catch a name?" Seb asked.

She shook her head. "No. He just said he was there to fix the pipe. I showed him where it was and left him to it."

"Do you think you could describe him to a sketch artist?"

She shook her head. "No, sorry. I was really busy that day because we had a bunch of temps in to help out for New Year's Eve. I was getting accommodations ready and checking people in all day. When he showed up, I was in the middle of sorting out a mix-up in lodging for a male and a female worker—we try to pair up men with men and women with women, and somehow they got mixed. I ran out long enough to show him the busted pipe and then went right back to straightening out that mess."

"Okay. Thank you for your help, Ms. Young. We appreciate it." He handed her a business card. "Call me if you think of anything that might be useful."

She gave him a rueful smile. "A handsome man gives me his number, but for all the wrong reasons."

Seb smiled back. "I think you have plenty of men interested."

"But not you. Or your friend." She glanced behind him at Jace.

"I'm taken. He's—"

"Not in the market," Jace cut in.

Her grin turned wicked. "Shame. You're pretty."

Seb laughed. "Ms. Young, I have no doubt you'll find some young man who will make you very happy. Have a good day." He motioned for Jace to follow.

"You find that bastard!" she called after them.

He gave her a thumbs up and broke into a jog.

"That sound like anybody on your radar?" Jace asked.

"Maybe. That guest at London's inn is about forty and blonde. I can't see him as a plumber, though. He's kinda fancy."

They reached the truck and Seb hit the button on his key

fob to unlock it. "He also didn't offer to fix the water heater when it broke."

"Maybe he's the one who broke it."

"Possibly. But the background check I did on him said he was the CEO of some development company. I think he's in the area looking to put up some condos or something."

"Way out there?"

Seb shrugged as he steered the truck from the lot and headed toward the city. "It's a pretty area and there's a lake not far away. He wouldn't be the first to want to build up the region. We have a lot of National Forest land, though, and it's hard to get people to sell the land that's been in their family for generations. We had one guy twenty-some years ago try to buy The Broken Bow from my parents. Even went so far as to claim there was a problem with the deed and that part of the land was still public after my dad said no. That ranch has been in my family since the 1860s and it's been added to with each subsequent generation. Legally. The guy had his day in court, though. It took two minutes for the judge to dismiss the case. We weren't the only ones he harassed. Our neighbors, the Nyderts, had trouble with him too."

"You haven't had any trouble with this guy, though, right?"

Seb shook his head. "No. If he's looking to buy land, no one has complained about him yet."

"And there isn't anyone else?"

"Maybe the hardware store owner. He's blonde and fit and has a bit of a thing for London, but he's in his fifties and doesn't seem the type. I ran that box and note London received, and it was wiped clean. There weren't any prints on the pieces of the hot water heater, either."

"You think they're connected?"

"Maybe. It seems a little odd, though. Why would he send

a gift one day, and the very next set up a potentially deadly explosion?"

"Maybe he wanted to be the one to fix it. Who did fix it?"

"The fire lieutenant, Declan Briggs. She couldn't get a plumber to come out quick enough and he volunteered."

"Maybe it was him."

"Not if it was the same man Emily Young saw. His hair is a dark auburn, and he's only a couple years older than London. It's always possible it's two different people too."

"But you don't think so, do you?"

Seb shook his head and stopped at a stoplight. "No. It's too much of a coincidence. I just need to figure out the connection."

Several turns later, he parked in the visitor's lot in front of the police station. Determined to get some answers, he and Jace strode through the front door. Seb flashed his badge at the front desk.

"We need to speak with the detective in charge of Amy Beckett's disappearance."

The sergeant manning the desk pulled his keyboard forward and typed the name into the system. "That would be Detective Ian Farley." He pushed a log book toward them. "Sign in, please. I'll call him and tell him you're here. Names?"

"Sebastian Archer, Boone County Sheriff, and Detective Jace Travers, Haskell PD." Seb picked up the pen and scrawled his name on the log, then handed it to Jace, who did the same.

The sergeant hung up the phone and the door to Seb's left buzzed.

"Down the hall. He's toward the end on your left."

They thanked the man and walked through the door. Boots echoing, they tread down the hallway. A man stepped out of an office several doors down.

"Sheriff Archer?"

Seb stopped in front of the detective and assessed him.

Dark eyes stared right back, doing the same. "Detective Farley." He motioned behind him. "This is Detective Travers. We'd like a minute to discuss Amy Beckett and Rebecca Carson."

"Not sure what I can tell you, but come on in." He turned around and walked back to his desk, sitting in the chair behind it. Seb perched in one of the visitor's chairs and looked around the small, cluttered office. Papers sat everywhere. They were piled on the desk, the bookshelf, even the floor. He had a sneaking suspicion now why Amy and Rebecca's disappearances were filed under voluntary. Judging by the stacks and the tired lines etched on his face, the detective was woefully overworked.

"We just came from Aspen Trails. The employee camp-ground manager told us that someone emptied Amy and Rebecca's RV of all their belongings."

"That's right. It's one reason we thought they'd just skipped town."

"But Amy's brother didn't think she would do something like that without telling him, and certainly wouldn't go this long without calling him. And why didn't he mention that all of her things were gone?"

Farley shrugged. "Honestly? I don't know as if we ever told him that and he never asked for her things. Probably assumed we had them in storage as evidence. And we see it a lot where families delude themselves into thinking a loved one is different from who they really are. We had no evidence Amy and Rebecca hadn't run away."

Seb bit back his frustration. "Did you at least dust the RV for prints?"

Farley looked at him like he had grown another head. "In a place like that? No. We'd get so many hits, it would widen our suspect pool, not narrow it."

"How about searching the woods behind the campground?" Jace asked. "We think Rebecca's body might be out there somewhere."

The detective frowned, his expression sharpening as he leaned forward. "Why?"

"Amy's the victim of a serial killer. We think Rebecca was collateral damage. The killer didn't want or need her, so he probably disposed of her as soon as possible. She's likely been out there in the woods since January."

Farley cursed. "You're sure about the serial killer thing?"

Jace nodded. "Amy was found down in Boone County. I'm from Nebraska, where the third victim was found. I came out here to help Sheriff Archer when he discovered the similarities between the murders."

Farley cursed again and picked up his phone. "I'll get a couple K-9s out there to search for a body. If he didn't bury her, I don't know as if we'll find much, though. The wolves would have gotten to her, along with the other small scavengers that don't hibernate. Dammit." He punched a series of buttons, then barked some orders down the line when someone picked up on the other end. Replacing the phone, he looked up at them.

"I hope you're wrong, but I also hope you're right about this. I hate to think we may never find her."

"Same here."

Farley sighed and leaned back in his chair. "I know you guys think I'm an inept idiot, but I'm not." He gestured at the state of his office. "I'm doing the work of three detectives, so when it looks like a duck and quacks like a duck, I rule it a duck. I don't have time to chase down ghosts."

Seb agreed. When resources were tight, you did what you could, but ultimately, other cases took precedence.

"Can you coordinate the search efforts and let us know if you find anything? We need to get back to Silver Gap."

"Yeah. I'll stay on top of things here. Let me know if there's anything else I can do."

"There is one other thing. See how far back Aspen Trails keeps security footage. The campground manager said a guest fixed the plumbing at the bathhouse just after Christmas. Try to find him and ID him."

"I can do that." He took the phone off the hook again. "You guys have a safe trip back. I'll let you know what I discover."

Not wanting to take up any more of his time, Seb and Jace nodded their thanks and left.

"I hope he finds something on that footage," Seb said as they made their way outside. "We could use a break."

"Agreed."

TEN

With a groan, Seb sank onto the small couch in London's living room. He was tired, but still too awake to fall asleep on the hard floor again.

He took a sip of the beer he brought upstairs to help him unwind. The house was quiet. All the guests were sequestered in their rooms and both London and Abigail were in bed. He picked up the remote and turned on the TV, hoping to find some movie he'd seen before so his brain could decompress. After he and Jace returned from Aspen, he shut himself in his office to work on all the things he'd neglected the last two days during this investigation. It was a late night, but he was caught up.

As he settled on a nineties action film, one of the bedroom doors opened. He looked over to see Abigail emerge from her room. He sat up and muted the TV.

"Hey, munchkin. Did I wake you?"

She shook her head and shuffled into the room to sit next to him on the couch. "No. I was still awake."

He took a sip of his beer and watched her over the bottle. She tucked her legs up under her and settled into the couch, eyes on the TV. She wasn't really watching it, though. Her eyes were glazed as she stared off into space.

"What's wrong, honey?"

She sighed and looked over at him. "Is Aunt London going to be all right?"

He frowned and turned to face her. "What do you mean?"

"I mean, she's getting weird packages and someone's tampering with the house—am I being paranoid to think she's in danger?"

He covered her hands with his. "No, you're not paranoid. I think something strange is going on too, but I won't let anything happen to her. Didn't you see the deputy downstairs earlier?"

She nodded. "Yeah. He sat in the living room all evening. Aunt London's not too happy about it, because the guests were starting to ask questions. She just told them all it was a precaution because she received some threats and that they were all safe. Are they safe? Are *we*?"

He squeezed her hands. "Yes, honey. That's why the deputy is there. Why I'm here. Not just for your aunt, but to keep everyone safe."

She bit her lip and looked down at their hands before looking back up at him. "Is it the killer who's after her? Is she going to end up like Amy Beckett?" Her voice broke on the last word and her lip wobbled as tears pooled in her eyes.

Seb's gut clenched. He'd never been very good with crying women. When his sisters cried, he usually steered them toward their mother and beat a hasty retreat, but he couldn't run away from this.

"Honey, I won't lie to you and tell you it's not the killer. The truth is, I don't know. But I *will* do everything I can to keep her safe. Your aunt means a lot to me."

"I know." She sniffed and rubbed away a tear that escaped. "But I can't stop wondering what happens if he is targeting her and he gets to her. You can't be there all the time, and no one will watch out for her like you. I can't lose her too."

Seb's heart stopped, then started back up double-time. How long had she felt this way? She hadn't shown any signs she was worried about her aunt, and he couldn't help but wonder what changed.

She sniffed again. "I keep seeing Amy's face. Ever since I learned her name, I can't stop thinking about her. How she looked when we found her compared to when she was alive. She was beautiful. And I can't help but wonder now if—if—" she choked on a sob and the tears fell in earnest, "if that's going to be London."

Seb scooted closer and gathered the girl into his arms. She rested her head on his chest and wrapped her arms around him. He hugged her tight as she felt like the small, scared child she had been when her parents died. He kissed the top of her head and stroked her hair as she cried silently against him. He had the same fear, but refused to give it a voice. If he let himself think about that he'd go mad.

"How can someone be so ruthless and cold-blooded?" she murmured, sniffling.

He brushed the tears from one cheek as he looked down at her. "I don't know, baby. Some people are just wired weird and they do terrible, terrible things. I'm sorry you had to see that woman like that. I wish I could take those memories away. I know you're scared something will happen to London, but I will move mountains before I'll let anyone take her away from you. You know that, right?"

She nodded and swiped at her face, her blue eyes still watery. "We're so lucky to have you. I wish London could see how much you love her and how you would do anything for her."

Seb felt his eyes widen at her mention of love, but before he could form a response, she started talking again.

"I don't know why she's still so against a relationship with you. She loves you too. I know she does, even if she's never admitted it. She's never moved past the idea that you only tolerate her because of my dad and me." She pursed her lips and glanced away, thinking. "I just wish there was a way you could convince her it's more than that."

Seb cleared his throat. "It's complicated."

She looked up at him and frowned so hard her brows touched. "No, it's not. She loves you, you love her. Just kiss her already."

"I did. Twice."

Abigail flashed a quick grin. "I know. She told me, but only because I pestered her. That's so exciting." Her tears vanished, for which Seb was grateful, but now he had a different problem.

"Honey, nothing has changed. Yes, we kissed, but we're still just friends."

Her frown came back with a vengeance. "Seriously? Ugh! What is wrong with you two?"

He couldn't help but grin at her disgruntled expression. "Maybe you should talk to her about this. I'm all for a relationship, but she's still fighting it."

Abigail rolled her eyes. "Of course she is. Okay, here's what we're going to do. Tomorrow at the party, you're going to get her to dance with you. While you do that, I'll hide a bottle of wine and a blanket around the side of the house, then you'll take her away from everyone and convince her that one, she's more to you than just your best friend's sister and my aunt, and two, that a relationship with you is the best thing that will ever happen to her."

He couldn't help but smile at her enthusiasm. She made it sound so simple. "I wish it was that easy."

"It is. You just need time *alone* together—where no one

can interrupt you. You should probably leave your phone with me."

He laughed and kissed her forehead. "You'd make a great strategic commander."

She pushed him back, giggling. "Or a lawyer like Maggie," she said, mentioning his youngest sister. She schooled her features into a serious mask. "I mean it, though. You need to get her alone tomorrow."

"How about I promise to *try*?"

She sighed. "I guess that's good enough." She glared up at him. "But you better try really hard."

He ruffled her hair and stood, holding out a hand. "I will. Come on. I'll tuck you back into bed."

She rolled her eyes again as she took his hand and let him pull her to her feet. "I don't need tucked in. I'm not a little kid."

He smiled. "Humor me."

"Fine," she said with another eye roll and an exaggerated sigh, but this time with a smile.

With a gentle touch, he steered her toward her room. She walked to the bed and climbed under the covers. He smoothed them out and kissed her forehead.

"Try not to worry too much about your aunt, okay? Leave it to me?"

She nodded.

"Good. Get some sleep. I love you, munchkin."

"Love you too."

He gave her shoulder a pat and left her room, closing the door behind him. He sat down on the couch again and stared at the muted television. His eyes flicked to London's closed door, his own worry and fear for her safety rising to the forefront. Abigail was right. He couldn't always be there to protect her, and it scared the shit out of him that something would happen to her when he wasn't around—even if he had someone here to keep watch or they got the security cameras installed. But those wouldn't stop anyone, only allow him to look for the person after the fact. And his deputies were good at their jobs, but he still didn't trust anyone except himself to keep her safe. She meant too much to him.

Anger, swift and dark, flared to life that someone would dare to threaten his sweet, beautiful London. It was unimaginable to think that what had befallen those other women could happen to her too. It also bothered him to no end that Abigail worried about it. She'd had enough death and fear and worry in her short life.

He let his head fall back against the cushions and shut his eyes against the riot of emotions. He wanted to wrap them both in a bubble and let nothing bad come near them. At least tomorrow he knew they would be safe. They would be surrounded by his family all day. The only person who would get London alone would be him. And as he had promised Abigail, he would do his damnedest to convince her they were worth it.

"Thomas, if you drop that cake, London will feed you to the single women's brigade," Tara shouted at her twin as he tripped on a rut in the yard when he turned to say something to them. The three of them were carrying cake boxes to the table set up in the yard at Lee and Jenny's.

"Is Rayna still in it?" he called back. "Because if she is, I'll drop this right now and let you put me at her mercy."

London gave him a devilish smile. "She was never in it. But Adelaide Martin is."

He bared his teeth and squinted. "Never mind. I'll walk like I'm a hundred feet off the ground on a tightrope."

She laughed. "Good boy."

"That woman is toxic. Why couldn't she stay in Denver?"

"Because her rich husband discovered he wasn't the only one warming her bed and cast her out," Tara said. "I still say her parents should have left her to fend for herself. At least they made her get a job."

"Yes, because her come-hither look is what I want to see every time I shop for groceries," Thomas retorted.

"Is that why you ask me to shop for you all the time now?" Tara said.

"Hell, yes. She accosted me in the cereal aisle once. Had me backed into the Lucky Charms and told me she'd like to lick my Blarney Stone."

London struggled not to drop her own cake boxes as she laughed. "She did not."

"Yes, she did. I about kissed Mrs. Chisolm when she turned down the aisle looking for oatmeal. If she's going to be here, I'm not going anywhere alone. Why did we have to invite her?"

"Because her parents are Mom and Dad's friends. We couldn't invite them and not Adelaide."

Thomas growled, but said nothing as they reached the area of the yard set up for the party. A large canopy covered two dozen eight-foot tables. Tara led them to the back patio where they set up all the food.

"This table is just for the cake, so set it up however you want," Tara said to London. She and Thomas set their boxes down on one end, and London put hers next to them.

"Sounds good."

"I'm going to go help Brady set up the hay maze for the kids," Thomas said.

"Okay. Thanks for helping me carry the cake."

"Sure. This grants me a save from Adelaide, right?"

London and Tara laughed.

"Yes," London said. "I promise to come to your rescue if she corners you."

He grinned and ran off to find his brother.

"So, what do you want me to do?" Tara asked, turning back to the cake.

"Let's get them unboxed and then we can assemble—"

"Tara!" A shout from the open back door cut off London's words. A moment later, Tara's sister Maggie poked her head outside. "Come tell Mom she needs to leave the meat alone. She wants to put a jar of relish on your pulled pork."

"What?" Horror filled Tara's voice. "It's not a hot dog!" She took two steps toward the door before turning back to London. "I need to go stop her before she ruins the food."

London laughed. "Please do. I don't want relish on my pork."

Tara scampered away and London could hear her yelling for Jenny to put down the jar.

Left alone, she flipped open the lid on the bottom layer of the three-tier cake she and Tara crafted over the last two days. Made of her signature flavor—and Jenny's favorite—chocolate cinnamon, it was covered in vanilla buttercream and a light blue fondant. Chocolate butter cream held the layers together in each tier for some extra flavor. When she had it fully assembled, beautiful burgundy and pink roses would cascade down the side.

She opened the other boxes and stacked the tiers in the center of the table. She pulled the last box closer and took out one of the larger roses. Knowing it would be hot today, she had made them all out of gumpaste.

"That looks amazing."

London looked up from arranging the flowers to see Seb standing at the end of the table.

"Thanks. It turned out pretty well."

He strolled closer. "Can I help?"

Her heart rate sped up as he neared, and her mind went to the conversation she'd overheard last night. She swallowed hard. "You can hand me flowers if you want."

He took a rose from the box and held it out to her. "Toothpicks?" he asked, noting the stem on which the flower perched.

She nodded and stuck the flower on the cake. "They hold better than buttercream in this heat."

"Where did you learn how to do this?"

She gave a half-shrug. "I learned to bake from my mom. The decorating I learned from YouTube."

He laughed. "Seriously?"

She smiled up at him and nodded. "Some of it I learned from a cake decorating book, but most of it came from YouTube, yes."

Seb ran a finger along the edge of one delicate flower. "Still, this is incredible. They look so real. You have a gift."

She blushed. "It's just cake."

"Beautiful cake." He held out the flower. Her fingers brushed his as she took the rose. Her eyes caught his, and she froze for a moment before turning back to the cake. She pushed the stick into the layer.

"So how was your trip? Did you get any leads?" She hadn't talked to him yesterday after he left for the day, other than a few brief phone calls to check in.

"Maybe. A lot of the seasonal employees live in RVs on the resort property. The manager of that campground said she remembered a guest who fixed the plumbing at the bathhouse when a pipe burst around the time of Amy Beckett's disappearance. She didn't see anyone else who was out of place. We're also searching for her roommate now. She disappeared at the same time."

"Oh, that's terrible," she said as she placed another flower.

"Yeah, well, everything about this case is terrible. I'm

hoping the resort still has the security footage from that far back and we can find the guy who made the repairs."

"Why wouldn't they have it? Isn't all that stuff digital now?"

He handed her another flower. "Mostly, but just like a DVD or a VHS tape, storage is limited. They may have erased it to make room for new footage."

"When will you know?"

"Soon, I hope. The detective handling Amy Beckett's disappearance was going to work on getting it this weekend."

London placed the last few flowers and stepped back to check her work. She made a couple adjustments to cover some holes, then nodded.

"Finished. I just hope it stands up to the heat. At least it's in the shade." She pointed up at the house which cast a shadow over the food tables.

She stepped forward to gather up the boxes, and he moved to help her.

"What are we doing with these?" he asked, arms full.

"I was going to put them back in my car. Tara's taken over the kitchen and there's no space for anything else."

She grabbed the smaller boxes and led the way through the yard to her SUV.

"I thought your parents were going to fly in for the party," Seb said as they picked their way through the grass.

"They were, but Dad caught a bad cold. Mom said they would try to come later in the year." She sighed. Her folks were a sore subject. She loved them, but they'd left a lot on her plate for her to deal with alone when Eddie died. London understood being back here was painful because of their memories of him, but she grieved for her brother too.

They reached her car, and she used the foot sensor to open the back hatch and set the boxes in the cargo area. Seb set his next to hers, and she shut the door.

As she turned to go back to the house, he reached out and took her hand, halting her progress.

"Wait."

She looked down at their joined hands, then up at him, confused.

"Come with me." He started tugging her away from all the cars.

"What? Where are we going?"

"Just—come on." He pulled on her hand, moving further from the party.

She dug in her feet. "Seb, I need to get back to the house and see what else Tara needs help with."

"Tara has a dozen other people to help her. Come on."

She bit her lip and cast a glance back at the house. The conversation she overheard between Seb and Abigail played through her mind. Was he getting her alone like he said he would? Was she really opposed to that idea?

The memory of his kisses flitted through her head. She wanted more of those, even if it wasn't wise.

"Okay." She gave in to the urge, recognizing she was fighting a losing battle.

His smile blinded her, prompting one of her own. He readjusted his grip on her hand and jogged across the yard toward one of the barns. As she followed along, she wondered if Abigail had hidden the wine and blanket yet.

They reached the yearling barn, and he pulled her inside the door. The large fans overhead whirred as they moved air around the large interior. The soft whicker of one of the young horses sounded over the fans, and a gray colt stuck his head over the door of his stall. Before she could walk over to pet him, Seb hauled her down the concourse to the supply room.

Her heart started to triple-time with anticipation.

Once inside, he kicked the door closed and leaned her

against it, trapping her body between it and his muscled frame. A shiver went down her spine. She grasped his biceps to steady herself, her fingers tracing the dips and lines of his arms. He felt so good.

She trailed her hands up to his neck, pulling herself closer. His hands slid around her waist to tuck her into his long, powerful body.

Just as she was about to raise her face for his kiss, his conversation with Abigail last night filtered back in, as did the doubt.

She slid a hand up between them and covered his lips.

He gave her a curious look. "Um, London?"

She dropped her hand and let out a huff, a little perturbed. "Before we—do anything, you should know that I overheard you with Abigail last night."

He straightened, his confusion turning to curiosity. "You did?"

She nodded.

"Okay. Why are you telling me this now?"

"Well, I can't help but wonder if the reason you're doing this is because you told her you would."

"I told her I would try. I never promised. I also wouldn't do this at all if I didn't want to." He let go of her and backed away. "Geez, London. What is it going to take for you to realize I'm serious about this? About us? I mean, do you really think I just see you as Eddie's kid sister? Or do you get that I see you as much, much more and are just too afraid to do anything about it?"

London's hackles rose at his accusatory tone. "Excuse me? I never said anything about being afraid of a relationship with you. It's always been about Abigail. I heard you with her last night. I know how much you love her. Do you really want to endanger what you have with her for a fling with me?"

"It wouldn't be a fling!" His voice thundered off the rafters.

Before she could react, he backed her into the door again and kissed her. London's anger morphed into need. Red-hot need, that speared her like a poker in the gut. She wove one hand into his hair and the other around his shoulders and kissed him back.

His hands roved over her hips, kneading her flesh through her flowy skirt. She pressed closer as the fire erupted between them, seeking a way to fan the flames that felt so good. Kissing Seb was unlike any other kiss she'd ever had. It was raw and real and had her ready to pop like a champagne cork.

When he drew back, they were both breathing hard. London's heart galloped in her chest faster than any of the young horses in the barn would ever run.

He leaned his forehead against hers. His warm breath fanned her face, making her yearn for another kiss. "Not just a fling. Never a fling."

She nodded in agreement and leaned in to kiss him again.

"Seb? You in here?"

Brady's voice echoed through the barn. Seb cursed under his breath and London heaved an annoyed sigh. So much for being alone.

Seb kissed her once more, his lips searing hers for a brief moment. "I swear, I will find a way to get us completely alone." He leaned around her and opened the door.

"Back here," he called. He took her hand and stepped through the doorway.

Brady rounded the corner and came to an abrupt halt when he saw her. His eyes flicked down to their clasped hands and a broad smile spread over his face.

"Sorry to interrupt. Thomas said he saw you come this way. We need another set of hands at the maze. My plans were a little more elaborate than I thought. We need someone to drive the lift and two people to unload if we want to get it done in time."

"Okay. Give me a minute and I'll head over there."

Brady's grin grew, but he just nodded and backed away before turning and jogging out of the barn. As soon as he cleared the door, Seb scooped her up and kissed her again.

Her feet left the floor as he swept her up to hold her tight. The blistering heat came back with a rush and she didn't fight it. Didn't even think about what it meant. She let go of all the doubt and worry and just let herself feel. When his tongue brushed the seam of her lips, she let him in, unable to remember why she ever thought this a bad idea.

He lowered her to the floor again, but didn't let her go. Instead, his hands started to roam. London moaned into his mouth when his fingers slid up her ribcage and feathered over her breasts through her dress. She arched into him, wishing he touched her bare skin.

She ran her hands down his chest, his thin blue t-shirt doing little to hide the firm muscles underneath. Her fingers dipped into the valley between his pecs and down over the hills of his abs. He sucked in a breath as she skimmed her hand over the waistband of his jeans. She could feel him pressing into her belly through his zipper. Heat pooled in her core.

He pulled back and broke the kiss. Leaning his forehead against hers, he looked down at her, chest heaving as he sucked in air.

"Later. We will finish this later."

She looked up at him through her lashes and nodded.

He straightened and released her, backing away. "I better go find Brady and Thomas before they come looking for me again. I'll see you in a bit."

London hugged herself, trying to stop her body from vibrating apart, and nodded.

The look in his eyes just before he turned away was

enough to melt her into a puddle of goo on the barn floor. It promised to set her on fire tonight.

A shiver ran up her spine as she watched him jog from the barn to find his brothers, back straight, long legs encased in tight denim.

The hum already running through her got louder.

She moaned and looked at the ceiling. It was going to be a long day.

London stuffed the last of her cake in her mouth and looked out over the crowd mingling in the yard. Lee and Jenny sat at the front of the crowd, laughing with the Martins.

To the side of the tables, Abigail's boyfriend Trent and his bandmates gathered, ready to play. Brady had constructed a raised dance floor and stage for the party-goers. He even added posts all the way around with lights strung across the top.

She scanned the crowd once more, looking for Seb. He had wandered off with Thomas after dinner to play corn hole. Not seeing him, or any of the Archer brothers, she moved away from where she stood near the house. She dumped her plate in the trash and stepped off the deck, weaving into the crowd to where the games were set up.

The first strings of a country song flared to life as she stepped past the edge of the canopy. Clear of the crowd, she saw Seb and Thomas standing with their backs to her as they tossed horseshoes with Brady and another man she didn't recognize, but based on his appearance, he looked like the man Tara described as the detective from Nebraska.

"London."

She turned at the sound of her name to see Ryan Marsters standing behind her. In dark jeans and a polo shirt, his muscular physique belied a man in his fifties.

"Mr. Marsters. Hello."

He offered her a hesitant smile. "Would you like to dance?"

She glanced back at Seb, who laughed at something Thomas said, oblivious to her presence.

"Um, sure," she said, turning back to him with a soft smile.

He held out a hand. "Call me Ryan, please."

She nodded and took his hand. "Ryan."

He led her onto the dance floor and pulled her into his arms as Trent and his band transitioned to a slow song.

"Are you enjoying the party?" she asked.

"Yes. The Archers always throw great parties."

London smiled. "They do. They're even better now that Tara's living here again. She ups the food game."

He grinned. "I had the barbacoa. It was amazing."

She nodded. "It was. I had a little bit of that and the pulled pork."

"I heard you had some trouble at the B&B. Declan came in for parts for your hot water heater. Said someone tampered with it. Everything all right out there?"

She sighed. "Yes. We had a little trouble, but nothing bad really happened. Seb's keeping an eye on things."

"Oh? Has he stepped up patrols out there?"

"He's staying with us at night and some of his deputies are spending their off hours there during the day."

He frowned, his expression serious. "It's that bad?"

"No. Honestly, I think he's just being a little overprotective, and because of his relationship with me and Abigail, his deputies are taking it more seriously. We're fine."

"If you need anything, you can call me too. I live on that side of town, so I can be there in just a few minutes."

"That's very nice of you. I'm sure we'll be okay, though."

"I hope so. I wouldn't want anything to happen to you. You're a lovely woman, London."

She rolled her lips inward at his words, getting the feeling he was working up the courage to ask her out.

"Actually, I think you're really great."

That sinking feeling got worse. She did not want to have this conversation, but couldn't think of any way to bow out without hurting his feelings.

"I admire you a lot—especially the way you stepped in to raise your niece when your brother and your sister-in-law died —and was wondering if you'd like to go to dinner with me. Maybe The Heartwood since you like Tara's food so much?"

Thankful for their proximity so he couldn't see the look of dismay on her face, she thought quickly. She had to find a way to turn him down nicely.

Taking a deep breath, she pushed back. "That's a very nice offer, Ryan, but I can't accept. You're a nice man, but I think our age difference is a bit extreme."

His face fell, the sweet hope leaving his eyes. He was so nice, and she hated to disappoint him.

"I know I'm a little older than you, but age is just a number."

"Not really. When we grow up shapes how we view the world. You're what, twenty years older than me? That's a lifetime of different experiences. I'm really sorry, but I think we're best as friends."

"Are you sure? We both grew up in small towns. You might find we have more in common than you think."

"No, I'm sure. I'm sorry."

He nodded. "Me too."

The song ended, and he stepped back. "Thanks for the dance. I'll see you later."

She frowned as she watched him go, upset she had so obviously disappointed him. But she couldn't see herself in a relationship with a man old enough to be her father, even if he was handsome and looked younger.

Strong arms slid around her waist and she jumped, relaxing as she recognized the now familiar hum provoked by Sebastian's touch.

"Hi," she said, turning her face up to look at him.

He dropped a quick kiss on her lips and smiled. "Wanna dance?"

She spun in his arms and looped them around his neck. "Yes."

"Good answer." He took her hand and stepped into the line of people, moving around the dance floor in a two-step. With a quick yank on her hand, he twirled her into his side.

She laughed in delight and followed his lead as the band played the upbeat song. London loved to dance, but rarely got the chance.

They made several circuits of the floor before the song ended with a flourish. She fell into Seb's side, winded, but laughing. The pace of the music changed again, and he pulled her against him. She sank into his embrace and rested her head against his chest, their clasped hands resting on his shoulder, each of them holding the other with one arm.

His warm breath ruffled the hair at her temple and she let out a contented sigh.

"I saw you dancing with Marsters. Do I have competition?"

She giggled and turned her face to look up at him. "No. He asked me out, but I said no. He's too old for me."

He bent closer. "Is that the only reason?" His voice was low and rolled over her. A shiver ran through her at the rich sound.

She shook her head. "No." The word came out on a soft breath and she tipped her face up. His lips met hers in a gentle touch. Liquid heat spread outward to put every cell in her body on alert.

Whistles and clapping broke through the fog in her brain as Seb pulled back. She looked past him to see his brothers and sisters as well as Declan, Macy, Rayna, and Seb's detective friend standing at the edge of the floor grinning widely at them. A different kind of heat spread over her face as she blushed.

Seb led her off the dance floor to their friends.

Macy fanned herself. "Girl. I don't know how you resisted him for so long. That was *hot*. Do you want me to ask Abigail to come back to my house tonight?"

"Ew," Maggie said, looking at her oldest brother, her nose wrinkled in distaste. "I did not want to think about that."

London blushed even as she coughed to cover up a laugh. "I think she mentioned something about going back to her friend Alexis's house, but thanks."

Macy waggled her eyebrows. "Either way, you two will be alone."

She pressed her lips together and cast a quick glance up at Seb, who looked as uncomfortable at the attention as she felt. She cleared her throat and changed the subject. "So, is there a reason you're all congregated here together?"

Thomas nodded. "We're rounding people up to play a game of softball. We were just waiting for you two to stop making googly eyes at each other so we could ask if you wanted to join us."

London narrowed her eyes at him. "You know that promise I made to you earlier? I rescind the offer." She looked around the yard, a wicked grin crossing her face when she spotted her quarry. "In fact, I see Adelaide now. I'm going to go ask if she wants to join us."

She spun away to do just that, but Seb grabbed her hand and pulled her back.

"There's no need to punish all of us for Thomas's tongue."

Her smile turned sly. "Who says she has to be on our team?" She sent a knowing look at Thomas, who blanched.

Seb's face split into a teasing smile and he turned to look at his brother. "Oh, I like that idea. We do need two teams of at least eight to play. We're still short six people."

"You guys are terrible," Rayna said. "Stop picking on the poor woman. She's just lonely."

"Yeah? Well, she can find someone else to assuage her loneliness," Thomas retorted.

Rayna rolled her eyes at him.

"So, if not her, who else do we ask?" Tara said.

"Anyone. Literally anyone," Thomas said.

London cast a glance at Adelaide again, who was now moving their way. "Uh-oh. I think we attracted her attention."

Thomas peered around her and groaned. "Shit." He pushed the detective forward. "Here. You're fresh meat. Let her shove her cleavage in your face."

Jace twisted his head to look back at Thomas, confusion all over his handsome face. "What? Is she seriously that bad? She's a grown woman, not some teenager stuck in hormone hell."

Before anyone could answer him, Adelaide was upon them.

"Hi. You guys look like you're planning something. What's up?"

"Nothing," Thomas said.

"We're putting together a softball game," Rayna said, casting a disapproving glance at Thomas. "Would you like to join us?"

Adelaide smiled and sauntered forward. "Well, I guess that depends. Whose team am I on?" She advanced on Thomas, who sidestepped behind Jace and Brady. She frowned at him, then looked at Jace.

"Well, hello. I'm Adelaide Martin. You're new." She held out a hand, fingers dripping red nails that looked like they hadn't ever seen a vacuum, let alone a softball bat.

Jace took her hand and shook it, offering the woman a smile. "Jace Travers. I'm a colleague of Seb's."

"You're a cop?"

He nodded.

She batted her eyes at him and tossed her long blonde hair over her shoulder, thrusting her chest forward. London heard Thomas bite back a groan of disgust, while Jace frowned.

"I do love a man in uniform." She stepped closer to him. "Can I be on your team?" She looked back at Seb. "And yours?"

London shocked herself and growled. She looped her arm through Seb's and glared at the woman.

Adelaide's simpering smile faltered at the glare on London's face. "You could be on the team too, London."

"Oh, thank you. I'm glad I have your permission." She rolled her eyes. "Do you want to play or not?"

Her eyes roved over the Archer men and all their friends, and she nodded.

London smiled at Thomas. "Now we only need five."

He groaned and scrubbed his hands over his face.

"Come on, Mags! We can't let them win!" Tara yelled from second base. Adelaide, who had proven to be not terrible at the game, stood poised on third, ready to run home as soon as Maggie made contact.

"Maggie can't hit the broad side of a barn," Thomas yelled from the outfield.

"You shut up! I can too."

London smiled from her spot on first base and cheered Maggie on. They had divided the teams by men and women. The girls only needed one run to win.

"He's right, you know," Seb said. He was playing first. "Maggie is a terrible hitter."

She had seen no evidence to the contrary today, unfortunately. She refused to accept that, though. "We'll see."

Brady wound up and tossed the ball toward the plate. Maggie swung and missed. London let out a sharp whistle. "That's all right, Maggie. You'll get the next one."

"She won't."

London poked her tongue into her cheek and looked up at him. "Want to bet?"

He straightened and smiled. "Any day. That's easy money."

"I was thinking something more interesting."

His eyebrows shot up. He peered at her over the top of his sunglasses. "Such as?"

She smiled, her expression coy. "How about who gets to be on top first?"

The clang of the bat hitting the ball sounded. London turned to see the ball on the ground headed toward her and took off for second base. Seb, stunned by her words, was slower to react and the ball flew right past him into the outfield.

London and the rest of her team whooped as Adelaide crossed home plate. She reversed course and ran to congratulate Maggie on her game-winning hit.

"No fair," Thomas said, interrupting their celebration. "You guys cheated."

"We did not," Maggie said. "I hit that ball fair and square."

"Not you. Her." He pointed at London. "She distracted the first baseman."

London held up her hands. "I was just making conversation."

Seb grabbed her around the waist and buried his face in her neck. "Distracting conversation."

London shivered as he nuzzled behind her ear. "Which we never finished."

She felt him smile against her skin. "I think it's time we did," he whispered in her ear.

Her knees wobbled, and she locked them to stay upright.

He pulled back and aimed a sinful smile at her.

"Get a room," Maggie said, walking past, the bat she hit the game-winner with sitting on her shoulder.

Abigail giggled. "I guess it's a good thing I'm going home with Alexis tonight."

London did her best to glare at her niece. "This is not an appropriate topic, young lady."

Declan walked up and put an arm over Maggie and Abigail's shoulders. "Ignore these two. You guys deserve some time alone. Come on, ladies. You can walk me to my car. I need to get back to the fire station." He steered the two women away.

Seb and London followed at a slower pace. As they made their way back to the main party, she noticed that many people had already left. The sun sat low in the sky and there was a chill beginning to permeate the air, reminding her it was still early June.

She noticed Jenny carrying platters of food toward the kitchen. Tara and Maggie were both headed her way.

"I'm going to go help your mother and sisters clean up."

He nodded. "I should help Brady and Thomas with the games. Don't leave without me."

"I won't."

He ran his knuckles down the side of her face and brushed her bottom lip with his thumb as he stared down at her. Her heart skipped a beat at the tender look in his eyes. He let his hand drop and backed away.

"Hold that thought."

For the second time that day, he walked away and left her wanting more.

ELEVEN

With nerves shaking her fingers, London inserted the key into the door from the garage, Seb behind her. Her high ponytail meant she could feel his breath against her neck, even from a distance.

She fought back a shiver and turned the knob, letting them inside.

"Let me just check the snack station in the dining room." She glanced at him, her anxiety about tonight making her feel jittery.

He nodded. "I'll go check in with my deputy and meet you upstairs." He left the room through the pocket door into the living room while London went through the door to the dining room.

She took a steady breath as she flipped on the light and walked over to the long buffet and mini-fridge along the wall where she kept a selection of snacks and drinks for the guests and looked through the contents. Abigail had filled it that morning, so it likely didn't need to be restocked, but London needed a moment to herself. When she had turned off her car and saw Seb walking into the garage, his long legs eating up

the ground as he strode toward her with purpose, the butter-
flies had launched an attack in her stomach. Going to bed with
him would forever change everything. There would be no
going back to their safe, simple friendship after this, and that
scared the daylights out of her.

Satisfied the snack station was well-stocked, she left the
dining room, flipping off the lights as she went. The living
room was silent, and she frowned. Where was Seb's deputy
who was supposed to be watching the house?

Instead of heading for the stairs, she went to the front
door and turned on the porch light, peering out through the
window to the side of the door. Seeing no one, she turned off
the light. Maybe he already left and Seb was upstairs. It seemed
quick, but if it had been a slow night, that wouldn't take long
for the deputy to relay.

She walked up the stairs to the family apartment and
pulled out her keys to unlock the hallway door and let herself
inside.

"Seb?"

Silence greeted her, and the living room was dark. She
flipped the light switch and gasped. The room was in complete
disarray. All the books were off the shelves, the TV tipped
over, and the couch cushions slashed, their stuffing sitting in
tufts around the room.

"Oh my God." Her purse fell from her numb fingers and
she walked further into the room. Through the open doors
she could see that her bedroom and Abigail's looked much the
same as the living room. She wandered closer to Abigail's
room and looked inside. It had been tossed, but not destroyed.
Her bedding was on the floor and things swept off her dresser.

She moved to her own room and couldn't hold back the
sob as she stepped over the threshold. It had taken the brunt
of the intruder's rage. Her bedspread and sheets were shred-
ded, and the springs pulled from the mattress to stick up like

spikes. The contents of her dresser and closets littered the floor, some of it ripped, and the pictures were off the walls, the glass smashed.

"Sebastian!" Backing out of the room, she ran out of the apartment and downstairs, tears flowing freely down her cheeks.

She ran through the living room, back to the kitchen, but there was no sign of him.

Her mind spun. *Where the hell did he go?*

Hands shaking, she pulled her phone from the pocket of her dress and called him. It rang several times before he finally picked up.

"Stay inside. I can't find my deputy and he's not answering his phone."

"Seb, the apartment's been trashed. It's a mess."

"What? Fuck. Of course it is. Is the rest of the house all right?"

"From what I've seen, yes."

"Okay. Gather all the guests in the living room. I need to know what they saw and heard."

London brushed her bangs out of her face and swallowed a hiccup. This was a nightmare. She wasn't going to have any guests left if this kept up. "Okay. Hurry."

"I will. Call 911 and have them send a crime scene unit."

He hung up and London dialed 911, requesting the CSI unit Seb wanted, then put her phone away. Taking a deep breath, she headed back upstairs to disturb her guests' evening once again.

Seb crept around the side of the house. When he'd gone into the living room and found it empty, he'd called the deputy who had volunteered to watch the house—Aaron Gentry—

but he hadn't answered. Concerned, he'd started searching the lower level of the house and had ended up outside. So far, the porch was clear as well as the front yard.

Rounding the back corner, Seb aimed the gun and flashlight he'd taken from his glove box ahead of him, the light cutting through the growing twilight. He walked up to the shed and tested the door. The padlock was shut tight, but noise from inside drew his attention.

He lowered his weapon and leaned an ear to the door. "Aaron? You in there?"

A muffled voice cried out, louder this time.

"Hang on. I need to check the rest of the property and get the key." Seb hurried away and checked the rest of the yard behind the house, but it was empty. He walked the back line where it butted up to the forest, but didn't see anything suspicious. Whoever had been inside was long gone.

He holstered his gun and ran back to the house, using the key London gave him the other day to get in the back door. Right away he heard raised voices from the living room. In four long strides, he was across the kitchen and through the pocket door.

His vision went red at the sight of Doug Brown standing over London, yelling in her face. Seb's long legs ate up the ground between them and he had Brown by the collar in an instant. He pulled the man away, lifting him off his feet as he spun him to the side.

"Hey! Get off me!"

"Buddy, you're lucky I don't punch you. What the fuck do you think you're doing?" He looked at London, her tear-stained face pale in the overhead light. Her full bottom lip quivered as she tried to keep her emotions in check.

Seb's blood boiled hotter, and he gave Brown a good shake. "Why are you yelling at her?"

"This is twice now something bad has happened. She needs better security. This whole place should be shut down."

"Did you not see the off-duty deputy in the living room all day? Now, sit down and shut up. You utter so much as a word without being asked, and I'm pretty sure you'll regret it." He let him go with a small shove.

Brown smirked and straightened his collar. "Yeah, right. You're a cop. You can't do shit to me if you want to keep your job."

Seb erased the distance between them in one quick move. He tangled his hands in the front of the man's shirt again and hauled him up so he was on his toes. "Fuck my job. You mess with London and my badge is nothing more than a shiny piece of metal. Get me?"

Brown blanched and had the good sense to nod and not say anything. Seb let him go again and pointed at an empty chair. Once the man sat, he turned to London.

"I found Aaron. He's in the shed, but it's locked. Where's the key?"

"It's upstairs on my key ring. I dropped my purse inside the apartment door. How did the shed door get unlocked?"

"My guess is whoever did this picked the lock. Keep everyone in here and I'll be back in a few minutes." He handed London his service weapon.

She frowned even as she took it. "What's this for?"

"Just in case dickhead over there gives you any more trouble."

"Seb, I'm not going to shoot him for running his mouth."

One corner of his mouth tilted. "I doubt you'll have too, but I feel better knowing you could." He leaned in and kissed her hard. "I'll be right back."

She nodded, and he ran up the stairs to retrieve her keys. Using his house key, he unlocked the apartment door and stepped inside.

"Whoa." She hadn't been kidding. It really was a mess in here.

He bent and took the key ring from London's purse, then closed the door and ran back downstairs past the group gathered in the living room and into the kitchen to go out the back door.

At the shed, he stuck his light between his teeth and found the padlock key. Tipping up the lock, he noted the scratch marks on it before inserting the key and opening it. He pushed open the door and removed his light from his mouth to shine it inside. Aaron sat in the middle of the floor, trussed up like a turkey, his hands and feet bound with duct tape and a piece slapped over his mouth.

Seb kneeled in front of the deputy and gently pulled the tape off his face.

"Ouch. That shit hurts."

"You all right? What happened?" Seb took a knife from his pocket and cut the tape binding the deputy's wrists, then moved to his ankles.

"Yeah, I'm okay." He reached a hand up to touch the back of his head. "I heard a noise outside, so I went out to investigate. I made it to the corner by the garage when someone ambushed me." He pulled his hand away, and it shone red in Seb's flashlight. "I woke up in here. Is everyone okay?"

Seb nodded and helped Aaron to his feet. "They're fine, but the family apartment's been torn apart. Come on. Let's get you inside so we can clean up that wound. You should probably go get checked at the hospital since you passed out."

Aaron stood, wincing. "I'm fine. Put me to work."

"Let's get you cleaned up first. Your head bled a decent amount." He guided the man out of the shed and toward the back door.

"Hurts like a bitch too."

Seb let them inside and headed for the living room. He

was pleased to see that Brown still sat in his chair. While he leaned back with a self-important look on his face, he was at least silent.

London rose from her seat when she saw Aaron. The others gasped at the sight of his blood-soaked shirt.

"Oh my goodness. Are you all right?"

"I'm fine, Ms. Scott. Just a bump."

She turned him around to inspect his head. "That's more than a bump. I'll go get the first aid kit. You might need stitches, though."

One of the female guests rose. "I'm a nurse. Can I help?"

London nodded. "Let me go get the kit. Why don't you take him into the bathroom off the game room and I'll meet you there?"

While the other woman led Aaron away, London walked toward Seb and passed him his weapon, then retreated to the kitchen to get the first aid kit.

Seb faced the rest of the guests. He pointed at Brown. "I take it from his behavior London filled you all in?"

The guests nodded.

"Good. How many of you, when you arrived, didn't see Deputy Gentry inside?"

One couple raised their hands.

"He was here when the rest of you came back?"

They all nodded, even Brown.

"What did you hear? Or see?"

"Just some thumps," Mrs. Strattman said. "Byron and I thought London had returned, and she was moving things around."

"Same here," one of the younger women said. "It wasn't really anything we wouldn't expect at a hotel."

Seb's mouth flattened into a thin line. He was afraid of that. "Did anyone look out a window and see anyone? Or maybe a vehicle you didn't recognize?"

Brown sat forward, his arrogant expression changing to a more thoughtful one. "There was a car parked on the side of the road when I came back. I didn't get a good look at it, but it looked like a truck or SUV. It was tucked behind some bushes."

Seb narrowed his eyes as he considered the man's words, trying to decide if he was sincere. He didn't trust Brown, and after the way he treated London, Seb wouldn't put it past the man to make trouble.

"What color was it?"

"Dark. Maybe dark blue or charcoal. I don't think it was black."

"Okay. You're going to show me where. Let's go. The rest of you hang out here for now. We need to sweep the rest of the inn. I have a crime scene unit on the way."

Brown rose, and Seb led him outside. "How far from the drive was it?"

"Maybe a couple hundred yards." He pointed to the right.

Seb started to jog down the drive, not caring that his companion was dressed in loafers and dress slacks. He reached the road, not stopping as he turned right. He looked back over his shoulder to see the other man keeping pace.

"Up there." Brown pointed to a clump of bushes on the opposite side of the road that were just visible in the low light.

Seb crossed over and walked onto the berm. He shined his light on the ground. The grass was depressed where a vehicle had driven through.

"How did you see this? Were you coming from this way?"

"No. I came back around sunset. The light was just right that it hit off the windshield. I could see part of the front bumper and the mirror."

He nodded, scanning the ground for any evidence, but all he saw was flattened grass. Turning back, he pointed his light in Brown's face.

"You want to tell me what you're really doing here?"

A slight widening of the man's eyes was his only tell. "What do you mean? I'm on business."

Seb stalked forward. "Land development, right?"

He nodded, standing straighter as Seb advanced.

"What land are you looking at?"

"That's privileged information." He crossed his arms and bristled.

Seb scoffed. "I'm not going to steal your sale. It's London's property, isn't it? That's why you're so tight-lipped."

"It's not."

"I don't believe you."

"It isn't, I swear."

"Then tell me where."

"I can't." An edge of panic entered his voice.

Seb grinned, knowing he had the man on edge. He stepped closer. "Fine. Keep your secret, but I will find out. I don't trust you. And if you dare speak one word out of line to London again, I promise you, my badge won't make one lick of difference."

Brown nodded, and Seb motioned him back toward the inn. They jogged back and reached the front porch just as the CSI unit turned onto the drive. He let Brown go inside while he waited on the team to get out.

"This is becoming a habit, Sheriff," the lead investigator, Katie Mitchum said, pulling a case from the van.

He walked down to her to help her carry her gear. "Tell me about it. This can end whenever it wants." He took the case from her as well as the next one she pulled out. She looped the strap of a duffel bag over her shoulder and shut the door. Her assistant came around front, carrying a camera case and two Tyvek suits.

He showed them inside and upstairs to the apartment.

Katie let out a low whistle and adjusted her glasses when she got her first glimpse of the destruction.

"Someone was angry."

Seb agreed. Whoever did this had been smart about it in their rage, though. While the place was ransacked, the furniture wasn't overturned other than the television, which would have alerted the guests to the intrusion. He couldn't help but wonder what set the guy off.

"Find me something, Katie."

She patted his shoulder. "I'll do my best." She stepped around him and motioned to her assistant. "Come on, Devin. Let's get busy."

Three hours later, London stood in the middle of her small living room and stared at the destruction around her. It didn't look any better than the first time she'd seen it.

Seb walked up behind her and wrapped his hands over her shoulders.

"Where do I start?" she asked. Her voice was rough. She was so overwhelmed and a little numb.

"How about we just do the bedroom tonight? We can get some sleep and tackle the rest tomorrow."

She nodded and crossed to her room in a bit of a fugue. The devastation in here was so horrible; every piece of fabric was torn, even her underwear.

Her eyes landed on a shirt near the closet. She crossed to pick it up. The tears she'd been holding in all night finally spilled over and a sob broke free.

Seb's arms were around her in an instant.

"Honey, it's okay. We can get you new clothes."

She held up the garment in her hands. "This—this was Eddie's." She'd found the hoodie when going through his things after his death. It had still smelled like him and she hadn't been able to part with it. Now it was ruined.

She turned and buried her face in Seb's chest and let the tears flow.

He held her tight, his hands making long strokes on her back.

"Why—why would someone do this?" She clutched Eddie's shirt to her face, feeling the softness against her skin and mourning all over again for what she'd lost.

His arms tightened, and he pressed a kiss to the top of her head. "I don't know, baby. I'm going to find him, though."

She sniffed and swiped at the tears on her face, inhaling Seb's scent and letting it soothe her frayed nerves. She was safe right now and wallowing in self-pity wouldn't help her or the situation.

Closing her eyes, she took one last, deep breath and pushed away, wiping the last traces of tears from her face. "Let's get this cleaned up. It's late."

He studied her for a moment, reaching out with one finger to brush over her cheekbone. "You sure you're okay to do this? I can call one of my brothers and have them help me. You don't need to be here."

Tears welled in her eyes once more at the gesture, but she blinked them away. "No. I do need to be here. I can't let this guy chase me from my home or make me afraid to live my life. Other than Eddie's sweatshirt—" she broke off as her throat closed with emotion. Swallowing hard to get rid of the lump, she continued. "Other than his shirt, I can replace everything else. I'll be fine."

He stared down at her for another moment, then nodded. "Okay. Let's get started, then. Why don't you go get some cleaning supplies—trash bags, the vacuum—and I'll start sorting through all this to see if any of it's salvageable."

She walked back to the main living area to do as he

suggested, feeling determined. No one was going to taint her home and pollute it with his rage. She wouldn't let him. This place was her sanctuary. It had helped her cope with Eddie's death. So, she was going to pull out her cleaning supplies and put it back to rights. She hoped word got back to the bastard that she was fine. That the break-in barely phased her. Let him stick that in his craw and chew on it.

Gathering the items they would need to make the bedroom habitable, she hauled her loot back to Seb and handed him a trash bag.

He pointed at a pile. "That stuff didn't look terrible. Why don't you look through it first, then move onto that side of the room?" He gestured toward the closet. "I'll keep going through things over here."

She nodded and bent to look at what he'd already sorted.

It took them two hours and ten trash bags, but they finally cleared the floor. London flopped onto the bare mattress they had flipped over to hide the exposed springs and wiped a bead of sweat off her temple.

"I think that's good enough. I'm ready to take a shower and go to bed."

"Me too. While you do that, I'll go clear a spot behind the couch."

She frowned. Why would he—? Her face smoothed out as she realized he intended to sleep on the floor again.

"Seb, you don't need to do that." She rose to go stand in front of him.

A muscle in his jaw ticked. "El, I know we talked about taking our relationship to the next level, but with all that happened tonight, we don't—"

She laid a finger over his lips to silence him.

"I want to. I'm tired of fighting us. Change is scary, but doing life without you is scarier. I like what's happened between us the last few days." She moved closer and wrapped her arms around his neck. His hands went to her waist, his fingers gripping her hips.

"You're sure? This isn't just a response to trauma?"

"I'm sure." She stepped back, trailing her hands down his arms to twine her fingers with his. "You know what we need to do first, though?"

He shook his head, desire making his eyes shine like black diamonds.

"Find new bedding."

He blinked, then laughed. "It might be more comfortable, yes." He let go of her hands to pull her close. "Although, a bed isn't required."

She gulped, her knees turning rubbery at the look in his eyes. Her entire body tingled as a hum of arousal coursed through her to pool in her core. If he could heat her up this much with just a look, sex would set her on fire.

Before he could kiss her and do just that, she pushed out of his arms and started for the living room. "If you can find the extra sheets that were in the bathroom cabinet, I'll go downstairs and get some spare blankets and pillows."

He blew out a breath, switching gears. "Yeah. Okay."

She fled. Not because she was afraid, but because she knew that the next time he kissed her, she wouldn't be leaving the apartment for a very long time.

Downstairs, she hurried into the utility room where she kept the extra bedding and pulled out a queen-size comforter. Arms full, she ran back up to find that Seb had already put the fitted sheet on the bed and was stuffing pillows into pillowcases. She set the blanket on the floor by the bed and picked up the flat sheet, billowing it out over the mattress.

"I can't believe he left these sheets alone."

Seb shook the pillow in his hands to settle it into the case, then threw it onto the head of the bed. He braced his hands on his hips and arched one eyebrow. "If they'd been in here, he probably wouldn't have."

London tucked the sheet under the mattress, then unfolded the comforter over top of it. "What he did destroy was enough. I'm going to have to go clothes and furniture shopping tomorrow. I don't know where we'll sit until a new couch arrives. At least he missed a few of my clothes, so I don't have to re-wear what I have on."

He pulled on one corner of the blanket to help her straighten it. "I'll go out to the ranch tomorrow after church and have one of my brothers help me bring over my couch. You can use it until you get a new one." Bed made, he walked around to her side to stand in front of her.

She frowned up at him. "What are you going to sit on? Or your guest, for that matter?"

Seb shrugged and wrapped his arms around her. "I still have my recliner. Jace can use that. And it's not like I won't be spending most of my time here anyway, even if there wasn't a psycho on the loose." He dipped his head and nuzzled the skin behind her ear.

A shiver ran down her spine and she sucked in a sharp breath.

"How about that shower now?"

She threaded her fingers into his hair and gripped the strands, using touch to keep herself grounded in reality.

"Okay," she said, breathless.

His arms clamped around her and he lifted her off her feet, then headed for the bathroom. Once inside, he set her down, then pulled his t-shirt over his head.

London's mouth went dry. Seb might be the county's top cop, but he was also a rancher, and it showed. Hard, sinewy muscles bulged beneath his tanned skin. She reached out to trace the line of black hair that split his abs and disappeared beneath the waistband of his jeans. The muscles jumped and flexed at her touch, and he growled, stepping back.

"Not yet." He leaned into the shower enclosure to turn on the water, testing the spray, while she just stood there and watched the play of shifting muscle in his back and arms. He wasn't the first man she'd ever seen without his shirt, but he sure was the sexiest.

He straightened and noticed her watching him. A naughty smile crossed his face, and he reached out to unbutton the front of her sundress. Mini-earthquakes rippled out from everywhere his knuckles brushed her skin until her entire body vibrated with need.

His eyes dilated with each button he unfastened, revealing more and more of her body to his gaze. When he reached her waist, he pushed the lightweight fabric off her shoulders and it slid down her legs to pool at her feet.

London felt like she was standing in front of a furnace, even though she was only in her bra and panties. Heat suffused her from head to toe until she was sure she would combust. She pulled the band from her hair and shook it free.

Seb's hands went to her waist and curved around her sides. His thumbs brushed the underside of her breasts and her nipples peaked as she shivered in delight.

"You're so beautiful," he said, voice low. He leaned down and took her mouth with his. The heat surged hotter, and she kissed him back. His hands found the clasp on her bra and popped it free, and he filled his hands with her flesh. London moaned as he made contact. His big hands were the perfect size.

She fumbled for his belt and bumped the hard ridge behind his fly. He jerked and groaned, and it spurred him on. He deepened their kiss, short-circuiting her brain and turning her fingers to clumsy sticks that could do little more than tug at his clothing. She whimpered with need and pulled back.

"Take off your pants."

He let her go to make quick work of his jeans, thrusting them and his boxer briefs down his legs. He stepped out of them, then hooked his fingers in the waistband of her panties and tugged. They dropped to the floor.

He wrapped his hands around her again, cupping her butt in his large palms, and lifted her against him, then stepped over the edge of the bathtub into the stinging spray of water. London moaned as his erection made contact with her belly. Once he set her on her feet in the tub, she reached down and ran her hand the length of it. Seb made a strangled sound in the back of his throat and pushed her against the wall. The cold tile hit her back, and she yelped.

It was like a cold bucket of water over his head. He pulled back to look down at her, his eyes hooded, but clearer than a moment ago.

"Too fast." He picked up her bottle of shampoo and turned her into the spray. "We're going to make this last."

Water sluiced over her head and down her breasts. London closed her eyes and turned herself over to the flames leaping at her insides as Seb soaped her hair, his strong fingers lulling her into an aroused, yet content state. It had been a long day full of ups and downs, and his ministrations helped to ease some of the tension. When his soapy hands drifted down her neck and over her chest, she moaned and the contentment fled. Desire spiked and her skin flushed with heat.

His erection brushed her backside, and she unconsciously leaned into him. His hands slid lower—down over her stomach to swirl in the curls at the apex of her thighs.

A high-pitched, breathy moan escaped her at his first touch on her core. He pushed his fingers deeper, running them through her curls, and her knees gave out. He tightened one arm around her waist while the other drove her to distraction. Water and soap ran in rivulets down her body, enhancing the effect of his fingers until she was a quivering, tingling mess of a woman, writhing in his arms as the most intense orgasm she'd ever had ripped through her.

Boneless and feeling like limp spaghetti, she sagged against his arm and let her head roll back onto his shoulder. She looked up at him and tried to smile.

His dark eyes stared down at her, the arousal in them making them look like pools of dark chocolate.

"Feel good?"

She nodded and reached one heavy arm up to hold his neck as he bent down to kiss her collarbone. Taking a deep breath, she tried to put some starch back in her legs. She pushed away and spun around, looping her arms around his shoulders and pressing her front to his. Her legs threatened to give out on her again, but she found some hidden well of strength and remained standing under her own power.

"It's my turn now." She thrust her hands into his hair and fused her mouth to his. She spun them so he was in the water and reached for the shampoo. Breaking the kiss, she poured some in her palm and lathered his hair.

"You're going to smell like me."

He licked a bead of water off the swell of her breast. London's heart two-stepped and she swallowed hard.

"That's okay. I plan to have all your scents all over me by the time we're done."

Holy hell! If she wasn't already lit up like a roman candle, she would be now. The image that provoked was enough to keep her humming for days.

She raked her nails over his scalp and his eyes rolled up. She scooped suds from his hair to draw them down over his shoulders, then ran her hands over his pecs, stopping only to swirl them lightly over his nipples. Down his torso, she continued, to wrap her hands around his manhood. He moaned and his head fell back. Soap slid down his tall frame as the water washed it away and London stood, transfixed as she watched the drops slide over his ropey muscles. She squeezed her hands in response to her own desire and he moaned louder.

"Okay, that's enough." He pulled her hands away and turned off the tap. Stepping out of the tub, he turned and grabbed her around the waist, lifting her over the side and onto his shoulder. She shrieked and held on to his shoulders. He clamped a hand over her hip and opened the door, then strode down the hall to her bedroom.

The room whirled as he swung her down and put her in the middle of the mattress. She bounced once, her limbs flailing as she landed. Before she even settled, he crawled over her.

Just as he was about to close the distance and kiss her again, he jerked back.

"Shit. Hang on."

"What?" The word wasn't even out of her mouth and he was off the bed and out the door. London stared after him in confusion. She heard the bathroom door hit the wall, then the sound of his bare feet slapping the hardwood as he came back to the bedroom.

He returned to the bed and held up a foil packet. "One day, if you're up for it, we'll make a baby, but not tonight."

Stunned at that thought, her mouth dropped open and her eyes went wide. She swallowed and looked into his dark eyes. They twinkled with happiness and desire.

"You've thought about having children? With me?"

"Of course. Haven't you?"

She nodded. "In a vague sense, yes. I just never thought it would actually happen."

He ripped open the condom and rolled it on, then shifted to crawl over top of her again. He settled between her legs and pushed a lock of wet hair off her cheek. His thumb brushed her cheekbone as he looked down at her.

"It will. We do this and I'm never letting go. You're mine, understand? No more of this 'we're just friends' stuff. I want it all, London."

Thoughts flew through her head as she continued to stare into his fathomless eyes, hardly able to believe what was happening. She had dreamed of being Seb's girlfriend since she was in her teens and discovered boys. But it had always been just that—a dream. Now, he was offering her everything, but did she dare accept it? What happened if it didn't work? She meant what she'd said earlier—she didn't want to do life without him. If they dove headfirst into a relationship and it later crumbled, he wouldn't be there anymore. Could she really live with that?

Although, considering she was lying under him, naked, was there any going back? If they didn't move forward, and she put a kibosh on this right now, their friendship would be awkward and there would still be this simmering, unfulfilled sexual tension humming between them.

Did she want to live like that?

As she looked up into his handsome face—the same one she'd looked into since she was a child—she knew she couldn't stop this. Not because it would be awkward, but because she was head over heels in love with this man and knew that if she didn't take this step, she would regret it and wonder what might have been for the rest of her life.

She flung her arms around his neck and kissed him, putting every emotion rolling through her head and heart into that touch.

He grunted in surprise and sank down, pressing her deeper into the mattress and took over the kiss. London let him. He seemed like he had a plan and she couldn't wait to find out what it was.

His hands trailed down her side to hold her hips. She could feel him pressed against her core and it was delightful.

He propped himself on one hand and rocked against her, toying with her breast with his free hand, plucking at the nipple, then rolling it in his palm. She arched her back, wanting to get closer to his touch. He leaned down and laved at her other breast, then sucked the bud into his mouth, biting the tip.

She moaned and wrapped her legs around his waist and gripped his hips. "Please."

Seb's throat worked, and he squeezed his eyes shut. His jaw flexed as he fought for control. She was past the point of waiting, though, and rolled her hips, increasing the friction.

Sweat popped out on his brow. "Slow down, baby."

She tossed her head on the pillow and rocked her hips again. "No. I want you. Now."

He opened his eyes and stared down at her, the pupils so huge, they swallowed up his dark irises. Holding eye contact, he slowly slid into her channel, stretching her walls and making her moan. He felt so good. So *right* seated inside her.

When he slid out and slammed back in, she couldn't hold back the shout of pleasure. She felt the jolt all the way to the ends of her hair.

That seemed to be his undoing. After that, he gave up on the slow, steady pace. London reached over her head to hold the headboard as her back arched and she met him thrust for thrust. Just when she thought she couldn't take any more, a white-hot light speared her behind her eyes and she shattered into a million pieces. She was sure her guests could hear her and know exactly what they were doing, but she didn't care. Sensations she'd never felt before bombarded her as she rode the waves of ecstasy ripping through her body. It left her bone-less and limp as she floated back down to earth.

Seb rolled to the side and flopped next to her. "Wow."

She managed a soft giggle. "Yep."

He groaned, his chest still heaving as he tried to catch his breath, then turned on his side, tugging the blankets over them and pulling her in close.

London closed her eyes as sleep pushed at the edges of her mind. She let it come, feeling sated and safe wrapped in Seb's arms.

TWELVE

"Do we really need *all* of that?" London crossed her arms and looked at the overloaded truck sitting in her driveway.

Seb gave her a sheepish smile and went around to the tail-gate. "I was going to just bring the couch, but then I remembered what your bed looked like—it kind of snowballed."

She eyed the furniture once more. "Your desk needed to come?"

"I need a place to work so I'm not stuck at the office so late. Your study has enough room for me too."

"You're moving in, aren't you? Not just until you catch this guy, but like, for good."

He lowered his desk chair to the ground, then walked over to stand in front of her.

A shiver went down her spine at his nearness. She could feel the heat radiating off him in the afternoon sun and smell the heady musk of sweaty man.

"And what if I am?" he asked, voice low and seductive.

All her nerve endings went on red alert and she swayed closer.

"I think that would be okay."

His head dipped toward hers, and a smile tugged at one corner of his mouth. "Good."

Inches separated them now as he hovered ever closer.

"Can you two make out later?" Boards clacked as Thomas dropped a stack of slats for the bedframe over the side of the truck. "I'd like to get out of the heat."

Seb straightened and cast an annoyed look over his shoulder. "Stop being a pansy. You won't melt." He ran a hand down London's arm, then turned to go help Thomas.

"Hey, between farm calls and work on the ranch, I'm out in the heat all the time. Doesn't mean I want to stand in it when there's air conditioning fifty feet away."

Seb rolled his eyes, before moving to help his brother unload the truck, still giving him a hard time. London grinned at their continued banter and picked up some of the slats.

They made quick work of carrying everything upstairs and London soon had an apartment full of furniture to replace the items Seb and his brothers carried out to the side of the house a couple hours before.

She tucked the sheet onto the bed and smoothed over the comforter just as Seb's cell rang. He looked at the screen and swiped to accept the call.

"Sheriff Archer."

London watched his face morph from concentration, to concern, then to worry as he listened.

"Okay. You have a CSU headed up there?" He paused. "Good. Send two officers around town to gather volunteers and have everyone meet at the trailhead. I'm on my way."

"What's going on?" she asked

Thomas joined them, having also heard Seb's end of the call.

"Adelaide Martin is missing."

Her eyes widened, and she covered her mouth. She took

several steps to the window and looked out over the lawn in disbelief.

"Are you serious?" Thomas asked.

"Yep. Her car was gone when her parents left for church this morning, so they thought she went somewhere last night with friends. When they got back this afternoon and she still wasn't home, they got concerned because she hadn't even called, so they tried some of her friends, but no one knew where she was. Her mother was finally able to locate her phone through their shared cell plan and they found it in her car, abandoned near the parking lot where we found Amy Beckett."

London spun around to stare at him, at the implications of that. He met her gaze, his eyes telegraphing his concern.

"We're mobilizing a search team. I need to go and help coordinate things."

"I'll call the family and we'll meet you up there," Thomas said.

"I'm coming too. And I'll see if any of the guests want to help." London headed for the door.

Seb snagged her arm. "You can't search."

She frowned. "Why not?"

He motioned to the now clean room. "There's some psycho targeting you. For all I know, Adelaide is missing as a ruse to draw you out. The last thing I need is to have you alone in the woods."

She stiffened at the thought that this was about her. Poor Adelaide. She didn't like the woman, but she would never wish any ill on her. Seb had a point, though. She couldn't knowingly put herself in a position where whoever was targeting her could get to her easily.

"How about I stay at the headquarters you set up and help run things? That would free up at least one of your deputies to help search."

He studied her for a moment before nodding. "But you stay in the tent. No wandering around by yourself."

She nodded.

"Okay, let's go."

~

Seb stared out over the forest in front of him and uttered a curse under his breath. Adelaide could be anywhere in that vast wilderness. Or nowhere. If she had indeed been kidnapped, her abductor may have left the car parked here as both a message and as a distraction. The scene felt staged, and he had a feeling they were wasting their time. He truly hoped he was wrong, and that she was just lost or had gone off with a boyfriend and didn't want to be found, but that could be wishful thinking on his part. Working had not been on his agenda today. He had planned to move his furniture into London's house and then spend the day getting her to test out his mattress.

He glanced back at the tent his deputies just erected. London stood in the middle of it, writing names and search quadrants on a whiteboard, her graceful lines highlighted by her snug t-shirt and hiking shorts.

Last night was amazing. It was everything he ever thought it would be. Explosive and mind-numbing. It was also hard to believe. They had been in limbo so long the abrupt shift left him a little off-balance. But it was good. Life already felt fuller.

Footsteps brought him out of his head and he turned to see Jace approaching.

Seb held out a hand. "Thanks for coming."

Jace shook it. "Of course. I'm here to help however I can." He looked around at their surroundings. "So, do you think we're dealing with our killer? I mean, she looks a lot like Amy Beckett. Same coloring, build."

Seb nodded. "I noticed. The location of her car didn't escape me, either. Abigail and Trent found Amy's body about a mile from here. I don't think Adelaide disappeared on her own."

"Sheriff!"

Seb looked up at Caleb's shout. The deputy beckoned him over to where everyone gathered at the tent.

"We're ready for the briefing."

"Showtime." He and Jace jogged over to the waiting volunteers. London pulled the board closer, then stood with the others.

Seb nodded his thanks, then flipped the board to show the map of the forest and a photo of Adelaide taped to the other side. "Our missing person is Adelaide Martin, age thirty-five. She's five-feet-seven inches tall, one hundred twenty-five pounds, and has blonde hair and blue eyes." He pointed to the map. "This is our search grid. We're here." He pointed to the red dot in the middle. "I know it's a lot of land, but don't get discouraged. Just concentrate on your section and take it grid by grid." He flipped the board back. "If you haven't already, find your starting quadrant and grid, then get a map from London. There will be one radio for every four people. Cell phones do work up here, but the coverage can be spotty, so keep that in mind and make sure you don't stray out of shouting distance from the person next to you. We don't need to search for our searchers."

A nervous chuckle ran through the group.

"All right. Let's get moving." Seb stepped back as the volunteers filed past to get their maps and double-check their search zones. Once everyone was out of the tent, he leaned back against the table and braced himself on his hands.

London walked over to stand in front of him. "You doing okay?"

He swiped a hand over his jaw and around to hold the

back of his neck. "Yeah. I just wish we could catch a break. This guy has turned the county into his personal playground and I don't have a fucking clue who he is."

She laid a hand on his chest. "You'll get him. We'll find Adelaide and you'll get him."

He covered her hand with his and tugged her closer. "Before she's dead? Before he gets to you?"

Her breath came out in a harsh puff and he could see the fear in her eyes.

Seb let out a rough sigh, annoyed with himself that he scared her. "I'm sorry. I'm not trying to scare you. I'm just frustrated. Mostly because I want to make sure you're safe, but I can't do that if I don't know what direction the threat's coming from. It could be anyone, and I don't know who to trust." He took her other hand and held them up near his shoulders, then placed a lingering kiss on her forehead.

She leaned into his touch and closed her eyes, some of the tension leaving her shoulders. He tipped his head down to rest his forehead against hers.

"So, you're sure that whoever killed that woman and kidnapped Adelaide is the same one who ransacked my house?"

He straightened and glanced over her shoulder to scan the trees as he thought about all the events that had occurred in the last week. "Not a hundred percent, but it's a hell of a coincidence if it isn't."

A shiver skated over her skin and she scooted closer to him, wrapping her arms around his waist. He tipped her face up to look into her pretty blue eyes. They shimmered in the muted light in the tent, looking more like silver pools. He wanted to get lost in their depths and forget about this case.

But he couldn't. Not if he wanted to find the bastard before he killed Adelaide and got to London.

"I won't let anything happen to you," he vowed, both to

188 ASHLEY A QUINN

her and to himself. He couldn't let it. Not now that he finally had her.

She slid her hands up his torso to link them behind his neck, pressing her body as close to his as she could get it. "I know."

He leaned down and pressed a soft, lingering kiss to her lips. Desire lit a slow burn in his belly and he wished again that they were back at the inn, testing out his bed.

But they weren't, and he had work to do. He pulled back and pressed another kiss to her forehead before letting her go. Footsteps on the gravel had him looking up to see more of the locals arriving to help search, including Ryan Marsters and several of the other business owners. To his surprise, he also saw Doug Brown bringing up the rear.

Seb stepped around London to greet them. "Thanks for coming, everyone. If you'll sign in, London will get you equipped with a map and a quadrant."

Ryan walked forward and held out a hand. Seb took it.

"Sheriff. This is some terrible business. Any word on Adelaide's whereabouts yet?"

"No. But we just started searching."

"Well, we're all happy to help." He looked back at the others with him, who all nodded.

"Good. London will get you set up."

Ryan nodded, and he and his group moved past. Seb stayed where he was and looked at Brown, who strolled forward, his hands stuffed in his pockets.

"Mr. Brown. I'm surprised to see you here."

"I want to apologize for earlier. I may act like a jackass from time to time, but I'm really not a bad guy, Sheriff. And I'd like to help search, if that's all right?"

Seb studied the other man. His blonde hair was perfectly combed, his skin tanned and smooth, but he was dressed for the wilderness—sort of—in jeans, a polo shirt, and tennis shoes.

"It's rough terrain out here. Can you handle it?"

Brown nodded. "I might be a businessman, but I run every day. I can handle the hike."

"Okay." Seb motioned to London. "She'll get you everything you need."

"Thanks." He moved past Seb to stand with the others.

Seb picked his radio up off the table. "London, I'm going to go call the media outlets and get a description of Adelaide put out. If you need to leave the tent, make sure you don't go alone, and if you leave the area, let me know?"

She nodded as she handed Brown a map. "Go. Be the sheriff. I'll be okay."

He knew that, but it didn't make walking away any easier. He couldn't shake the feeling that something was amiss.

"Girl, my feet hurt," Tara said as she sank into one of the folding chairs. London plopped down next to her with a groan.

"Mine too."

They had just finished feeding the last group of volunteers and were exhausted after having been on their feet all day.

"I don't know about you, but I'm going to go home, take a hot shower and flop into bed. Naked." Tara peeled her sweaty t-shirt away from her breasts and fanned herself.

London twisted her ponytail up into a bun and secured it on top of her head. Even though it was dark, they were hot from standing over the grills.

"We still have to pack all this back up." She motioned to the two charcoal grills Brady brought to the site, and three tables worth of food and supplies locals donated for the search effort.

Tara moaned. "The grills can stay, since we'll probably need them tomorrow still. Hopefully, they'll find her and we won't need them past that. But we do need to pack up the food or this place will be overrun by bears. You know, I don't like Adelaide, but this is terrible. She might be a bitch, but she doesn't deserve this."

"I know. And it's awful to say, but I don't think they'll find her. I think Seb's right—he'll either find her when he finds the killer, or she'll turn up dead somewhere."

"I think you're right, but I hope you're wrong."

Headlights lit up the tent as two vehicles pulled into the lot.

"That's probably Seb." London rose from her seat and walked over to the food tables, covering dishes and closing bags.

Tara grabbed the coolers, dragged them over to the tables, and began piling dishes inside. London stacked paper products and cups into boxes.

"What can we do?" Seb asked, stepping into the food tent.

London glanced up to see Jace file in behind him. "Start carrying things out to the cars. I don't know about you guys, but I'm ready to go home."

Jace picked up the cooler Tara just filled. "Bed sounds fantastic."

Seb stacked two of the boxes and hooked several grocery bags over his fingers. "Agreed."

The four of them made quick work of cleaning up the tent. Fifteen minutes after the men arrived, they were closing the flaps on the tent and making their way to the vehicles.

Tara started to walk toward Seb's truck when he stopped her.

"Jace will take you home, Tara. I'm going back to the inn with London."

Her eyes widened and flicked to Jace's red truck before going back to her brother. "Oh. Okay."

It was all London could do not to laugh at Tara's deer-in-the-headlights expression when she turned to say goodnight.

London hugged her. "It's just a car ride home. You're not marrying the guy," she whispered, then pulled back to smile at her.

Tara rolled her eyes and grinned. She turned to Jace. "All right, hot stuff. Let's go." She headed for his truck.

Jace arched an eyebrow and one corner of his mouth quirked as he stared after her. "I guess we're leaving. I'll see you tomorrow at the station," he said to Seb, then nodded to London and jogged off.

"It's too bad he won't be around much longer. He'd be good for your sister."

Seb frowned as he fell into step beside her. "Jace? And Tara? You think she likes him?"

She nodded. "I haven't seen her so animated about a man since she came home. He irritates her, but mostly because she finds him so attractive."

They climbed into Seb's truck and he started the engine. "I don't want to think about my sister's love life." He shot her a heated look in the dim light of the dashboard. "I'd much rather think about ours."

London blushed and giggled. "Put this truck in gear, then."

"Yes ma'am." He shifted into drive and turned them around.

Anticipation licked at her blood as he drove, and she tried not to squirm in her seat. Memories of the night before played on a reel in her mind. She couldn't wait for a repeat.

By the time he turned onto the road the inn was on, she

was already so worked up he wasn't even going to have to touch her to set her off.

"What the hell?"

Seb's quiet exclamation shifted her focus, and she looked at him.

"What?"

"There's something in the road."

She peered through the windshield into the darkness. There was a shadow ahead, but she couldn't tell what it was. As he drove closer, she gasped and her heart stuttered in her chest.

"Is that—?"

"My lilacs!" All the bushes along the road line had been ripped out of the ground.

Seb stopped the truck in front of the obstruction and London clambered out, running toward the destruction.

The horror that met her was almost unfathomable. Her beautiful lilacs laid across the ditch and on the roadway, their fragrant blossoms scattered all over the asphalt and their roots dripping dirt, exposed to the night.

Tears welled in her eyes, spilling over, and she slapped her hands over her mouth to hold in the wail. Seb's hands closed over her shoulders.

"Why?" she choked out. "Why would someone do this?"

"I don't know, honey."

She shrugged off his hands and stepped toward one of the bushes. Bending down, she stroked one of the soft petals and breathed in its heavenly scent. Shock left her brain foggy.

He squatted next to her. "I'm sorry, sweetheart. Is there a chance we can save them? I doubt they've been out of the ground long. Someone would have seen this and reported it."

London sniffed and turned watery eyes on him. "I don't know. I'm not even sure how we'll right them to get them back in the ground."

He stood. "You leave that to me. Take some pictures of the damage. I'm going to make some calls and get us some help."

Hope lit her chest at the optimism in his voice. She rose and pulled her phone from her pocket and began snapping pictures of the downed plants while Seb stepped away.

She knew it was silly to be so upset over some flowers, but the lilacs were as much a part of the inn as the house itself. They were what drew her to the property in the first place. What gave it its name. She looked forward to their blooms every spring. It made the house and grounds feel fresh and new. One of her favorite things to do in the spring was to open all the windows and let their light scent fill the rooms. It was better than any air freshener could ever be.

Seb's shoes crunched on the road as he approached again. She looked back as he strode toward her, a determined set to his jaw.

"My dad, brothers, and Jace are on their way. Brady's bringing straps and chains. We should be able to get them upright using those and the trucks.

London sniffed and wiped her face. "I hope so. It will take years to replace them if we can't."

He took her hand and guided her back to the truck. "Come on. Let's go see if any of the guests heard anything suspicious."

"I'm just glad Abigail decided to stay another night with Alexis. I don't want her anywhere near the inn right now." She climbed into the vehicle and leaned against the door.

Seb started the engine. "It might not be a bad idea for her to go stay with my parents for a bit."

A smile lit London's face. "She'd like that. Lee and Jenny spoil her."

"It would give us some time alone too." He waggled his eyebrows at her and a sexy grin spread over his face.

She laughed. "Are you going to be like this all the time now?"

He smiled back at her and shrugged as he parked the truck out front. "I won't apologize for wanting you. Ever. Especially after it took me so long to get you."

She opened her door and got out. "Out of curiosity, how long have you had feelings for me?"

He came around to stand in front of her and traced the line of her hair at her temple with one finger. "I've thought you were pretty since you were a teenager, but I've wanted more since Eddie died. It made me realize what you meant to me. The timing just didn't feel right then, though."

She nodded. "I know what you mean. I still hope we're not making a mistake by not waiting until Abigail is an adult, but I'm tired of hiding what you make me feel."

He tipped her chin up and lowered his head. "Honey, Abigail is more of an adult than most adults. No matter what happens between us, she will be fine, and my relationship with her will be fine." He sealed his mouth to hers in a searing kiss. London's knees went weak, and she grabbed fistfuls of his shirt to hold herself upright as she returned his kiss. She would never get enough of this. Even when she was ninety, she would crave his mouth on hers.

Seb broke the kiss and growled. "As much as I want to continue this, we need to go find out if anyone heard anything."

London sighed and let go of his shirt. She smoothed out the wrinkles and stepped back. "I'm not going to have any guests left after this event. I already lost the two couples who checked in mid-week and the Strattman's decided to move on early. They were supposed to stay through Tuesday."

"I know this is rough, but it won't last. I'm hoping I get some results tomorrow on the trace evidence we recovered from Amy's body, and that the detective from Aspen can get surveillance footage on their mystery plumber."

She unlocked the front door and pushed it open. "See, you're not totally without leads."

He closed and locked the door behind them. "I know. I just hate the waiting game. Especially this time."

Tears threatened again at the tenderness on his face, but she blinked and turned toward the stairs. She was done crying. "So, how do we want to do this? Bring them downstairs to the living room again? Only the two couples are here. I didn't see Mr. Brown's car in the lot when you pulled up."

Seb frowned and London wonder what that was about, but he didn't give her a chance to ask.

"Let's just knock on their doors. No need to completely disturb their evenings."

She led him up the steps to the first occupied room—a couple on a second honeymoon. The man answered the door and told them he heard what sounded like a loud engine, but then nothing.

The second room belonged to a young couple taking a break from the city. They helped search earlier and hadn't been back long. The woman said the road was clear when they came back about thirty minutes before Seb and London, and they heard nothing. London didn't find that strange, though. Their room was on the back side of the house and in the middle. It consistently got the most compliments because it was so quiet.

As they went back downstairs, the first set of headlights turned into the drive and lit up the living room. Seb opened the door again, and London saw Jace pull to a stop next to Seb's truck. Tara hopped out of the passenger side.

"This shit is getting ridiculous," she said. "We didn't even make it back to the ranch when you called." She walked up the porch stairs and into the house to envelop London in a hug.

London clung to her, grateful for the support. "Thank you for coming."

Tara released her. "Of course. We're going to fix those pretty bushes and tomorrow Seb and Jace and every other member of the sheriff's department will find the jackass who thinks this is fun." She gave her brother and Jace the stink eye, promising hell to pay if they didn't do as she said.

Seb held up his hands in surrender. "Trust me, I'm doing everything I can."

London grabbed Tara's hand and tugged her toward the kitchen. "We know," she said, cutting Tara off before she could get wound up. London loved the woman, but she could have a bit of a temper and be fiercely protective.

"Let's go get some coffee started. I think we're going to need it." She knew she did. After the long day she already put in running logistics for the search and feeding everyone, she was exhausted. Now, she had to replant her bushes in the dark. She just wanted to close her eyes and make the entire day disappear.

I wonder if there's still any whiskey in the cabinet?

THIRTEEN

Rain dripped off the edges of the tent, its soft plop onto the ground a soothing patter to the tension roiling through Seb's mind. A cold, damp wind blew, bringing a chilly dreariness to the day to match his mood. The search teams went back out at dawn, and now, at just after three in the afternoon, there was still no news on Adelaide's whereabouts. The lack of clues was wearing on everyone.

Seb turned up the collar on his jacket and sank into a chair for a moment. His feet ached from being on them all day, not to mention most of the night. It took them a couple hours to right the lilac bushes and get them back into the ground. He hoped they survived. London would be devastated if they didn't. She had put so much work into cultivating those plants and making them into the lush, full bushes they were.

The trill of his cell broke through the soft sound of the rain. He took it from his pocket to see Alex Randall's number on the screen. Anticipation shot through his veins, reinvigorating him. He swiped his thumb over the screen.

"Sheriff Archer."

"Seb, it's Alex. I finally got the trace back on the sediment from Amy Beckett's back. It was a mix of dirt and rock, but there was also some pollen in there. I had the lab run it and we may have something. It's from an extremely rare plant called Weber's Draba. It's only found in a few places in the county along rocky shorelines in high altitudes."

Seb's heart rate kicked up. That was a solid lead. "Really? I don't suppose you can tell me where?"

"No, but Rayna Nydert might. If she can't, I can give you the number for a botanist at the University of Colorado. But I'd try Rayna first. If anyone around here knows where that stuff might grow, it'll be her."

"Okay. She's out here searching, so I'll call her in and ask. Thanks, Alex."

"You bet. Let me know if you need that botanist's number."

"I will. Thanks." Seb ended the call and picked up his radio, calling Rayna back to the tent. He tried to temper his excitement. The lead could get them very little. But it was still something.

While he waited on Rayna, he called Detective Farley in Aspen. Seb listened to the phone ring several times and just as he resigned himself to leaving another message, the man picked up.

"Detective, it's Sheriff Archer. Have you any headway on getting that security footage?"

"Actually, yes. I was going to call you here soon. The footage is on a server at a data farm. The resort manager was working on getting it for me, so I should have it tomorrow."

"Good. We've had a development here. Another woman's been kidnapped. The sooner you can get and review that footage, the better. I need a lead."

Farley's dismay came through the line loud and clear on a harsh sigh. "Yeah. Okay. I'll call the manager back and see if he can put the screws to the data farm people. As soon as I know anything, I'll let you know."

"Thanks. I appreciate it. What about your search for Rebecca Carson?"

"Nothing. We've scoured the forest around the campground. All we did was startle a bunch of birds and anger a bear."

Dammit.

"Okay, if you uncover anything, be sure to let me know."

"Yep. Keep me posted on your missing person, and if there's anything else I can do up here, give me a shout."

"I will." Seb thumbed off the call with a little more force than necessary as frustration clawed at his insides. This case just didn't want to give him anything.

Movement from the woods had him looking up to see Rayna emerge from the trees. She had her inky hair pulled back and hidden beneath her hood, showing off her high cheekbones and violet eyes. Even clad in a bulky, shapeless rain slicker, her curvy form was obvious. She was a stunningly gorgeous woman—not to mention one of the nicest people he'd ever met—and his brother was an idiot for screwing things up with her.

She walked into the tent and set her lightweight pack down on a chair, then pushed back her hood. "What's up?"

"I got some new information on Amy Beckett's murder that I need your help with."

She frowned, curious. "Me?"

"Yes. Trace came back showing some pollen in the wounds on her back from a rare plant called Weber's Draba. Dr. Randall said it only grows on the rocky shores in high alpine areas. Do you know where we might find it around here? I think it could lead us to the murder scene."

"Oh, wow. That's a lucky break. It only grows in a few locations and only in this part of the state. I don't know all the locations offhand, but there's a database I can access that will tell us where it's been seen." Her brow dipped as a thoughtful frown crossed her face. "We may not need to look at it, though. There's a high lake near here, and I've seen Weber's there before."

That excitement he'd been trying to tamp down got a little louder. "What's the quickest way there?"

"We can take an ATV from here. There aren't any roads, but the terrain isn't too rough for an off-road vehicle."

Seb lifted his phone and punched in the number for dispatch.

"Sheriff's depart—"

He didn't let the dispatcher finish. "It's Archer. I need you to send Katie Mitchum up to the search site. I have a lead on Amy Beckett."

"Right away, Sheriff."

Seb disconnected the call and looked down at Rayna. "Can you access that database from here?"

She nodded.

"Do it. Write down the locations. I have a feeling the one near here will be our crime scene, but just in case it's not, I'd like to be able to immediately move on to the others."

Without a word, she moved to the table and pulled a pad of paper and a pen toward her. Seb turned to stare up the mountain. For the first time since this all began, hope lit his chest that maybe they were finally on the right path.

The drone of the ATVs broke the solitude on the mountain as Seb and his team climbed higher. It hadn't rained on this side of the mountain and they kicked up dust as they moved. He glanced at the sun. Though bright, it was beginning to dip as the afternoon waned. He hoped they were nearing the lake

Rayna remembered. They would already be setting up lights if they found the crime scene up here, but he didn't want to work into the middle of the night.

They crested a ridge and Rayna slowed. Seb pulled up beside her and looked at the vista in front of him.

"Wow."

She looked at him and grinned. "Right?"

"How did I not know this was here?" Surrounded by mountains dotted with snow, the lake surface shimmered in the sun. Pristine, it reflected the surrounding scenery like a mirror.

"It's fairly remote, so it doesn't get many visitors."

"Except our resident herbalist out scouting for rare plants." A broad smile spread over his face.

She beamed up at him. "Yeah. Except for her."

"So, where is this stuff?"

She gestured toward the lake. "It'll be along the shore line. It grows in the crevices between the rocks. And it'll be practically in the water. It likes to be wet."

He motioned her to lead the way. "We'll follow you."

Much slower than the pace they had kept up the mountain, Rayna led them around the perimeter of the lake. Before they left, she told them what to look for, so Seb and his men scoured the shoreline looking for the tiny yellow flowers.

A sharp whistle drew his attention away from the water. He turned to see Gentry point up to the sky. Vultures circled to the west.

Dread settled heavy in Seb's gut. It could just be a dead animal, but he didn't think so. He pulled up next to his deputy.

"Take Reeves and go check the area. I'll keep searching the shoreline with Rayna and Katie. If you find something, radio it in."

Gentry nodded, then waved to Reeves. The two men

peeled off. Seb gave the circling birds one last look before going after Rayna, who had stopped about a hundred yards away.

"What did you find?"

She pointed to the water. "Weber's. Katie wants to have a closer look." She gestured to the criminologist who had already climbed off her ATV and was busy pulling items from her bags.

"Can we help?" he asked.

"Not really. Just stay close in case I need a hand."

Seb twisted off his quad's engine and swung his leg over. Katie handed him several items to hold, then picked her way over the rocks toward the shore, taking pictures as she went. He followed, careful to step where she had, so he didn't disturb any potential evidence.

"Anything?"

She squatted and took several pictures in rapid succession, then looked up at him and shook her head. "No. I don't see any crush evidence, and there are no blood smears. We haven't had enough rain—or snow up here—to wash it away." She straightened and moved around him. "This isn't your murder scene."

"Let's keep moving. There's more than one place around this lake where Weber's grows," Rayna said.

Seb nodded, handing Katie back her vials and bags. She quickly stowed them and they set off again. This had to be the place. It felt right. Especially with the vultures.

He glanced up at the sky again. The huge black birds floated on the air currents, giving the idyllic setting a sense of foreboding.

A quarter of the way around the lake, Rayna stopped again. This time, Katie picked her way over the rocks with just her camera and left all her supplies in the bags on her ATV. As she made her way down to the shoreline, she paused and frowned, then squatted and aimed the camera between some rocks.

"Sheriff, grab those evidence bags."

His heart skipped. He hurried over to her ATV and retrieved the requested items, then picked his way over the rocks to reach the shore.

She pointed down and Seb saw crushed flowers as well as some dark smears on the rocks. She let her camera hang around her neck and took the evidence collection case from him. Taking a swab from the kit, she dabbed at the streaks on the rocks, then using a pair of tweezers, she plucked some of the tiny flowers and bagged them.

Seb's radio crackled to life.

"Sheriff."

He took it off his belt and depressed the mic. "Go ahead." He looked up to see Reeves standing on his ATV, waving his arms.

"You need to send Katie over here," Gentry said. "We found a body. But it's not Adelaide."

Seb shared a look with the women. Rayna looked shell-shocked, while Katie just looked resigned. She put the evidence she'd collected into her case and snapped it shut, then stepped away from the lakeshore and stowed the case on her quad.

"We need to mark this spot. I'll have more of my team come up here and we'll comb over it better. We'll need them anyway to deal with the body."

He brought his radio up. "Reeves."

"Yeah, boss?"

"Head back down the mountain until you get a cell signal and call in the calvary. Full CSU and Dr. Randall."

"On it." The whine of an ATV in the distance echoed off the mountains as Reeves put his quad in gear and took off.

Seb looked back at the women to see Rayna building a mound out of nearby rocks to mark the location.

"Go," she said. "I'll catch up."

He nodded, then looked at the CSI. "You ready, Katie?"

She climbed onto her ATV and revved the engine in response. He hopped on his own and led them across the plateau to where Gentry sat waiting.

He glanced up again as they pulled to a halt. The vultures were directly overhead now.

Parking his quad, Seb went to stand next to his deputy. A yellow tarp lay on the ground ten feet away, held down on the corners by rocks.

"We covered her because it's getting windy," Gentry said to Katie.

She nodded and removed some long, thin pieces of metal from her bag and a bundle of rope.

"That was good thinking, deputy. Help me create a wind-screen, will you?"

As she lifted the tarp to create the screen, Seb got his first look at the body. Scavengers had ravaged it already. Holes peppered her flesh and her torso was torn open, jagged edges of flesh hanging to hide the gaping hole where her organs used to be.

He glanced at her face, trying not to stare at the horror that greeted him. Empty eye sockets stared upward through the dark strands of her hair. Her teeth shone white through her cheek and fluid leaked from the holes on the sides of her head where her ears once sat. He couldn't say for sure because of the destruction from scavengers, but she matched Rebecca Carson's general description.

Seb looked away, his stomach protesting the gruesome sight, and stared at the mountain with unseeing eyes. Why would the killer keep her? Why didn't he kill her soon after they disappeared? What value did Rebecca hold?

One thing was certain, though. Whatever his reason for keeping Rebecca Carson alive—if this was indeed her—he did not hold the same regard for her that he did for his other victims. This woman had been thrown into the wilderness like trash, not cherished like Amy Beckett.

He sighed and stepped forward to help Katie collect evidence.

FOURTEEN

London rinsed the last dish from breakfast and stared out the window at the yard. Sunlight streamed through the trees, chasing away the shadows and warming the air. It was a stark contrast to yesterday's cold, wet, miserable weather and to the heaviness weighing on her heart. There was another body in Dr. Randall's morgue, and Adelaide Martin was still out there somewhere.

She set the bowl on a towel to dry and hung her dishrag over the sink divider, then dried her hands. With her guests dwindling down to just one couple and Doug Brown, breakfast this morning had been simple. The only blessing in that was it gave her enough time to run to town to pick up some supplies to stake her lilacs. They were doing surprisingly well, but a couple of them had started to lean.

Exiting the kitchen, she walked upstairs to get her purse and car keys. On her way back down, Mr. Brown's voice caught her attention as she walked past his room. He sounded angry.

Seb's dislike of the man made her pause, curious herself about why he was really in town. She didn't normally spy on her guests, but Brown's attitude as well as his reticence to talk about his business kept her from caring. She'd been contemplating asking him to leave, but now that all her other guests had left, she needed the income.

She edged toward his door until she stood next to the jamb.

"I'm trying to find out more, but it's not like I can just waltz in and ask. They've closed ranks because of these murders, so there's always someone around."

What? She leaned closer, trying to hear more. What was he talking about? And to whom?

"I understand you want information, but I can't give you any at the moment." He paused and London held her breath. "Look, if you really want it that damn bad and think you can get it faster than I can, you are welcome to come out here. I'm sure she would love to see you." There was another brief pause. "I'm not threatening you, just stating facts. There's a reason you hired me."

There was? *What the hell was going on*? She thought he was a land developer, but that didn't sound like a land deal.

"Yes, as soon as I know anything I will call."

She heard Brown growl and something clatter onto a flat surface. Realizing he was off the phone, she hurried away in case he came out of his room. Her mind spun as she made her way downstairs and into the garage to her car. What was he looking for and who was the "she" he mentioned? She'd had a feeling he was shady, but this confirmed it.

Once out on the road to town, she hit the button on her steering wheel to activate the hands-free on her phone.

"Call Seb."

She tapped her fingers on the wheel as she waited for the call to connect.

"Hey, hon. What's up? Everything all right?" Seb's deep voice rumbled through the interior of her car.

"I'm fine. I'm actually on my way into town."

"By yourself?"

She could practically see the deep frown on his face.

"Yes. It's two miles, and it wasn't planned. I'll be fine. I didn't call to talk about my day, though. I think you need to take a deeper look at Doug Brown. I walked past his room on my way out of the house and I overheard him on the phone. He said something about how he can't look for something because there's always people around. It doesn't sound like he's your killer, but he's definitely up to something."

"Yeah, I've been quietly poking around in his background since the break-in Saturday. Once I did, his identity didn't hold up. I don't know who he really is, but he isn't Doug Brown."

London frowned. "Why didn't you tell me that? He could be dangerous and he's been staying in my house!"

"I didn't tell you because I didn't want you to kick him out or for him to catch on that we knew he wasn't being truthful and then hightail it to parts unknown. I needed him here because he was a suspect in my case."

Anger simmered at his words. "So, basically you didn't trust me to keep it a secret. Give me some credit, Sebastian. I'm not an idiot."

He sighed. "I know you're not and I never said you were. I'm just not used to divulging information about an active case. It can jeopardize the investigation."

"So, you used me."

"Would you stop putting words in my mouth? Why are you snapping at me?"

"Because you don't trust me. You're treating me like I'm the kid sister again."

He growled. "I do not want to have this conversation over the phone. Where are you headed?"

"The hardware store. I need stuff to stake those bushes."

"I'll meet you there." He hung up, leaving London staring at the speaker, seething.

She was so angry. He kept telling her he didn't see her like a kid, then turned around and deliberately kept her in the dark.

She took the turn into town and in less than a minute pulled into a parking space in front of the hardware store. As she shut off the engine, Seb's cruiser came to a halt next to her. He was out of the SUV and pulling her door open before she could even grab her purse.

Eyes flinty, he stared at her. "Where is this coming from? I said I was sorry, and I meant what I said. I'm not used to having people close to me involved in my investigations."

She pushed against his chest so she could get out of her car. He backed up enough, so they stood toe to toe.

"All along, you've said you don't see me as Eddie's kid sister, but when it really counts, what do you do? You treat me like the kid sister. Which is it, Seb? Am I the woman you're dating or the annoying tagalong?"

His shoulders sagged, and he exhaled a sharp breath, head hanging as he gathered his thoughts. When he looked up, his expression was serious, but not angry.

"I never meant to make you feel like the tagalong. I haven't felt that way about you in a long time. It honestly was me just conducting my investigation like I always would. I weighed the risks of not outing Brown and decided he wasn't a threat to you."

Her eyes widened as she remembered their exchange the night someone ransacked her apartment.

He held up a hand. "I didn't know he wasn't who he said he was until after the break-in. I dug a little deeper after that. And he and I had a nice little conversation about him checking himself around you when we went looking for where that vehicle sat. Trust me when I tell you he backed down like the little chicken shit he is and will not be a problem anymore."

London rolled her lips in, her eyes searching his. She wanted to believe him, but it was so hard after she spent years as the kid sister. He and Eddie had pulled this stuff all the time, keeping her in the dark about things they decided she didn't need to know.

Seb took her hands and took a step forward so his front lightly brushed hers. Heat suffused her skin, and she fought the urge to sway into him. She tipped her head back to see his face.

He looked down at her. "I will make more of an effort to keep you informed, okay? This relationship is an adjustment for both of us. I didn't think before I acted and I'm sorry." He reached up and ran a hand through her loose hair, cradling the side of her head. "Now, can we please agree to put the whole kid sister thing to rest?" His eyes darkened, and he leaned closer. "I most certainly do not think about my sisters the way I think about you."

Her knees turned to water, and she fell against him, looping her arms around his waist. "That's good. Because I'm really glad you aren't my brother."

A low chuckle rumbled through his chest and he leaned down, pressing his mouth to hers. London reveled in the feel of his kiss. They lingered a moment, savoring the contact, before breaking apart.

"I need to get back to work. Who's hanging out at the house?"

"Alaina Wilder, actually," she answered, knowing he meant which of his deputies was on volunteer guard duty. "She helped me make breakfast this morning."

He smiled. "Yeah? Good. She's great. She'll keep a good eye on the place. And you."

London rolled her eyes. "I hate that I have a babysitter."

Seb arched a brow. "Who you shucked to come to town on your own."

Her grin was sheepish as she blinked up at him, trying to look innocent.

A low chuckle broke free, and he shook his head. "Go get your stuff, then go straight home. And text me when you get there."

Her smile turned genuine, and she nodded.

He leaned down and kissed her forehead, his fingers skimming the side of her face. "I'll see you tonight."

London drew a deep breath, his scent washing over her. She buried the memory of it deep so she could bring it out later when she was stressed.

She pushed out of the circle of his arms and closed the car door. "Will you be home in time for dinner?"

"I'm not sure yet. It'll depend on what I get from Dr. Randall and Katie Mitchum."

"Okay. Well, I threw a roast in the slow cooker this morning, so it'll keep."

"Sounds good." He placed a quick kiss on her lips, then walked around the front of her car to his cruiser. "Don't forget to text me."

"I won't." She shooed him into his car. "Go do police stuff."

He grinned and climbed into the vehicle. London walked toward the store and waved as he pulled out. Turning to go into the store, she couldn't help but smile, glad they'd had that talk. She just hoped he meant what he said and kept her informed.

Seb walked into the morgue and made a beeline for the cabinet with the peppermint essential oil. This body smelled worse than the last one. The odor permeated the entire space with its putrid scent of decay. Seb fought the gag, fighting to break free from his throat. He dribbled several drops of the oil in his mask and slapped it over his face.

When he turned around, Alex stood over the exam table, a smirk showing over his mask. Jace stood across from him, a mask over his face too, an amused twinkle crinkling the corners of his blue eyes.

"What?" He frowned, then his face cleared as he realized they were teasing him about the smell. "Oh, come on. It's not like you two didn't do the exact same thing."

Jace chuckled and raised a hand. "Guilty."

Alex shook his head. "Wimps."

He turned to the body and pulled back the sheet. Flies rose to buzz around them and maggots crawled over the corpse's decaying flesh. Seb felt his breakfast roll over in his stomach.

"She's in pretty terrible shape," Alex said, grabbing the overhead light to better position it. "Predators and insects have really taken a toll on her. I already took samples of the larvae and the flies and sent them over to trace. Katie should have more info for you on all that."

"Cause of death?"

"Blunt force trauma." He turned the head and moved the light in closer. "See the fractures there?" He pointed to the areas of the skull peeking through the matted and crusted hair. "He hit her over the head with something. Probably a rock, judging by the irregularity of the wound."

"You know what I don't understand?" Jace said. "Why did he keep her? We know Amy Beckett is the woman he wanted, so why did he bother to keep Rebecca Carson alive for so long?"

"Cooperation, maybe?" Alex said.

"Maybe," Seb mused. He'd already thought long and hard about this. "Or it was just easier to keep her alive and dispose of them both at the same time. Less chance he'd get caught."

"Well, whatever the reason, he killed them both very differently," Alex remarked. "Amy Beckett's death was almost reverent, whereas this woman's was violent and abrupt."

"Is there anything else we should know?"

"I found some other trace on her clothes. Saw dust. A couple stray hairs that look like they might be from an animal. But since we found her in the mountains, those probably came from whatever scavenger fed on her. I sent it all to Katie."

Seb stepped back from the table and motioned for Jace to follow. "We'll go talk to her then."

Alex grinned behind his mask. "You just don't want to hang out with the stench."

"Got it in one, Doc." Seb laughed and headed for the door. "Call me if there's anything else." He chucked his mask into the trash on his way out the door.

"Hey, maybe we can do lunch later," Alex said.

Seb glanced back to see him hold up what was left of the intestines.

The doctor grinned. "Hot dogs, maybe."

Jace barked out a laugh, while Seb just shook his head. "You have got one sick sense of humor, Alex. We'll see you later."

Alex waved with a laugh.

"So, where to?" Jace asked.

"The criminology lab. It's next door, adjacent to the police station." Seb led him through the halls of the hospital basement and up a set of stairs. They exited into the courtyard, then walked around the side of the building and down the sidewalk.

"Your set up here is nice. Having the police department and the crime lab right next to the hospital. I've never seen it like that."

"We had a levy on the ballot a few years ago to build a new emergency services complex. The old station house was falling down around us, the crime lab in it tiny, and the fire department desperately needed a bigger building. The ground next to the hospital was vacant and already city owned, so they built it here. When I came back to town, it was already in service, but I remember touring the old buildings in high school. They were crap then. I was glad to hear the people in the county wanted to upgrade."

"I wish they'd do that back home. I have a bucket sitting in the middle of my office floor to catch the drips every time it rains."

Seb wrinkled his nose. "No wonder you don't want to go back yet."

Jace grinned. "This town definitely has its advantages. Thanks for inviting me into the investigation today, by the way."

"Not a problem. I'm glad you've stuck around. With the search still on for Adelaide, I can use the extra hands."

They reached the two-story brick building next to the hospital. Seb waved his ID badge over the reader and let them inside.

"Hi, Sheriff."

Seb smiled at the office manager, Melody Carlisle. "Hi Melody. We're here to see Katie."

She nodded, already picking up the phone. "I figured. She came in bright and early this morning to get a jump on the evidence from that latest victim. I passed her in the break room when I came in and she was already on her third cup of coffee and mumbled something about murderers messing with her sleep."

"That sounds like her," he said with a laugh.

Melody turned her attention to the phone, telling the person on the other end they were here, then replaced the receiver. She handed Jace a visitor's badge and pushed the log book toward them. Seb scrawled his name on it. He handed the pen to Jace who did the same, then pinned his badge to his shirt. Seb crossed to the door to the left of the reception desk and swiped his ID again. The door buzzed, and they were in.

They passed several offices before they reached the main lab. Seb glanced through the room and spotted Katie's messy bun toward the back. Threading between the tables, they made their way over to her.

Hunched over a microscope, her translucent pink-frame glasses on top of her head, she peered through the eyepiece at the slide below. Seb and Jace stopped several feet away in her field of vision, but she kept staring through the microscope.

Seb cleared his throat. "Katie?"

She looked up, frowning at the interruption, and pulled her glasses back down over the bridge of her nose. "Oh, it's you. If you've come for an update, I'm still testing things. The preliminary results on the larvae and the flies match the time of death Dr. Randall surmised. I don't have DNA back yet on the tissue samples he sent me. I think he put in for Rebecca Carson's dental records, which will probably be a more definitive match than her DNA anyway since she didn't have any close family." She pushed away from the table, her rolling chair clacking over the tile floor as she glided to the opposite table where she picked up a stack of papers from the printer.

"The hair was from a bear. I also ran the saw dust the doc found tucked into the fold of her pant cuff." She held out the papers. Seb took them and glanced down, but let her explain. "It's pre-treated pine. I also found some paint in her hair and ran it through the mass-spec. Sherwin-Williams Knitting Needles. You find me that can of paint and I can match it."

Anticipation that they might have a decent lead sent Seb's blood pulsing faster. "This is good. It gives me a place to start."

She shook a finger at him. "Don't be so sure. I ran a search.

There's over twenty Sherwin-Williams locations within fifty miles, and that doesn't include the local hardware stores, like ours, or the big box stores that carry the paint."

Seb waved the papers. "It's still a place to start. Hopefully, our guy messed up and bought the paint and wood locally and Mr. Marsters will have a record of it. Thanks, Katie. Call me if you get anything else."

She rolled back to her microscope. "Yep. Now go away. I'm busy studying the dirt sample from under the victim's nails." She shooed them with one hand as she put her glasses back on top of her head and peered down through the scope, but a smile tugged one corner of her mouth.

He couldn't help but grin back at her. "Yes ma'am." Backing away, he and Jace walked out of the lab.

"Is everyone in this town a little—off?"

Seb laughed. "Pretty much. Come on. We have another stop to make."

"Hardware store?" Jace asked as they signed out on the log book.

"Yep."

"Will he give you anything without a warrant?"

Seb tipped his head back and forth. "Maybe. I hope so. We don't have enough for a warrant. Like Katie said, that paint could have been bought at any number of locations."

The two men jogged back to the police station parking lot. They climbed into Seb's cruiser and headed for the shopping district a few streets over. In minutes, Seb was pulling into a parking space out front of the hardware store for the second time that day. As he climbed out of the SUV, he took out his phone and checked his texts, frowning when he didn't see a message from London. She should have been home by now.

Jace rounded the front of the car and Seb held up a finger as he called her. She picked up on the third ring, out of breath.

"I just got home. I ran into the coffee shop to get a latte on my way back and got to talking to Macy. I'm fine."

"Didn't we just have a conversation about keeping each other informed?"

"For the record, I did call Deputy Wilder. I didn't want to disturb you with a bunch of texts because I knew you would be busy."

Seb rocked on his heels, finding it hard to stay angry at her when she was just being considerate. "You're never a bother and I'd rather know you're safe."

He heard a grunt and then the slam of a car door. "I'm sorry. I'll text next time." The clatter of boards hitting the ground punctuated her words.

"Thank you. Did you get everything you needed?"

"Yep. I just unloaded it all in the front yard. I'm about to go get my tools and put these in. My poor bushes look terrible."

"The stakes should help. Keep your phone on you and if anything feels weird, you go inside."

"I will."

He could almost hear the eye roll and it made him grin.

"Alaina's going to come out and help me, so you can rest easy."

"Good. I need to go. Be safe."

"Yep. See you tonight." She hung up before he could say goodbye. He stared down at the phone and shook his head. Stubborn woman.

"Everything okay?"

He looked up, stuffing his phone back in his pocket. "Yeah. Just checking in with London."

Jace started for the door and Seb followed.

"I take it you two finally stopped pussy-footing around?"

Seb gave him a half-smile and opened the door. "Yeah."

"Good. Now I don't have to listen to your sister moan

about how you guys need to get your heads out of your asses."
Jace stepped inside.

A quick laugh burst from Seb. "That sounds like Tara. Or
Maggie. We're talking about Tara, though, right?"

Jace nodded. "She spent a good deal of the party Saturday
watching you two and telling me she was going to lock you in
a room together until you 'did it.'" He air-quoted.

Seb rolled his eyes as he walked toward the counter. "Of
course she did." He turned his attention to Ryan Marsters,
who stood behind the front desk, watching them.

"Hi, Mr. Marsters. We have a couple questions for you. It's
regarding the recent murders."

He straightened, running a hand through his light blonde
hair as his expression grew serious. "Oh? What can I help you
with?"

"Has anyone bought pre-treated pine and Sherwin-
Williams Knitting Needles paint in the last month?"

"Son, this is a hardware store. Do you know how much
paint I sell even in this small town?"

Seb sighed. He was afraid of that. "I know it's probably a
lot, but anything you can remember would be useful."

Marsters eyed him skeptically, but turned to the computer
and brought up a different screen. "I can search by paint, but
not by what color. And it won't tell me who bought what."

"That's fine. I'm just hoping it'll jog your memory a bit."

He nodded and moved his fingers over the keyboard, then
hit enter. A list popped up.

"That's a lot of paint," Jace said.

Marsters nodded. "You wouldn't think it, but people
change the color of rooms all the time. Or they paint a porch,
or a fence—you get the idea."

"Okay. Can you print that, then look up lumber sales and
do the same?"

He hit a few keys and a printer beneath the counter sputtered to life. "Just an FYI, the lumber list will be even longer. This is a ranching community."

"It's all we've got, Ryan, and we need a lead."

His expression was grave as he nodded. He hit print again and the printer spit out more paper. Ryan picked up the stack and held it out.

Seb split the stack by item and handed the paint list to Jace. They set the papers side by side and began going through the purchases and calling out dates.

"The fifteenth?" Seb looked up at Ryan. "There was lumber and paint sold at the same time. Do you remember who that was?"

The store owner frowned down at the pages, trying to read them upside down. "Of May?" He tilted his head back and looked up at the ceiling as he thought. "Millie Perdue. She made me cut a bunch of one-by-eight planks and two-by-fours so she could build her cats a new tower. It took forty-five minutes, because she wanted to draw it out and explain it so I knew exactly how to cut the boards."

Seb grinned. That sounded like Millie. She was a nice older woman, but very particular. Her yard was immaculate, and she always had the best rose bushes in the county. "That is not our killer." He looked back down at his print-out.

Jace pointed at a more recent date. "What about this one?" He looked up at Ryan. "Last Thursday."

"Thursday? Wood and paint..." Ryan's voice trailed off as he thought. "Wait." His face cleared. "Declan Briggs bought both. He got the parts to fix London's water heater, but he also bought some lumber and a gallon of paint. And it was Knitting Needles. He said it was for Macy."

Seb fought to keep his expression composed. He did not want to suspect his friend, but there were too many coincidences piling up for him to ignore. He scraped together the papers. "Can we keep these?"

Ryan nodded. He looked like he wanted to ask questions, but Seb was not going to speculate. He would rather go straight to the source. "Thanks for the info. If you can think of anyone else who's bought both in the last few months, let me know."

"I will, Sheriff. Is there any word on Adelaide?"

Seb shook his head. "Not yet, I'm afraid."

"I sure do hope you find her soon. I'll be back out on the mountain as soon as the store closes this evening."

"We appreciate it and I'm sure Adelaide will too. Thanks for your help." Seb held up a hand in farewell and backed toward the door as he talked.

"Anytime." Ryan waved back.

On the sidewalk, Seb stopped in front of his SUV to gather his thoughts. He didn't want it to be Declan. They had become good friends the last couple years since Seb's return to town. He didn't want to think the man he knew could be capable of such heinous acts.

"You okay?"

Seb pushed away from the cruiser. "Yeah. Let's go talk to Declan."

Because of Adelaide's disappearance, Declan was on the mountain heading up the search. Seb wound his cruiser out of town and up the highway to the trailhead, his gut churning the entire drive. By the time he turned into the parking lot, acid made his stomach burn.

He swallowed hard and climbed from the vehicle, his feet feeling like lead as he walked toward the search tent.

Declan saw them coming and smiled. "Hey guys. What brings you by? I didn't think you were searching until later."

"We're not." Seb sucked in a breath and came to a halt a few feet away. He propped his hands on his hips, his expression serious. "Deck, we need to talk."

Declan straightened. "About what? Has there been more trouble at the inn?"

Seb shook his head. "No. This is about Adelaide."

A frown formed between his brows. "Adelaide? What about her? I know you didn't find her unless she showed up in town." His eyes widened. "Oh, God. Did you find her? Is she all right?"

"No, we haven't found her. I was hoping you could give us some insight."

Declan frowned. "What? How would I know where she is?"

Seb sighed and pinched his brow. "Dr. Randall and the crime lab found saw dust and paint on Rebecca Carson. The same paint you bought last week."

His eyes went wide. "Wait." He pointed at his chest. "You think I had something to do with Adelaide's disappearance? With the murders? That's sick. You know me, Sebastian. I would never hurt anyone, especially not like that."

Seb held his hand out, placating. "I'm just following the evidence. It led me here. I have to ask."

Declan crossed his arms. "Fine. Ask."

"Where were you New Year's Eve?"

"New Year's Eve? I went skiing. It was my weekend off, and I needed to blow off some steam."

"Where did you go?"

"Aspen."

The dread knotting Seb's stomach got tighter. "What resort?"

"Aspen Trails."

Seb muttered an oath under his breath. "I'm sorry, Declan, but you're going to have to come into the station with us."

"What? You can't be serious."

"I am. If you come voluntarily, I won't have to handcuff you."

"Handcuff me? Are you serious? I didn't kill anyone."

Seb glanced at Jace. Shock and disbelief colored his face, mirroring Seb's feelings.

"Whether you did or not, I still need you to come down to the station and answer some questions. I hope to God what you say is true, but right now the evidence points to you. I have to take you in for questioning. I'm sorry."

"I can't believe this," Declan muttered, his jaw set and his blue eyes dark with anger.

"Me either. Are you going to come willingly or are you going to make this hard? Please don't make it hard, Deck."

Eyes flashing fire, Declan picked up the radio clipped to his shoulder and radioed for one of Seb's deputies to come man the tent. He set it back down and looked at Seb and Jace, the blue of his eyes cold and hard. "I'll come, but only because I don't want you walking me out of here in cuffs for anyone to see. This is insane."

"Agreed, but I have to do my job. I can't ignore what the evidence says just because you're my friend, no matter how much I think it's all a load of shit."

His shoulders sagged slightly and some of the anger left his eyes. "Yeah. Okay. Let's go get this over with."

Seb gave a curt nod. "And then I'll buy you a beer—or ten —once we get all this sorted out."

Declan walked past him and Jace toward the cruiser. "How about the whole fucking bar?"

"Yeah," Seb muttered. He scrubbed a hand over his face and followed his friend around front. He would probably owe him that after this was all said and done. Even if he cleared Declan's name, the man's reputation would still take a hit. He just hoped the city council would understand and he wouldn't lose his job.

The three of them climbed into Seb's SUV, and he pointed the cruiser toward town. The ride back to the station was filled with stony silence. He glanced in the rearview mirror and saw Declan seething in the backseat. He couldn't blame him for being angry. He would be too, but Seb would be remiss if he didn't question him.

He turned into the lot at the police station and parked in his space. The three of them got out and Seb let them into the building through the back door. Inside, they bypassed the offices and the rooms where Abigail and Trent spent time last week, and stopped in front of a room marked, "Interrogation."

"Really?" Declan said, looking at the label.

Seb twisted the knob and opened the door. "The conference rooms don't have recording devices. Go have a seat. I need to go get some things, then I'll be in."

Declan stepped past him. "If I'm going to be in here for hours, can I at least get a water?"

"I won't be very long, but I'll bring you one when I come back."

He got a grim nod. The chair legs scraped the ground with a loud screech and Declan sank into the chair, folding his muscular arms over his chest and glaring at the mirrored wall.

Seb closed the door and sagged against it. He looked at the ceiling and groaned. "This is ridiculous."

"I don't know him as well as you do, but I'm inclined to agree. He doesn't seem the type. He also doesn't match the description of the man who fixed the campground's plumbing. But are you sure he didn't do it?"

Seb looked back down at Jace. "Yes. I will eat my badge if he's our killer." He pushed away from the door and headed for his office. "God, this is insane. The D.A. is going to love that we have a suspect and will push to file charges so he looks good in the eyes of the public—never mind that he's got the wrong guy—and once the press hears we have a person of interest and they learn it's a decorated firefighter, this will be all over the news. This whole thing will blow up and I'm going to have reporters teeming at the front doors, wanting the latest." He groaned again. "Macy's going to kill me. After her brother does for ruining his life."

Jace patted his shoulder. "Let's get his story first. Maybe we can clear him quickly and no one will be the wiser. You don't even need to call the D.A. yet."

"I can't hold him off long. He calls every day for an update on the case. So does the damn mayor."

Seb's phone rang. "See?" He pulled it out of his pocket, expecting to see the number for either man, but instead he saw London's smiling face.

He slid his thumb over the screen. "Hey, hon. Is everything okay? I can't really talk right now."

"Sebastian Lee Archer, tell me you did not arrest Declan."

Seb pulled the phone away from his ear to stare at it a moment before answering. "I didn't. I brought him in for questioning. How the hell do you know that? We literally just got to the station."

"Seriously? It's a small town and Macy's café is down the street. Someone saw him go in with you looking pissed and told her. She called me to ask what I knew. Why did you bring him in for questioning?"

He sighed. "I can't really discuss it. It's an active investigation." A headache bloomed behind his eyes and he rubbed at his forehead.

"Sebastian." Her tone was low and threatened to make his life a living nightmare if he didn't give her something.

"All I can tell you is that there's evidence that led me to him. I don't believe it, either, and I can't see him as the killer, but I have to do my job and check him out."

"Well, at least you don't think he's capable of it, but I wish you didn't have to bring him in. Aargh! Why do you have to

be such a good cop?" She hung up, leaving him staring at the
phone again.

He looked at Jace, who had a bemused expression on his
face. "London's mad?"

"Yeah. But she understands." He put his phone away.
"Let's get this show on the road." He stepped into his office
and swiped the file for Amy and Rebecca's murders off his
desk as well as a legal pad and a pen.

"Can you get Declan's driver's license photo and send it to
Detective Farley? Have him go talk to Emily Young and see if
she remembers him."

Jace grinned. "Oh, he'll love that."

Seb chuckled. "Don't give him a head's up. Let him
discover the joy of Ms. Young all by himself. And call Caleb.
Have him get a search warrant for Declan's house and car."

"Got it." He spun on his heel and headed for the empty
desk in the bullpen Seb assigned him while he was here.

Taking a deep breath, Seb strode back down the hall, grabbing a bottle of water from the break room on his way to
interrogation. He opened the door to find Declan sitting the
same way he left him.

He held out the bottle. Declan took it and snapped off the
lid, downing half of it in a few swallows. Seb sat down across
from him and pressed a button on the table to record the
interview, then clicked his pen before reading Declan his
rights.

"Tell me about Aspen."

Declan arched a brow. "What about it?"

"When did you get there?"

"The thirty-first."

"You went alone?"

He nodded. "Yes."

Seb sighed and sat back, tossing his pen down. "Come on,
man. I'm trying to clear you. Help me out here."

Declan dropped his arms on the table and the stubborn-
ness left his face. "Fine. What do you want to know?"

"Tell me about your trip."

He paused a moment, gathering his thoughts. "It was last
minute. We'd had that really bad fire on the west end of town.
The one that killed that family?"

Seb nodded, remembering. That was an awful night. A
family of five perished when their Christmas tree caught fire.
They hadn't had any working smoke detectors.

"I needed to get away. Reset and try to put it behind me. I
had New Year's Eve and New Year's Day off, so I called around
to see if any of the resorts had an open room. Aspen Trails had
a last-minute cancellation, and I jumped on it. I got there
around noon and headed straight for the slopes. I didn't even
check in until late—probably seven or so. After I dropped my
bag in my room, I went down to the restaurant to get something to eat."

"What did you have?"

He thought for a moment. "Hell, man. I don't know.
That was six months ago."

"Did you have anything to drink?"

"I probably had a beer maybe two."

"Any dessert?"

Declan shook his head. "I don't think so, no."

Seb opened the folder and took out a photograph of Amy
Beckett. "Did you see this woman there?"

He looked down at the picture. "Maybe." He stared a
moment longer. "Yeah. Actually, I think I did. She was
tending bar. I didn't talk to her, though. Is that Amy
Beckett?"

Seb nodded and put the photo away. "You didn't have any
other interaction with her? You didn't see her in some other
part of the hotel?"

He shook his head. "No. After I ate, I went back to the

ski slopes and stayed out until they closed them down at eleven. Then I went to my room and ordered room service. I didn't come out again until morning. My lift pass was good all day on the first, so I checked out and stowed my stuff in my car, then skied until late-afternoon before coming home."

"What time did you get home?"

"Around nine."

"Did you talk to anyone? A neighbor, maybe?"

"No. I called Macy, though, to see how her New Year's went. We talked for fifteen minutes or so, then I checked my work email to see if there was anything pressing I needed to deal with in the morning. Once I was done with that, I took a shower, watched the news, and went to bed."

"Did you stop anywhere on your way home?"

"No. I filled up my car before I left for Aspen, so I came straight home."

Seb opened the folder and took out Rebecca's picture. "How about this woman? Did you see her while you were there?"

Declan looked at the photo for a moment and shook his head. "No. I've never seen her."

There was a knock on the door and Seb turned as Jace poked his head in. "His lawyer's here."

A frown creased Seb's brow. He glanced at Declan, who looked equally perplexed.

"Who?"

Jace pushed the door wider to expose Seb's sister, Maggie, who grinned at him from ear to ear. She waggled her fingers at him. "Hi."

Declan laughed and propped his elbow on the table and rested his chin in his palm.

"You're his lawyer? Who the hell even called you?" Seb asked, his voice conveying his incredulity and annoyance.

She strode into the room, her heels clacking on the floors in a smooth staccato, and stopped next to Declan. "Macy."

"My sister hired you?"

Maggie nodded.

"To defend me?"

Again, she nodded.

"Have you even passed the bar yet?"

Her open, teasing expression slammed into a frown. "Yes. Last year."

He held up his hands. "Don't get so touchy. I just want to make sure you're not going to make things worse."

She smacked his shoulder and glared. "Well, I'm all you've got for now, and unless you want to spend the night here, you should probably shut your mouth." She turned her attention to Seb. "You. You should know better than to question someone without their lawyer present."

He held out his hands. "He wanted to talk. He wants to clear his name as much as I do."

She squinted at her brother as if gauging his truthfulness, then pulled out the chair next to Declan and sat. "All right. What has he said so far?"

Seb quickly summarized what they had discussed.

"So, what do we still need to clear him?"

"I'm waiting on security footage from the lodge. Everything is circumstantial at this point, but I do have enough to get a search warrant."

Declan's face clouded over again.

"I know and I'm sorry. Again. This would be different if you had a solid alibi. I could verify it and let you go, but you went alone."

"Was there anyone you spent a lot of time with while you were there?" Maggie asked.

Declan crossed his arms again. "There were a couple of

other guys there on a guys' weekend and I skied with them some."

"Did you get their names?" Seb asked.

"There were three. Jim, Austin, and Dan. They said they were from Denver."

"You get any last names?"

He shook his head. "No."

"Can you get those?" Maggie asked Seb.

"Maybe. Depends on what we can get from the lodge. I may need to go back up there." He sat forward and folded his hands over the folders. "Look, I believe you. I just have to prove it."

Declan held out his arms. "Tell me what you need. You can search anywhere you want. I have nothing to hide."

"Declan, that's not wise," Maggie said.

"Why? I didn't touch either of those women. They won't find anything they haven't already because Amy and Rebecca were never anywhere near my car or house."

"I also don't need his permission, Mags."

"No, but you also can't hold him. Do you have any more questions?"

"Yes." He opened the second folder and took out the photos of the other three women he had attributed to this killer. "Do you know any of these women?"

Declan sat forward and peered at the photographs. "No," he said with a slow shake. "None of them look familiar. Who are they?"

"Other potential victims."

Declan's eyes widened. "Nope. No. That's *five* women, Seb."

"I know, which is why this sucks so much." He growled. "Where were you in November?"

"What does that have to do with Amy and Rebecca?" Maggie asked.

"It doesn't. Jace's victim was found around Thanksgiving."

"Well, that should clear me. I was here," Declan said. "I spent the day with Macy at a shelter, then she cooked us dinner. She even dragged me Black Friday shopping the next morning."

"And that weekend?"

"I worked Saturday, and Sunday I spent running errands."

"Okay. Let's go back to your trip to Aspen. Did you notice anyone paying particular attention to Amy while you were in the restaurant? Or anyone who seemed—off?"

Declan inhaled a deep breath and put both elbows on the table, scrubbing his hands over his face as he thought. "Not really. I didn't spend much time in the lodge. I was there to ski and get my head back on straight. The only reason I remember Ms. Beckett at all is because she had on this ridiculous gold top hat with streamers around the brim and several light necklaces looped around her neck."

"And you never saw Rebecca, correct?"

"Right. So, can I go back to the search now?"

"You should probably stay away from the search until we clear you, but you're free to leave," Seb said and shuffled the pictures back into their folder.

"Can I at least go get the fire station's SUV and take it back to the firehouse?"

Seb nodded.

Maggie stood. "You know where to find us if you think of something else. Come on, Deck. I'll drive you back to your car."

He rose, as did Seb, who punched in the code to exit the room. Maggie swept through the door, Declan on her heels.

Seb caught his arm on the way out. Declan looked at him with a frown.

"I'm sorry about this, Deck."

Declan's face softened, and he nodded. "I know. You're just doing your job. I just wish you didn't have to waste your time on me. I didn't touch those women. Any of them."

"For what it's worth, I believe you. If you really want to help your case, have Maggie take you out to the ranch for the next few hours and go riding with her. I have a warrant in the works to search your house and vehicle and it'll go a long way with the D.A. if, when we find nothing, he can't argue that you had time to dispose of stuff."

Declan nodded. "I'll do that. Just don't trash my house, please."

Seb's mouth quirked. "We'll do our best not to."

"Thanks." He sauntered away after Maggie who stood at the end of the hall, one hand on her hip, staring at them with her lawyer face on.

Seb grinned at her and waved. She was cute when she tried to act all grown up. She would always be his baby sister, though, no matter how professional she acted or looked.

She glared harder at him, no doubt guessing what he was thinking, then spun on her heel and marched out the door as Declan reached her.

He heaved a tired sigh and went to his office, sinking heavily into his chair. The folders hit the desktop with a splat. He leaned forward, bracing himself on his elbows, and ran his hands through his hair.

This sucked.

FIFTEEN

"Hey, Sheriff?"

Seb looked up from his search of Declan's bookcase as his radio crackled to life. He pushed the button on the side. "Yeah, Bering."

"You need to come down to the fire station and look at what I found." His voice sounded grim, even over the radio static. Seb felt the bottom drop out of his stomach.

"What? What did you find?"

"Just come look."

He sighed and headed outside to his cruiser. "On my way."

The drive was short, and he soon pulled into the fire station and parked beside Declan's SUV. He noted that the vehicle Declan drove to the search site was parked in the lot. He hoped the man followed his advice and stuck close to Maggie for a while.

He walked up to Caleb who opened the back door on his cruiser.

"I found this inside his SUV. It was stuck down between the cargo area and the backseats." He held up a clear evidence bag. It contained a gold necklace with a small diamond pendant.

Seb took the bag and looked at it a little closer. It looked familiar. "I've seen this somewhere."

Caleb shrugged. "It's not uncommon. A lot of women wear diamond pendants."

He frowned and turned the bag over, looking for any identifying marks. Seb agreed that many women did wear jewelry like this, but he had seen one recently. He just couldn't remember where.

"Have you asked Macy if it's hers?"

"Haven't had a chance. I just found it."

Seb jingled the keys inside his pocket. "Let me go ask her."

Caleb cocked a brow. "Are you sure you wouldn't rather have me go? You're not exactly her favorite person right now."

He huffed out a breath and shook his head. "No. I'll go. Better that she's only pissed at me and not the entire department."

Caleb held up his hands. "She's all yours, then."

He offered his deputy a grim smile. "Thanks." Spinning away, he went to his cruiser and climbed in, pointing the vehicle toward Peppy Brewster. He hoped he could get in the door without Macy flinging a hot cup of coffee in his face.

He found a space near the café and got out of his SUV and strolled down the sidewalk. He pulled open the door, trying to look nonchalant and non-threatening.

"Sebastian Archer! You have a lot of nerve coming in here right now."

He held up both hands in surrender as he faced the woman behind the counter. She stood ramrod straight. Twin spots of color bloomed on her cheeks and her blue eyes flashed fire.

"I know. I didn't come for coffee, though. I need to ask you a question."

"So, ask."

He looked around at the two occupied tables. Both customers had looked up from their screens at Macy's exclamation.

"Can we talk in your office?"

She huffed and locked the register. "Fine." She spun on her heel, leaving him to follow her through the door to the kitchen.

Seb suppressed a groan and went after her. This was not going to be a pleasant conversation.

He passed through the compact kitchen where she made her baked goods, to the back of the restaurant and the small office. Macy stood next to the desk, vibrating with anger.

Not wanting to get too close, he stopped in the doorway. "I'm sorry about all this. I'm just doing my job."

"I know, but it doesn't change the fact that I'm pissed at you for even thinking Declan could be capable of such a thing."

"For what it's worth, I think he's innocent. But I still have to investigate him. My evidence is pointing straight to him."

"Someone's framing him. Declan would never hurt anyone. He saves people for a living, for God's sake!"

"I know." Seb reached into the cargo pocket on his pants and pulled out the necklace Caleb had taken from Declan's SUV. "Do you recognize this necklace?"

Macy took the bag and looked at the pendant, turning it over, before handing it back and shaking her head. "No. It's not mine. I don't own anything like that."

"Do you know anyone who does?"

"London and Maggie are the only ones of my friends who I can see wearing something like that. It's too flashy for Tara, and Rayna only likes the earthy stuff. Why? What does this have to do with Declan?" Her eyes widened, and she stared at the bag. "Wait. That's in an evidence bag. Did that come off one of the victims?"

"I don't know whose it is. We found it in your brother's car. I was hoping it was yours."

She shook her head and massaged her temples. "God. This is a nightmare."

"Has Declan dated anyone lately? Is there a girlfriend it might belong to?"

Again, she shook her head. "No. He's been single since he and that woman he was seeing from Colorado Springs broke up last fall."

Seb remembered her. She'd been nice enough, but hadn't been willing to move to the boonies and give up the nightlife in the city. Declan hadn't wanted to live in the more urban and touristy area, so they called it quits when the long-distance thing had gotten to be too much.

"Would she have worn something like this?"

"Maybe. She was a little high-maintenance, so I could see her wearing it. I don't have her number."

"That's okay. I'll ask Declan. Thanks, Macy. I'll get out of your hair now."

He turned to go, but her soft voice stopped him.

"This is bad, isn't it?"

Seb stopped and looked back. "If I don't find another suspect soon, yes. It could be very bad for him. He's the only person I can link to the murders, even though it is a stretch."

Tears welled in her eyes and Seb moved into the office and enfolded her in a hug.

"I'm so sorry, Macy."

She took a shaky breath and sniffed, leaning back so she could see his face. "I know you are. And I'm not really mad at you."

He smiled at her. "I know that too."

She nodded and pushed away, wiping at her face. "Go.

Find the person who really did this and clear my brother's name."

He hesitated. "You sure you'll be okay? I can call London and stay until she gets here."

"I'll be fine." She shooed him out with a wave of her hand. "Scram."

"Okay. Call me if you need anything. Day or night."

"I will. Thanks, Seb."

He nodded and left her alone in her office to gather herself. Once outside, he leaned against the door of his car and texted Maggie a picture of the necklace, then called her, hoping that wherever they were on the ranch, they had service.

It took four rings, but she finally picked up.

"We're out riding, just like you suggested. Are you done with his house so he can go home?"

"Not yet. I just sent you a picture. Can you show it to Declan and ask him if he's ever seen it?"

"Now, why would I want to do that?"

"Just do it, Maggie. Or I'll have to have you bring him back in. Please," he tacked on. His sister was notoriously stubborn, and she was right. As his attorney, she didn't have to show him the photo, but he was hoping she would so they could avoid a second round in the interrogation room.

She huffed and he could imagine her rolling her eyes. He heard the creak of leather as she handed Declan the phone.

"I've never seen that necklace before," Declan said. "Where did you find it?"

"In your car."

"What?" Declan's tone was sharp. "Seb, I don't know how that got there. I haven't had a woman other than Macy in my car since I broke up with Lilah."

"Are you sure it wasn't hers?"

"If it was, I never saw her wear it. She had another one she wore a lot. It was three stones stacked, not a single stone like that one. Did you ask Macy?"

"Yeah. She said she's never seen it, either."

Declan's sigh was loud and long. "This is getting scary. I think someone's trying to set me up."

"I agree." He refused to believe Declan could murder anyone, let alone five women. "Stay with Maggie. Under no circumstances are you to be alone right now. Even if you have to move in with Macy, you stay with someone."

"Yeah. Okay."

"Good. Put Mags back on."

He heard more creaking as they passed the phone.

"Yeah, Seb."

"Keep an eye on him. Make sure he doesn't go anywhere alone. If someone is trying to frame him, we don't want to give the killer an opportunity to set him up."

"Okay. I'll be glue. Let me know if you find out anything else."

"I will. And Maggie, you know that if I find out this necklace is from one of our victims, I'll have to arrest him."

Her voice was solemn when she answered. "I know."

Seb sighed. "I'll keep you posted."

"Find this bastard, Sebastian."

"I'm trying. Bye."

"Bye."

He hung up and tapped the phone against his forehead, then let out a frustrated growl. Pushing off the car, he climbed inside and headed to the old part of town where the Martins lived. He'd try them first, and if they didn't recognize the pendant, he'd call Jack Beckett. Part of him hoped the necklace was Rebecca Carson's. He doubted anyone would be able to identify it if it was hers, which meant Declan stayed out of jail.

A pang of misgiving bounced around in his stomach as he drove. What if he was wrong and Declan really was the killer?

Could he be that bad of a judge of character? Or was Declan just that good of an actor?

But his reactions to the photographs of the women were genuine. Seb doubted he knew any of them other than the brief encounter he had with Amy. The thing that bothered him most, though, was how Amy ended up here if Declan wasn't their guy. Why would the killer target Declan? Was the guy a local? And what were the chances that two people from the area were at the same resort on New Year's Eve?

Seb released another frustrated breath and pulled into the Martin's driveway. Whatever the answer to those questions, they would have to wait. He got out of the cruiser and walked up the porch steps of Luke and Susan's house.

His boots echoed on the wooden porch. He rapped his knuckles on the screen door and waited. Footsteps sounded inside and he could see Susan hurrying to answer. She no doubt was hoping her visitor had news. He had asked either her or her husband to stay home in case there was a ransom demand. Luke, a retired miner, had been unable to just sit around, so Susan waited at home for a call Seb was sure would never come.

She pulled open the door, her expression hopeful but wary. "Sheriff. Do you have news? Did you find her?"

"I'm sorry, Susan, no. I have a question for you, though."

She pushed the door open wider. "Come in."

Seb stepped inside.

"What did you want to ask?"

He took the necklace out of his pocket and held it out to her. Before he could ask, she gasped and took the bag from his hands.

"That's Adelaide's!" Her shocked eyes met his. "Where did you find it?"

Heaviness pooled in Seb's gut. "Are you sure it's hers?"

She looked back down at it and turned it over, then

nodded. "Yes." She showed him the back of the pendant. "See the mark? It's from Belton's in Colorado Springs. We bought this for her when she graduated college. We were very proud of her and she knew that, so she wore it a lot. Where did you find it?"

"Declan Briggs's SUV."

Her eyes widened. "What? Why would Declan have it? They were in the same grade in school, but I don't think they've had much to do with each other since Adelaide came home. She hasn't had much to do with any of the people around here her age—man or woman. I was amazed to see her playing softball with you all at Lee and Jenny's party. She's not exactly well-liked."

Seb masked his shock at her candor, but not quick enough.

She waved a hand at him. "Sheriff, I'm under no illusion that my daughter doesn't have an attitude problem. We spoiled her because she was our only child—one that we tried very hard for. I love her, but she can be rude and snide and mean when she doesn't get what she wants. I don't blame a man like Declan for shunning her. Or your brother, Thomas, for that matter. Did you ask Declan why he had her necklace?"

"Yes. He says he's never seen it and doesn't know how it got into his car. Mrs. Martin, we have evidence linking Declan to the recent murders and now Adelaide's abduction."

Her face turned white and her hand quivered as she brought it up to push back her bangs. She frowned at him. "Are you sure? I mean, he's such a nice young man, despite his upbringing. I can't imagine him doing something so awful."

"I can't either, ma'am, but that's where the evidence points. Now, you're sure this necklace is Adelaide's?"

She nodded. "One hundred percent."

That heavy ball in his stomach got bigger and dread made

his shoulders sag. "Okay. Thank you for your time, Mrs. Martin. I will let you know as soon as I find out anything else."

"Thank you, Sebastian." She laid a hand on his arm. "I'm sorry about your friend. I have a hard time believing it's him. Whatever the case, I hope you find the truth."

"Me too, ma'am." He touched the bag to his temple in goodbye and backed toward the door. "I'll see myself out. Let me know if you have any questions or you hear from Adelaide's abductor."

"I will. You take care."

"Yes ma'am." Seb opened the screen door and stepped back onto the porch, his footsteps heavy as he walked back to his cruiser. His next stop was not one he wanted to make, but he had no choice now. Inside his car, he snapped his seatbelt in place and backed out of the drive with lead in his heart, on his way to city hall to talk to the D.A.

London peeked out the window when headlights cut through the darkness in her bedroom. Seb's truck rolled to a halt behind the garage stall where Abigail normally parked. She watched as he turned off the engine and climbed from the vehicle. His weariness was apparent even from her vantage point.

Pushing off the sill, she donned her robe and house shoes and grabbed her keys, exiting the apartment. Out of habit, she tread lightly so as not to disturb her guests, but it wouldn't have mattered if she'd run down the hall in her cowboy boots. Doug Brown was the only one left. The other couple checked out that afternoon, deciding the atmosphere was too stressful for the relaxing vacation they hoped for.

She ran across the living room, startling Alaina Wilder, who elected to stay until Seb returned. She sat up in the chair she'd been sprawled across and the book she was reading dropped to the floor.

"What? What's going on?"

"Seb's home." London continued through the pocket door to the kitchen, flipping on lights as she went. The interior door to the garage opened when she was halfway across the room.

She took one look at the misery in his eyes and flew to him. He tucked her in close and held her tight. London could feel his muscles quiver from the stress of the day as he continued to hold his emotions in check. She pulled back, framing his face in her hands, and looked into his eyes. She hadn't seen him so beaten up and discouraged since Eddie died.

Knowing he needed her, she took his hand and led him back the way she'd just come. Alaina stood in the doorway, her face stoic as she took in her boss's haggard appearance. She stepped back to let them pass, but Seb tugged on London's hand and paused in front of his deputy.

"Thank you for staying, Alaina. I'm sorry I'm so late."

She waved off his apology. "Not a problem. I'm sorry about Declan. Hopefully, it'll all turn out to be a coincidence and you can let him go."

"I hope so too." He walked past her, pulling London with him. "Go home. Get some rest. I'll see you in the office tomorrow."

She nodded. "Goodnight, Sheriff."

London's heart broke at the sad smile that crossed his face. Together, they crossed the quiet living room. Alaina gave them a soft wave as she exited. Seb twisted the door locks behind her and London shut off the living room lights. He took her hand and led her up the stairs. At the door to the family suite, London inserted her key into the lock, letting them inside. She reached for the light switch, but Seb's hand on hers stopped her.

Without a word, he took the keys from her and tossed them onto the table next to the door. He pushed it closed and locked it, then wrapped his arms around her hips and lifted her, carrying her to her room. She pushed her hands into his hair and pressed her forehead to his, trying to take away some of the sadness from his day.

With a tenderness she felt all the way to the marrow of her bones, he laid her on the bed. She watched through the darkness as he shed his utility belt and laid his sidearm on the nightstand. He perched on the edge of the bed and removed his boots and socks. His uniform shirt came next as he tugged it up over his neck in one smooth, fluid motion. When he stood to unbuckle his pants, she rose to her knees and brushed his hands away. His quick intake of breath was his only reaction.

She slid her hands inside the waistband of his cargo pants and his boxer briefs and pushed them down past his hips. They slid to the floor with a quiet swish. She took a condom from the nightstand and quickly sheathed him. He moaned again when her fingers closed around him, then raised his hands and, with just his fingertips, opened her robe and flicked it off her shoulders. The silky material slid down her arms and pooled on the bed around her. London didn't wait for him. She grasped the hem of her sleep shirt and pulled it up over her head, leaving her in just her panties. He hooked his fingers in them and pushed them down, then latched onto her mouth, making her moan.

London threaded her fingers into his hair and held him close. His hands wrapped around her back to ghost up her spine, leaving a trail of goosebumps in his wake. She tugged on his neck, pulling him down with her to the mattress. He broke their kiss to trail his mouth down her neck and over her breasts. Each whisper of his kiss on her skin ratcheted her need higher until it burned white hot. She raked her nails over his scalp and he moaned into her flesh.

"Please, Sebastian."

His hands stroked the skin on her outer thighs as he trailed his fingers over her hip bones and down her legs. With a gentle nudge, he pushed them apart and settled between them. He brushed her hair back and stared down at her in the darkness. In the low light, his eyes glittered with emotion.

"I love you."

Her heart stopped, then did a little flutter before it started racing in her chest at his tender admission. Tears welled in her eyes. She blinked them back and raised her head to place a gentle kiss on his lips, cradling his face in her hands. "I love you too."

He kissed her again, this time full of passion. London's need hit new heights, consuming her. She wrapped her legs around his waist and let it take over. He slid inside her, sending her to a new plane. One filled with heat and light, and a pleasure so intense it wanted to rip her apart.

In an instant, it did just that. She shattered into a million tiny pieces of pure ecstasy. Seb's shout came on the heels of hers. She tried to wrap her arms around him and ride out the wave, but couldn't make her muscles work. She sank into the mattress, sated and limp.

Seb shifted, so he wasn't lying directly on her and tucked her into his side, throwing a leg over hers. His body relaxed and he let out a long sigh. London felt the moment he let all the stress of the day go and fell asleep.

She stroked his eyebrow and ran her fingers up into his thick, dark hair, staring at his handsome face in the moonlight coming through the window. He looked younger asleep. All the worry lines around his eyes smoothed out and his mouth relaxed. Her heart ached for the pain he'd gone through today.

It couldn't have been easy to arrest Declan for murder and kidnapping. Even if Seb didn't believe he did it. She was sure he thought Deck viewed it as a betrayal of trust, and he probably did, even if he understood that Seb was only doing his job.

Leaning forward, she pressed a tender kiss to his temple, then scooted down to settle against his side on her pillow. She snuggled closer and shut her eyes, praying tomorrow would be better.

Sixteen

London hummed to herself as she washed the breakfast dishes. With only one guest, herself and Seb in the house, it was a quick process. Once she finished, she planned to head up the mountain and help with the search again. They were going into day three now, and the prospect of finding Adelaide alive was growing slimmer and slimmer.

She shut off the faucet and shook the excess water from her hands. As she reached for the towel, she glanced out the window. Something near the tree line caught her eye. Leaning forward, she squinted against the morning sun. Tall and pale, it swayed against a tree.

What was that? Had the deputy watching the house today arrived and decided to do a sweep of the property first?

It moved with a lurch and London gasped.

"Oh my God!"

She broke into a run, yanking open the back door and flying across the yard to reach the figure that emerged from the woods.

"Adelaide! Oh my God!" She caught the other woman as

she collapsed, her full weight sagging against London's taller frame.

"London?" Adelaide's voice was weak. She looked up, eyes glazed with pain and confusion.

"Yeah, it's me." She took stock of the other woman's condition. Naked as a jaybird, she was dirty and bruised. Dried blood marred her creamy skin from hundreds of tiny cuts. Her hair, normally so perfectly done, was a mess—tangled and sticking out every which way with twigs and leaves woven into the disheveled strands.

Jesus. What had she been through to get here?

"Let's get you inside. Can you walk?"

"If—if you help."

London nodded. "Okay. Come on." She readjusted her grip, helping the other woman stand more upright, and together, they made their way to the house. Twisting the knob, she pushed open the door, and they stumbled inside. London led her over to the small kitchen table and eased her down onto one of the wooden chairs.

"I'll go get you a blanket." She turned to do just that, but Adelaide's hand on her arm stopped her.

"Water. Can I have some water first?"

"Oh. Yes. Yes, of course." She changed direction and filled one of the glasses she'd just washed, then handed it to Adelaide. The other woman drank eagerly.

"Slow down. You don't want to throw it back up."

Adelaide took one more hearty sip, then set the glass down and nodded.

"I'll be right back." London ran out of the kitchen to get a blanket from the linen closet in the laundry room.

She dashed back, unfolding the warm cloth as she crossed to the table. She wrapped it around the other woman, who sighed as it touched her skin.

"Thank you."

London squatted in front of her and tried to push some of the matted hair away from her face. "Are you okay?"

Tears welled in Adelaide's eyes. "No." Her whisper was broken. She swallowed hard, sniffing, and continued. "I was so scared."

"Who took you?" London prayed she wouldn't say Declan.

"I don't know. All I saw was a shape in the dark. He drugged me." She craned her neck and London saw a small bruise. Adelaide's tears started again and London patted her knee through the heavy blanket.

"Okay. I'm going to call for help now."

Adelaide nodded and leaned back in the chair, closing her eyes.

London rose and pulled her phone from her shorts' pocket. She dialed 911 and relayed to the dispatcher that Adelaide Martin was safe in her kitchen. After she hung up, she called Seb.

"Hey, babe—"

She cut him off. "Adelaide just came out of the woods at the house. She's in my kitchen."

There was a brief pause as he digested what she'd just said.

"What? Is she okay?"

"Sort of." London moved away from the other woman and lowered her voice. "She's pretty beat up. There are bruises all over her arms and legs. And—and around her throat." She swallowed hard at the thought of what that meant and took a deep breath before continuing. "She's covered in cuts too, but I think those might be from brambles. Her feet are a mess." She glanced at the bloody footprints on the floor from the door to the table. "She's pretty dehydrated too. I already called for help."

"Okay. I'm on my way. Just keep her comfortable."

Her head bobbed. "I will." She hung up and tucked the

phone back in her pocket, then walked back to Adelaide and pulled out the chair next to her.

Adelaide opened her eyes. They were bleak.

London's heart lurched, and she reached out to grasp the fingers holding the edges of the blanket together. "I'm so sorry this happened to you. Do you remember anything about who did this? I know you said you were drugged, but were you lucid at all? Even a little?"

She closed her eyes in thought, and a tear leaked out, rolling down her cheek. "He smelled like sawdust. And I remember being cold because he took all my clothes. He—he —" she broke off on a sob, and London could fill in the blanks. She felt her own tears spring up.

She blinked them back and squeezed Adelaide's hand tighter. "What do you remember about him other than his scent?"

"He was strong," she whispered. "So strong." She drew in a shaky breath. "I tried to fight him off, but I was too loopy from the drugs. I think I might have scratched him once, but I'm not sure."

"Did he ever talk to you?"

"Once. When he came in and held me down and—" she pressed her lips together on a muffled sob.

"Shh. It's okay. You're safe now. Do you remember what he said?"

Adelaide sniffed. "He called me by another name. Coraline. And told me I was his—that I'd always be his."

London closed her eyes for a brief moment. *What a sick bastard.*

"How did you get away?"

"He took me to some old shack in the woods. It was in bad shape. I remember seeing stars through the cracks in the roof before he climbed on top of me and blocked them out. He— wrapped his hands around my neck." A torrent of tears rushed down her face and her voice broke again. "After that I don't remember much else until I woke up. I don't know how long I walked or how far. I just knew I had to get away. In case he came back."

London covered her mouth in horror. A few tears escaped her eyes, and she turned her head, wiping them away. Sniffing, she picked up Adelaide's water glass and held it out. "Here. Take another drink."

Adelaide took it and sipped the water. London heard sirens and relief rushed through her.

Thank God.

The sound got louder as they turned into the driveway. She rose to go meet them, giving Adelaide a reassuring pat on the hand. When she opened the front door, the ambulance crew was climbing out of the truck, laden with bags.

"Did she really just walk into your yard?" the older of the two men asked.

London nodded.

He shook his head and motioned his partner forward. "I can't believe they think Declan did this. He was my partner for years before he promoted to lieutenant. Stuff like this always made him mad. He wouldn't hurt anyone like that, let alone a woman."

"I agree, but the evidence says otherwise."

"Then he's being framed."

"And Seb will prove that. We just need to be patient." She turned and led them into the house, pointing at the pocket door. "She's in there."

She hung back, giving them room to work. The younger paramedic shined a light in Adelaide's eyes while the older one eased her arm free of the blanket to take her blood pressure. London was sure it was probably off. The woman still looked shellshocked.

Heavy footsteps sounded on the porch and the front door

flew open. London turned to see Seb burst into the house. In four long strides, he was at her side, his mouth agape as he caught his first glimpse of Adelaide.

"Oh my God." His voice was soft, but there was no mistaking the shock in it. "She looks awful."

"I know. She's pretty lucid, though, which is good. She told me she doesn't really remember much. He drugged her and raped her." She drew in a deep breath. "And strangled her. I think he meant to kill her and thought she was dead when he left."

"Fuck." Seb's curse was soft, but emphatic. "Well, thank God she wasn't. Her parents would be devastated."

"I just hope she can handle the trauma. What she went through—" London broke off and blinked away tears threatening to spill over.

Seb wrapped an arm around her shoulders. She looped hers around his waist and tucked her head into his chest, glad he was there to lend some support.

"Did she say anything else?"

"Just that he called her Coraline and took her to some broken-down shack in the woods. And that she thinks she scratched him."

That made him straighten. He dropped his arm and retreated to the door. "I'll be right back."

London frowned, but didn't say anything as he loped out the door. A moment later, he came back in with an evidence collection kit.

"What are you doing?"

"I'm going to clip her nails. If she scratched him, there might be DNA under them."

London's eyes widened. "That could exonerate Declan." Or condemn him.

His expression was hopeful. "Yep."

He stepped past her and walked over to Adelaide. The

paramedics, nearly finished with their assessment, moved off to the side. Seb crouched in front of her.

"Adelaide, London said you told her you might have scratched your attacker. I need to clip and scrape your nails."

She held out a shaky hand "Anything. I just want you to catch who did this to me."

He removed the pulse oximeter from her finger, then had her rest her hand over the edge of the table. Using nail clippers, he clipped her nails into a small paper sack, then scraped under the edges, making sure it all fell into the bag. He repeated the process with the other hand.

"Is there anything else you remember about the man? Hair color? Height? Build?"

Some of the shock had faded from her eyes and she stared at a point over his shoulder, thinking. "He was average height, I guess. I was really loopy, so it's all bits and pieces. Some things, like the smell of sawdust and the stars, stick out. It was so dark, though. He was strong. That I remember." Her eyes connected with his. "I wish I could tell you more."

"That's okay. You're doing great. Did you recognize his voice when he spoke to you?"

She shook her head. "No. He whispered it. I just remember thinking, why is he calling me Coraline? My name is Adelaide."

"Okay. I'll let these guys get you to the hospital. Myself or Deputy Bering will be by later to talk to you again after you've rested." He patted her hand. "I'm glad you're safe, Adelaide."

Her eyes welled. "Thank you. Will you call my parents? They're probably so worried."

He nodded. "They are, and yes, I will." He stood and stepped out of the medics' way. They helped her stand, making sure the blanket stayed wrapped around her and led her out of the kitchen. Seb and London followed, helping to carry the medical bags. It didn't take long before the ambulance pulled away, headed for the hospital.

"What happens now?"

Seb frowned after the retreating vehicle before looking down at her. He held up the bag with Adelaide's finger clippings. "I already called off the search. Now, I'm going to call Mr. and Mrs. Martin, then take these to Katie Mitchum in the crime lab and have her expedite the DNA. Hopefully, by tomorrow morning, we'll know if I have the right man in jail."

"You don't." London was adamant about that. She had known Declan since she was in grade school. He had been the annoying older brother who always liked to pick on her and Macy. He wasn't a killer. Or a rapist.

"And now, hopefully, this will prove that." He gestured to the evidence bag in his hand.

She pushed him toward his cruiser. "Go. Get that bag to Katie. I'll go talk to the Martins."

His brow puckered as he opened the door. "You sure? It's not your job to talk to the families."

"I know, but I want to."

"Okay." He bent and placed a quick kiss on her lips. "Be careful. Let me know where you go after you talk to the Martins."

She nodded. "I'll probably go find Macy. Let her know what's going on."

"Sounds good. Love you." He climbed inside and started the engine.

"Love you too." It was still a thrill to hear those words come out of his mouth. She closed his door and stepped back.

He waved as he turned around and headed down the drive. London backed toward the porch, watching him go, then turned and ran back inside to get her purse and keys, anxious to tell the Martins their daughter was safe. As she reached her car, her phone rang. She answered it without looking as she fastened her seatbelt.

"Hello?"

"London, it's Ryan Marsters. Your faucet is in."

She punched the button on the remote clipped to the visor and the garage door rumbled up behind her. "Oh. Good. It'll be later before I can come get it. I'm on my way to the Martins' right now. Adelaide wandered into my backyard this morning. She's battered, but she's safe."

There was a moment of silence.

"Oh." The shock was evident in his voice. He cleared his throat. "That's great. I'm glad. How about I just bring this by tomorrow, then? I can install it for you too. I know how eager you are to have it."

London turned out of her driveway, only half-listening. "Sure. That sounds fine."

"Good. I'll see you about nine? I don't have to open the store until ten, so that should give me plenty of time to get it installed."

"Sounds great. Thanks, Ryan."

"You're welcome. Drive safe and give Adelaide my best."

"I will." She said goodbye and hung up. She pressed a little harder on the accelerator. Considering the circumstances, Seb would forgive her for speeding this once.

Thankful the town was small, she turned into the Martin's drive a few minutes later. The engine was still winding down when she scrambled out of the car and ran up the steps. She banged on the door.

Through the window, she could see Susan Martin hurrying to answer it.

"London?" she said as she pulled it open. "What's going on?"

"Adelaide's alive. She wandered into my yard this morning. She's in rough shape, but she's alive and going to be fine."

The older woman stared at her wide-eyed, mouth agape for a moment before her eyes filled with tears. A sob broke free and the dam burst. She fell into London's arms, sobbing.

London wrapped her up and held on tight.

"Oh my God! Oh, thank goodness." The older woman straightened and wiped at the tears on her face.

"Get your purse. I'll drive you to the hospital."

Susan sniffed, wiping away more tears. "Yes. Oh, this is wonderful news." She scrambled back inside and returned within moments, clutching her handbag. London ushered her into the car and pointed the vehicle toward the hospital on the other side of town.

"Was she able to tell you anything about what happened to her?"

"Not too much," London hedged. She didn't want to stress the older woman out by telling her about Adelaide's ordeal. "She was drugged, so she doesn't remember much."

"Oh, my poor baby." Tears welled again, and she sniffed them away. "I suppose that's good, though. I'm trying not to think about what she went through." Susan took her phone out of her bag. "I need to call Lucas."

London listened as she relayed the news to her husband, who said he would meet her at the hospital. She ended the call just as London pulled up to the emergency room doors.

The older woman opened the door and turned to get out, but paused to lay a hand on London's arm. "Thank you."

London smiled. "You're welcome. I'll check on you all later."

Susan waved and got out, hurrying toward the doors. London pulled away with a smile, happy Mrs. Martin wasn't mourning her only child.

～

The hushed sounds of a hospital ward greeted London as she stepped off the elevator several hours later. After dropping off Mrs. Martin, she went to Macy's to break the news and keep her from storming the jail, demanding her brother's release. They just needed to be patient, and she was sure he would be a free man by lunch tomorrow.

She adjusted the bouquet of lilacs in her arms and knocked on Adelaide's hospital room door before poking her head inside. Adelaide and her mother both looked up. Susan smiled at her.

"London, hello. Come in, dear." She waved London into the room.

"How are you feeling?" she asked Adelaide, moving into the room. She set the vase down on the window ledge.

"Better. Thank you."

Susan stood. "Here. You take my chair."

"Oh, you don't have to get up, Mrs. Martin."

"Nonsense. I'll just go get some coffee and let you two chat." She picked up her purse from the floor and left the room.

London watched her go, then looked back at Adelaide who stared at the lilacs London brought.

"Those are so pretty. I was always so jealous of your inn. Of the success you had."

London frowned and sat down in Susan's vacant seat. "What? Why would you be jealous of me?"

Adelaide turned her head. "Because you were a success. I graduated college and floated from job to job, trying to find the 'right' one. I realize now that I just hated marketing. I only went into it because I thought it would be a lucrative career." She glanced down at her hands. "It might have been if I'd actually applied myself to it." She scoffed. "I've made such a mess of my life. I married my husband because he was rich, because of his lifestyle. I still wasn't content. Our marriage was empty, which is why I slept around."

"Did you ever love him?"

She shook her head. "He was pleasant. At first, anyway. Then he just got mean. He never hit me, but he'd belittle me. Tell me I was worthless."

London's heart clenched. The poor woman. "I'm sorry to hear that. You're not worthless."

She looked at London with sad eyes. "Are you sure about that?"

"Yes." London's voice was emphatic. "Look, I know we haven't really been friends, but I'd like to change that. I think you could use a friend."

"You don't want me as a friend. Not now that you're with Sebastian. His brother hates me. It'll just cause problems. Besides, I don't have anything to offer you as a friend."

London waved a hand. "Thomas is a bit of a blowhard. He'll come around. Especially if you make an effort to change."

A ghost of a smile crossed her face, giving London a glimpse of the old Adelaide. "But he's just so damn scrumptious."

London giggled. "All the Archer men are handsome."

"True."

"And you have plenty to offer. You're an intelligent woman. And I think you're ready to change. To be a better person. I want to be friends with anyone who has such a desire to work on herself. Tell you what. How about when you've recovered some, you come over for lunch? You can help me brainstorm a way to bring business back to the inn."

The first genuine smile she'd seen from the other woman blossomed over her face. "It's a deal. Thank you, London. I can't say that enough."

London swallowed around the lump in her throat. "You're welcome. I'm just so very glad you're okay."

She sat there a while longer, getting to know her new friend, happy she was safe and already starting to heal from her ordeal. She just hoped Seb could catch the man who'd done this and give Adelaide some real peace.

SEVENTEEN

The sound of the doorbell echoed through the house, and London shut the lid on the washer and pressed the buttons to start it up, then headed for the foyer. She peeked through the window and saw Ryan Marsters standing on the other side.

He saw her and waved, a sack hanging from his fingers and a box in his other hand.

My faucet. She had forgotten all about it until now. Turning the lock, she opened the door.

"Hi, Ryan. Come in."

He stepped inside.

"I still need to clean out under the sink. I forgot you were coming."

"That's all right. I'll help." He smiled at her and she found herself smiling back at his open, polite face.

They waved at Deputy Bering as they crossed the living area. London shoved open the pocket door and motioned Ryan inside. He set down the faucet and the other items he brought on the counter. She opened the cabinet doors under the sink, crouched, and began taking things out. Ryan squatted next to her to help.

"I didn't realize I had so much crap under here. It's probably a good thing I decided to replace the faucet. Gives me a good reason to clean this out."

"I don't want to look under my kitchen sink. I'm sure there's stuff that's been under there since I moved into that house."

She chuckled and stuck her head inside to get the items at the back.

"So, what do you make of this business with Adelaide? I can't believe it."

London scooted back with her armload of goods and set them on the floor. She brushed her hair out of her face and shrugged. "I know. It's crazy. I'm just so happy she's safe. We had a good talk yesterday afternoon at the hospital. It's nuts, but the whole ordeal helped her see herself in a different light. She took stock of her life and decided she wanted a change. I told her I'd help her in any way I could. She seemed pretty lost."

He patted her shoulder. "You're a good person. I don't know if I could be as considerate to someone like her."

She frowned. "Why? Deep down, I think she's a good person. And she's done nothing to me, personally. Even if she had, she seemed sincere in wanting to change. It wouldn't be very Christian of me if I didn't give her another chance."

Ryan reached into the cupboard and shut off the water. "Forgiving and becoming her friend are two very different things. The Bible says nothing about having to do the latter."

"No, but I want to. She doesn't have any, and she's lonely. I think she needs a friend. Someone who won't judge."

He picked up a wrench from the canvas sack he'd brought along and leaned into the cabinet again. "Like I said, you're a good person. Better than me." He looked back at her. "That's one of the things that drew me to you—your morality."

Her cheeks reddened, and she opened her mouth to politely change the subject, but he held up a hand.

"I know. You're with Seb. I won't ask again. I just wanted you to know that."

London smiled. "You're a nice man, Ryan. One day, some lady will come along—who's closer to your own age—and appreciate that."

She stood and dusted off her hands. "I have a few other things I need to do. Will you be all right doing this by yourself?"

He nodded. "This is easy. Not like changing out frozen pipes or plumbing a house. I should be out of here in about forty-five minutes or so."

"Sounds good. Holler if you need me."

He gave her a thumbs up and stuck his head back under the sink.

London wandered out into the living room. She needed to vacuum in here and dust, then restock the snack station in the dining room and clean Mr. Brown's bathroom.

Caleb stood as she crossed the room on her way to the utility room to get the vacuum.

He tipped his head toward the kitchen. "Why is Ryan Marsters here?"

"He's changing out my faucet. I've been waiting on it for over a month and he volunteered."

"Oh. Okay." He rocked back on his heels and looked around.

London grinned. "Are you bored?"

His shoulders slumped. "God, yes. I'm sorry. I like you and I'm happy to help out by watching the place, but I'm not used to just sitting around."

She laughed. "Come with me." She led him into the utility

room and motioned to her cleaning supplies. "You can vacuum or clean a bathroom."

He grabbed the vacuum. "I know I should be chivalrous and take the bathroom, but I don't even like cleaning my own."

She grinned. "That's fine. I have gloves." She took a caddy off the shelf on the wall that held her bathroom supplies. She picked up two rolls of toilet paper also.

"You want just the living room done?"

"If you're feeling ambitious, you can do the game room too. I have a vacuum upstairs to do Mr. Brown's room."

He rolled the sweeper toward the door. "Works for me."

"Thanks, Caleb," she called after him. He lifted a hand, waving off her thanks, and left the room.

She grabbed a mop to add to her stash and followed him out. At least so long as she was busy, the time would go faster. She just hoped the DNA results came back soon so Declan could get out of jail.

Seb walked into the crime lab determined to camp at Katie's desk until she gave him some results. He'd visited Declan last night and told him the news. The man had been disappointed he still wasn't free, but buoyed by the fact that they got DNA from Adelaide's nails. Seb also managed to talk the D.A. into holding off on filing formal charges with the recent developments in the case. He wanted those damn results so he could let his friend out of his cell and start looking for the actual killer.

Katie held up a hand as soon as she saw him approaching. "It's still processing."

"How much longer?"

"A few minutes."

He growled.

A dark frown split her brow. "Don't look at me like that. I can't work any faster than the process."

He sighed and leaned against the table behind him. "I'm sorry. I just want to look for the actual killer instead of chasing the suspect I know is innocent."

"You don't know that. You just want to because he's your friend."

Seb crossed his arms. "I'll tell you the same thing I told our guest detective—I will eat my badge if Declan is our guy." He shook his head. "You don't know him, Katie. You didn't grow up around here—haven't seen him on the job. He's not a killer."

"But Adelaide wasn't killed. Just abducted and raped," she pointed out.

"Right, but it was the same guy. There are too many similarities and it's too much of a coincidence for there to be two such violent offenders operating in this area at the same time."

She shrugged and refreshed her computer screen. "Maybe. I'm just saying that not everyone is what they seem."

He had a feeling she spoke from experience. Before he could reply, though, she hit the refresh button again, and the computer pinged. Seb shot forward to peer over her shoulder.

"What's it say?"

"Give me a second." She hit a few keys on the keyboard to bring up the assay. To Seb, it just looked like a bunch of fuzzy bands.

"It's not a match." She spun around to look up at him, an enormous smile on her face. "Declan didn't kidnap Adelaide."

"I knew it! Okay, can you find a match in the database?"

"That might take a little while." She spun back to the computer and pulled up a different screen, typing furiously. "You can go. I'll call you if I find anything." The printer shot to life and she pointed at it. "That's for you."

He took the paper from the tray. It was the DNA results. Disappointed he couldn't go arrest the real killer right now, he realized he still had something else to do. "Fine. I'll go talk to the D.A. and get Declan released."

"Good idea," she murmured, engrossed in her search.

Seb's mouth pulled in a small smile and he shook his head. At least she was dedicated.

He left the lab and headed for the courthouse to talk to the D.A. Daniel Kerr. A short drive later, he parked his cruiser in front of the three-story building and jogged inside. He waved at the security guard and bypassed the elevator in favor of the stairs. Taking them two at a time, he burst through the door and nearly ran over a law clerk, his arms piled high with briefings.

"Sorry," Seb muttered, hurrying past. He reached the end of the hall and stopped at the desk outside Kerr's door. Emma Quentin, the D.A.'s long-time secretary, smiled up at him.

"Hello, Sheriff. You look out of breath. Is everything okay?"

"I'm fine. I need to talk to Dan. Is he in?"

"Yep. Let me see if he's free." She picked up her phone and hit a button.

"Mr. Kerr, the sheriff is here to see you." She paused a moment, then smiled and hung up the phone. "You can go in."

"Thanks."

Seb rounded her desk and pushed open the door.

"Seb. What brings you here so early?" The D.A. smiled and motioned him forward.

"I just came from the crime lab. Declan's not our abductor." He held out the paper with the DNA results.

Dan took it and read it, then looked up. "Good. I'll reduce the charges and get him over to the magistrate for bail."

Seb frowned. "What? He didn't do it, Dan. What are you going to charge him with?"

"Accessory to kidnapping. We still found her necklace in his car."

"Because someone planted it."

"I'm not discounting that possibility, but right now, I have no evidence of that."

"Sure you do." Seb pointed at the paper the D.A. held. "And whatever happened to innocent until proven guilty?" He stepped forward, anger making his face and voice hard. "Don't use him just to make yourself look good. He was not involved in any of this. Adelaide said there was one man."

Dan crossed his arms and glared. "This is not about me. It's about justice for those women."

"Bullshit. It's an election year for you. If you let Declan go, you have to admit you were wrong, and that makes you look bad."

"It makes you look bad too."

"I don't fucking care! I will not railroad an innocent man. If I'm wrong, I'm wrong and I'll own that. You need to do the same. Release him. All charges dropped."

Still, he hesitated.

"Come on, Dan. You know Declan. He had nothing to do with this."

Dan sighed and leaned forward, moving the computer mouse to click on the screen. "Fine. I'll send over the release form now." He glanced up as Seb. "But if it turns out he was involved in this in any way, I will make sure it's you who takes the hit, not me."

Seb shrugged. "Fine by me. I'm not wrong." He spun on his heel and marched out of the office before he did something to land himself in his own jail.

"Bye, Sheriff," Emma said as he walked past.

He waved at her, not looking back. He was going to be there to let Declan out as soon as the order cleared the system.

London's rubber gloves snapped as she peeled them off and put them back in the caddy. She deposited the whole lot on the shelf and moved to the sink to wash her hands. Using the towel draped across the bar on the front of the sink, she dried them off, then left the utility room.

Caleb had finished vacuuming and disappeared. She looked out the window as she crossed the living room, but didn't see him. He was probably walking the perimeter to stay busy. She entered the kitchen and saw Ryan leaning over the sink, assembling the new faucet.

"That looks great and you're not even done."

He turned his head and smiled. "You picked a good one, that's for sure."

She crossed to the pantry and started stacking boxes in her arms to refill the snack station. When she emerged, she had her arms full.

"When you're done, I have some sausage and pancakes left from this morning if you're hungry."

"Oh, that sounds great. I only had a protein bar for breakfast."

London made a face. "Seb likes those too. I don't know how you guys stand them. I think they're gross."

He laughed. "They're quick and I don't have to cook it."

She rolled her eyes. "True enough. Let me fill the snack station and I'll warm it up for you."

"Thanks. It's appreciated. I don't get many home-cooked meals. My sister was an excellent cook. I didn't inherit that gene."

She smiled. "Well, I fed my last plumber. I can't very well neglect you when I fed him."

He nodded. "Was that Declan?"

Her smile faded, and she nodded. "Yeah. I'm hoping he gets out this morning. Seb found DNA under Adelaide's nails. They're supposed to get the results back today."

Shock crossed his face, and he straightened. "Really?"

She nodded.

"They got DNA?"

"Mmm-hmm. Those talons of hers came in handy." She walked away before he could respond, her arms getting tired.

She dumped her load on the buffet as she heard the back door open and close. She paused and listened, expecting to hear Caleb say hello to Ryan, but only silence met her ears. Curious, she hurriedly stuffed packages into their designated cubby holes, then bent to look in the fridge. It was full, so she gathered her load again and headed back into the kitchen.

To her surprise, it was empty. Ryan's tools sat spread out on the counter still, and the new faucet was on its side at the edge of the sink.

Unease crept up her spine.

She heard a thud outside and moved toward the door, snagging a screwdriver off the counter. Worried that Ryan was hurt, she opened the door and peeked outside.

There was a man on the ground, all right, but it wasn't Ryan.

"Caleb!" She rushed toward him and crouched at his side. He bled profusely from the back of his head.

She pressed her fingers against his neck, praying he was still alive. A weak pulse met her touch. She reached for the phone in her back pocket, but the sound of a pistol cocking behind her made her freeze.

Fear made her muscles sluggish, and she slowly turned her head. Ryan stood a few feet away, aiming a handgun at her.

"Drop the screwdriver and stand up."

She hesitated a moment, and he cocked his head at her.

"I don't want to hurt you, but I will if you make me. It's time for you to come home now. Drop it."

What? She *was* home. Her fear intensified and she did as he asked. The tool thudded into the grass. She stood and faced him.

"It was you? All along, it's been you?"

He nodded. "You should have just agreed to a date. I wouldn't have had to hurt him." He gestured to the unconscious deputy. "Or Adelaide. I didn't want to hurt her. She wasn't the right one. You are."

"Me?" London's voice shook.

"Yes." He stepped closer, still holding the gun on her. His eyes took on a bit of a faraway cast, and he reached out to run a finger over her cheek. She fought back the shiver of disgust, not wanting to give him a reason to hurt her before she could escape.

"My Coraline. I found you again."

Her eyes widened as she realized he was projecting another woman onto her. Judging by the look on his face, he now thought she was someone else.

He grasped her chin and sealed his mouth to hers in a crushing kiss. London squirmed in his grip. He backed off, but took hold of her arm and started around the side of the house, his gun pressed to her side.

Her heart thudded in her chest and her breath came in rapid pants. Tears trickled down her face, clouding her vision. "Where are you taking me?"

He paused at the back door to his SUV and stroked her face again. "Somewhere no one will find us, my dear. We'll be all alone and able to rekindle our love. It's been so long."

Something she read in a book once, about how a woman survived an abduction by playing along with her captor, filtered into her freaked out mind. She licked her dry lips and took a deep breath.

"I know and I'm sorry. Why don't we go back inside, and I'll make us breakfast? We can sit down and talk. Catch up," she said, playing along with his fantasy.

He paused and frowned at her, seeming to consider her offer, before shaking his head. "No. We have to get out of here. That cop never stays away for long." He opened the back door and thrust her inside.

London hit the seat and tipped onto her side with the momentum. He pointed at the floor. "Put those on."

She looked down to see a set of zip-tie handcuffs at her feet and thought fast. "Why? I thought you loved me. Why would you want to tie me up?"

"I do, but you like to run away. It took me three decades to find you this time."

London knew her eyes were as wide as saucers, but she couldn't help it. Something he said to her when she picked up her sconces pinged through her brain like a pinball. "Ryan. Who am I to you?"

He frowned and motioned to the cuffs again. "Don't be ridiculous, Coraline. You know who you are. You're my sister. And my bride. Now put those on."

Her hands shook as she reached for the cuffs.

Oh my God, oh my God, oh my God. He had murdered his sister, probably because she rebuffed his advances, and now he thought she was Coraline. He'd had a complete psychotic break.

God help her.

EIGHTEEN

The bars clanked as Seb rolled the door back and smiled at his friend. "The D.A. dropped your charges. You're free."

Declan rose from the cot, banked hope on his face. "For real?"

Seb nodded. "Yep. The DNA came back. It confirmed what we've been saying. It's not a match to you."

"Finally." Declan brushed past Seb to stand in the hall outside the cell. "You owe me a bar, remember? But I'll settle for a night of drinking at one."

"I know, and I promise we'll do that, but it'll have to wait. Katie's trying to match the DNA to someone in the database as we speak. I'm hoping she gets a hit soon."

"Has there been DNA in any of the other cases?"

Seb shook his head. "No. He's been very meticulous until now." His phone rang, and he took it from his pocket. "It's the detective from Aspen." He answered it, praying he had something good to report.

"Detective Farley. Tell me you have something."

"Maybe. I showed your suspect's picture to the campground manager. She didn't recognize him. Said—and I quote —'if a hunk of meat like that came around here, I'd definitely take notice.'"

Seb didn't bother to hide his grin. Declan cocked his head and gave him a curious frown. Seb held up a finger.

"I also flashed it around the lodge. No one recognized him. I did find him on the security footage when he checked in and when he checked out. He popped up in the restaurant for dinner and breakfast too."

"What about our mystery plumber? Did you find him?"

"I think so. I brought the campground manager and the concierge that handled the complaint at the campground in and had them go through the footage. I'm glad it was that poor bastard who had to sit with her and not me. I've never been so glad to be married in my life."

Seb chuckled. "Yeah, she's a character."

"Understatement of the year, my friend. Anyway, they found a man they think was him. I just emailed you the picture. It's pretty grainy. I tried to find a better view, but they couldn't be sure of his face. What you've got is it."

"It's more than I had two minutes ago. The suspect I had in custody has been cleared. The DNA we got from Adelaide Martin didn't match."

"Well, then I really hope someone recognizes the man in the footage."

"Me too. Thanks, detective."

"No problem. Let me know if you need anything else."

The men exchanged goodbyes and Seb switched to his email app.

"What did he say?" Declan asked.

"He got a still of a potential suspect and emailed it to me." He opened the email and clicked on the attached photo. A grainy image filled his screen, and he stared hard at it. It was too blurry for him to really make out any of his features.

All he could tell was that he was about average height and blonde.

He showed the picture to Declan. "Recognize him?"

Declan took a hard look at the picture and shook his head. "He looks familiar, but I can't tell you where I've seen him before."

Seb thought the same thing.

His phone rang again and his heartbeat quickened as Katie's name flashed across the screen. He answered it and put her on speaker. "Yeah, Katie. What do you have?"

"Sheriff, you need to come over here. Right now."

Her tone brooked no argument. Adrenaline poured into his veins. "On my way."

"I'm coming with you. I want to know who framed me."

Seb didn't bother to argue. It would take too long to dissuade him, and Seb didn't want to wait, either. He ran out of the jail, into the main area of the station. Jace looked up from his desk as they ran past.

"Hey. Where are you going?"

"Katie's got something. If you're coming, you better keep up." Seb didn't pause on his way through the bullpen. Jace fell into step behind them, and the three of them pushed through the side door and dashed across the grass to the crime lab next door. He swiped his ID to get inside, stopping only long enough for them to scrawl their names on the visitor log.

Their shoes thudded on the hard floor as they hurried down the hallway to Katie's lab. Inside, she looked up as they entered and motioned them over, her sleeves pushed up, flashing her colorful tattoos in the harsh light.

"What did you find?" Seb asked, nearly skidding to a halt.

"So, I found a match. *But* it's only a partial. It came back to a woman who was murdered nearly thirty years ago in northern Nevada. Coraline Marsters."

"Holy shit," Declan said.

"There's more. She was discovered in an abandoned house, on a bed, wearing a wedding dress and clutching a handful of wildflowers. It wasn't in NCIC because the department that handled the case was too small to upload things back then. I only know the details because I did an internet search on her name and a news article came up that revisited the murder about ten years ago. It's still unsolved."

Seb slammed his hand down on the table. "Son of a bitch. I knew I should have paid more attention to him after he asked London out, but he seemed too old to be the killer. And he honestly didn't give off any creeper vibes. Dammit. Okay. Email that to Kerr's office. I'm going over there now to get a warrant." He looked at his watch. "Marsters should open the store soon. We can get him there." He spun on his heel. "Great work, Katie," he called over his shoulder.

"Catch the asshole!" she called back.

The three men ran to Seb's cruiser in the police station lot and piled in. Seb resisted the urge to turn on the siren. He needed to rein himself in before he did something stupid because he wasn't thinking. They shouldn't have any problem getting Ryan Marsters into custody. He hadn't released to the public that they got DNA from under Adelaide's nails, so the man should open his store as usual.

He parked in the same space he had the last time, and they hurried inside. Because he had Jace and Declan with him, this time he had to wait as they went through the metal detectors and received visitor badges. He leaned against the security desk and tapped his foot. Energy hummed through him with the anticipation of finally ending this nightmare of a case.

Declan and Jace clipped their badges on and Seb took off for the stairs again. The three of them pounded up the concrete and metal structure to the third floor. There was no law clerk near the door this time when they burst out, but they did startle several attorneys in a conference room across from the stairs.

"Back again?" Emma said as they approached her desk.

"Yes. Is he in?"

"Yes, but he's working on a brief and doesn't want to be disturbed."

Seb shook his head and walked around her desk. "He'll want to be disturbed for this."

"Wait." She stood "Sheriff, you can't go in there!"

Seb ignored her and pushed the D.A.'s door open. Kerr looked up, startled, then frowned.

"Sheriff. What's the meaning of this? I asked not to be interrupted." He glanced at Declan, a hint of fear showing on his face.

Declan smiled, a devilish gleam in his eyes.

A corner of Seb's mouth ticked up for a moment. The D.A. deserved to sweat a bit after trying to railroad the other man.

He schooled his features and pointed at the computer. "Check your email."

"What? Why?"

"Katie matched the DNA. She got a partial match to a cold-case murder from almost three decades ago out of a tiny town in northern Nevada. It belongs to Coraline Marsters."

"Marsters?" Kerr's frown turned to shock as he made the connection.

Seb nodded. "Ryan Marsters is our killer. I need a warrant for his arrest as well as a search warrant for any property in his name and his car."

Declan crossed his arms and glared. "I told you I didn't have anything to do with this."

"It would seem so, Mr. Briggs." He looked at Seb. "I'll get the warrant to the judge. You'll have it within half an hour."

"Which judge?"

Kerr ran a hand around his neck and clicked on his computer screen. "Um, Brandt. He's on today."

Seb nodded. "We'll be at his chambers waiting." He touched Declan on the arm as he backed toward the door. "Come on."

Declan waved at the D.A. and followed Seb and Jace out of the room.

Emma waited on the other side of the door, an angry frown on her face. Seb held up his hands.

"I'm sorry. It couldn't wait. I won't do it again, unless it's completely necessary."

She wagged a finger at him. "Make sure you don't. This is a civilized office, Sheriff."

"Yes, ma'am." He fled before she could scold him anymore.

"So, now we wait, right?" Jace said as he followed Seb down the stairs to the second floor.

"Yep. Hopefully, it won't take too long to get the warrants. This is a high-profile case, so it should go through quickly." They came to a halt outside Judge Brandt's chambers.

His law clerk arched a brow at him. "Something I can do for you, Sheriff?"

Seb nodded at the young man. "You can go in and tell Judge Brandt that Kerr is sending him some warrants for Ryan Marsters. He abducted Adelaide Martin and killed the two women we found in the mountains. I want those documents before the ink dries on his signatures."

The young clerk swallowed hard, his eyes going wide, and nodded. "Yes, sir." He turned and fled into the judge's chambers.

Seb sighed and leaned against the wall.

"You okay?" Declan asked.

"I should be the one asking you that question."

Declan grinned. "I'm a free man and I got to terrorize the D.A. I'm great."

Seb and Jace chuckled.

"I'm sorry, Deck. You shouldn't have had to go through any of this."

"I don't blame you, I blame that sick fuck, Marsters. You probably shouldn't let me be alone with him when you take him into custody."

Seb scoffed. "I probably shouldn't be either. Not after everything he's done to London."

Jace patted Seb's shoulder. "We'll stick with you."

"Thanks. I appreciate it."

Jace nodded.

Seb took out his phone. "I need to arrange a team." He swiped his thumb over the screen and called his desk sergeant to get things in motion. Wilder was good at organizing. She'd have that team ready to go when he had the warrant in hand.

The thirty minutes passed quickly as Seb spoke to different members of his staff to get ready for the raid on Marsters' properties. He had just hung up the phone when the judge's chambers opened and Judge Brandt stepped out. The older man was trim and tan, his pressed slacks and tie perfectly straight.

He stopped in front of Seb and held out two folded packets of paper. "Here you go, Sheriff. Go get the bastard."

Seb took the documents and gave a curt nod. "Yes, sir."

He stuffed the warrants in the pocket on his pants and took off for the stairs again. They rendezvoused with the rest of his team in the police lot, and just after ten-thirty, Seb led a procession of cars through downtown to the hardware store.

He and Jace stepped from the cruiser, adjusting their vests. Declan stayed in the car.

Seb looked around at the assembled team. He motioned to Gentry to head around back, then to Jace and the other deputy who would make entry with him through the front. "Let's go."

The three of them advanced on the door, weapons drawn. Seb's expression turned grim as he realized there was no one in the store. He tugged on the door and found it locked.

He pressed the button on his mic. "Gentry, is the back door locked?"

There was a pause, then a crackle of static. "Yes, sir."

"Fuck." He turned to Jace. "He's not here."

He turned his head to speak into his radio. "Everyone back to the vehicles. We're going to his home address. Reeves, you stay here in case he shows up."

Boots pounded against the asphalt as everyone hurried back to their cars. Seb slammed his door shut and put the vehicle in gear, hitting the siren.

"What's going on?" Declan asked.

"He's not here."

"What? The store's supposed to be open."

"I know." Seb's gut churned. Maybe they'd gotten too close and spooked him. He could be a state or more away by now.

Or, he could be in hiding, waiting to grab London.

He punched a button on the steering wheel that connected his phone to the car's audio system.

"Call London."

The sound of ringing filled the interior. After five rings, it rolled to voicemail. Seb cursed and hit the button to disconnect, then the one to place another call.

"Call Bering."

More ringing filled the car, but it too rolled to voicemail.

Seb's heart thundered in his ears and his stomach twisted. He gunned the engine.

"You thinking what I'm thinking?" Jace said.

"Yep. I hope to God we're wrong." This was not happening. London was fine. Just out of cell range, or she'd left her phone inside. Maybe they were working on the bushes and neither of them could answer.

He prayed harder than he had ever prayed as he rocketed through town.

"Radio Gentry. Tell him to keep going to Marsters's house."

Jace did as asked, but Seb barely heard him over the sound of the siren and the blood pulsing through his ears. The drive felt like it was light years instead of just a few minutes, but finally the drooping lilac bushes came into view.

The SUV's tires spun as he turned into the drive. Caleb's truck sat in the driveway.

Seb parked across the drive and all three men exited the vehicle. He went around back and lifted the rear hatch. He reached in and took out another vest and handed it to Declan.

"Put that on."

Declan lifted it over his head and strapped the velcro without a word. Seb rummaged through the cruiser's contents and took out extra ammo clips as well as a rifle and a shotgun. He looped the rifle over his shoulders and handed the shotgun to Declan as well as a box of shells.

"What's the plan?" Declan asked. He set the box on the bumper and began loading shells into the gun.

"You and I will go through the front. Jace, you go around back to make sure he doesn't run out."

Jace looked around. "I have a feeling he's not here. It's too quiet."

Seb concurred, but didn't want to think about what that meant yet. He handed Declan a spare radio, then slapped a magazine into his rifle.

"What channel?"

"Five."

They all set their radios and Seb shut the hatch. "Let's go."

On light feet, they made their way to the house. Treading

softly, he and Declan ascended the porch stairs and positioned themselves on either side of the door to wait on Jace's signal.

"Seb, I found Bering. He's dead."

"Goddammit." Seb's harsh whisper cut through the quiet. He glanced at Declan, whose eyes were wide.

"Copy. Hold your position. We're going in." He released the mic and pulled out his house key, unlocking the door. He stepped back and brought his rifle up. "You open the door and follow me in. We go on three. One...two...three."

Declan twisted the knob and pushed the door in. Seb stepped into the doorway. Silence greeted him. He turned to his right, toward the game room.

"Wait here."

He left Declan standing by the stairs and made his way into the lounge. It, too, was empty. He crossed the room and advanced into the utility room. Glad that London's key was a master key, he unlocked the door. The running dryer was the only sound. He glanced at the dial. The load was almost done, which meant she'd been here just over an hour ago.

He jogged back to the living room and pointed at the kitchen. Declan fell into step behind him.

"The dryer's running so we didn't miss him by much," Seb said as they moved.

Rifle at the ready, he entered the kitchen. The faucet was in pieces, tools and the contents of the cabinet beneath the sink scattered all over the counter and floor.

That's how he got in.

The backdoor hung open and he could see Jace standing just outside. Seb walked over to the garage door and went inside. London's car sat in its bay, but the garage was void of people.

He stepped back into the kitchen and let his rifle hang.

"We can check the rest of the house just to be thorough, but I don't think he or London are here."

"Agreed. I'll go look upstairs. You go check on your deputy."

Seb nodded and stepped out the backdoor. Jace pointed to Seb's right, and he turned to see Caleb sprawled on his back on the ground, a pool of blood beneath his head. A large wrench laid a few feet away.

Sorrow and rage warred in Seb's chest as he walked over and crouched next to his friend. He pressed his fingers to Caleb's neck, confirming what Jace had already said. Bering was dead.

"He took his gun." Jace motioned to Caleb's empty holster.

Great. If Marsters wasn't armed before he was now.

"Did you see any sign of London?"

Seb rose, shaking his head. "Declan's checking upstairs, but I think he took her." He got on the radio and called Gentry.

"You got anything at Marsters's house? The inn is empty."

"Negative, sir. No one's here, and I don't see any signs he held anyone captive. We checked the basement and the cellar. Both are empty."

A string of curses that would shame a sailor flew out of Seb's mouth. Taking a deep breath, he brought the mic back up. "Okay. Regroup at the station. We need to form another search party."

He let the radio drop, then released a yell at the heavens. He picked up a rock from the ground and threw it toward the trees as hard as he could.

Jace laid a hand on his arm. "Hey. Cursing God won't bring her back. I need you calm and we need a plan."

Seb released a harsh breath, his chest and shoulders heaving. He scrubbed his hands down his face and around his neck, locking them briefly on the back of his head before tossing them back to his sides. He blew out another, softer breath. "Yeah. Okay." He got back on the radio and called for the coroner and another deputy.

"Come on. Let's go round up Deck and go back to the station."

Jace patted him on the shoulder and the two of them jogged back inside. Declan came down the stairs as they reached the living room.

He shook his head when he saw them, his mouth set in a grim line. "It's as empty as the rest of the house."

Seb was disappointed, but not surprised. "We're regrouping at the station. They're out there somewhere. We just have to figure out where."

Declan held out his hand. "Give me the keys. You're in no shape to drive."

"I'm fine."

"Bullshit. The woman you love was just kidnapped by a psychotic serial killer and one of your deputies is lying dead in the grass out back. Give me the damn keys."

Rather than waste time arguing, he handed them over. "Fine. But don't either of you try to sideline me when we search."

Jace's mouth tilted. "We'd have to lock you up for that."

"Damn straight."

A siren sounded and Seb gave thanks the inn wasn't far from town. They met the cruiser out front. One of Seb's rookies climbed out of the car.

"What do you need me to do, sir?" The young man was eager, which Seb appreciated.

"Secure the site and show the coroner and crime scene units out back when they get here. Deputy Bering's dead."

The young deputy's face blanched. "What? Oh my God."

Seb put his hands on the man's shoulders and gave him a slight shake. "Do your job, deputy. I'm counting on you."

That snapped the kid out of his shock and he nodded. "Yes, sir."

Seb looked at Jace and Declan and tipped his head toward his car. "Let's go."

As they climbed into the SUV, Seb said a silent prayer for Caleb's soul and another one that they would find London before Marsters did to her what he'd done to Adelaide and Amy.

Nineteen

London shivered in her shorts and t-shirt as Ryan hauled her deeper into the mineshaft. When he'd pulled up to the mine entrance her heart sank. There were miles of tunnels underground. He could hide her in any number of them, moving her around indefinitely. A search party would never find her.

She swallowed her fear and tried to get some more information. "How far are we going?"

"We're almost there, Cora. I have a nice spot set up for you. I think you'll like it."

London stomach flip-flopped, and she fought the bile that rose in her throat as she thought about what that meant. She couldn't help but remember what Adelaide said.

They walked another hundred yards into the mine, when it opened up into a larger cavern. Ryan walked over to one side and she heard a generator start up. Lights popped on all around them and London took in the room.

The ceiling was low. Only about seven feet, but the cavern stretched for a hundred feet or more. Along one wall sat a large cage, bolted into the rock. Inside was a full set of furniture, from a bed to a couch to a table and chairs. Her eyes widened as she took in the makeshift prison.

He took hold of her arm and led her over to the cage. London struggled a bit.

"Ryan, please. Don't lock me in there. I'll be good, I promise."

He shook his head. "No. You've run away too many times. I can't trust you. Maybe once you've realized you belong with me, but not now."

A key ring jingled as he pulled it from his pocket. He inserted one of the keys into the padlock and opened the door. London planted her feet as he tried to push her inside, but he was too strong for her and she stumbled through the doorway.

He stepped inside with her. She backed away, unsure what he intended to do. If he tried to rape her, she would fight tooth and nail, gun be damned.

He seemed to realize she wasn't going to cooperate and stopped. A sweet smile spread over his face. "I'll let you get settled in a bit, and we'll spend some time together later. There's food in the cabinets over there and in the little fridge. I also stocked some books for you. Romances, just like you always used to read."

London's stomach heaved at the thought of reading one of those books while she was trapped in this hell.

"Give me your hands." He pulled a pocket knife from his pants and flicked it open.

Hesitantly, she held up her arms. He sawed through the tough plastic and the cuffs snapped. She rubbed at her sore wrists and stepped back.

"There are extra clothes in the wardrobe if you'd like to change, including my favorite dress. I'll be back later. I have a surprise for you."

No way in hell was she putting on that dress. She stood there and watched as he backed out of the cage and locked the door. She didn't move until she could no longer hear his foot-steps echoing off the granite walls.

When she was sure he was gone and out of earshot, she began searching her prison for anything she could use to get out of here. Her first stop was the small kitchen area. The little island contained some plastic ware, paper plates, and napkins. The items in the small pantry were all boxed or bagged, and there were only water bottles and yogurt in the fridge.

She shut the door with a huff and looked around, her eyes landing on the bed. Maybe she could pull off a spring and use it to pick the lock. She pushed the mattress off the bedframe, but it was just a few bars welded together.

"Dammit," she whispered, tears welling in her eyes. She walked over to the couch and tipped it over. There were springs underneath, and she pulled on several, trying to dislodge one, but she needed a hammer to break one free and there was nothing heavy enough in this damn cell to use as one.

Frustrated, she kicked over the small wastebasket next to the couch. It bounced off the wall with a clang, and she sank onto the ground. Sobs pushed past the lump in her throat and she gave into the despair choking her. She needed a miracle to get out of here.

"Come on. There has to be someplace around here where he'd hide her that we haven't thought of," Brady said, staring at the map. "There aren't many abandoned buildings in the mountains that are so secluded he wouldn't risk someone stumbling over them."

Seb sat at the conference table, his head in his hands as the others talked around him. He'd called his brothers and put the word out that Ryan took London. Within half an hour, he had thirty people—both civilian and law enforcement—crammed into his tiny conference room.

Tara stepped forward and pointed at the map. "What about the mines? We used to go there all the time when we were kids. They're remote and the Department of the Interior as well as local departments have really cracked down on the kids trespassing in the last few years. They don't get many visitors anymore."

Seb's head popped up, and he stood. He crossed to the map and looked at the locations of the mine entrances. The southern one was near where Abigail and Trent found Amy Beckett and within a couple miles of the high lake where they'd recovered Rebecca Carson's body.

"Do we have a map of the shafts?"

"I'll go look," Gentry said, and hurried from the room.

Declan stepped forward and pointed at one of the entrances. "This one caved in last year. We keep track of that stuff for search and rescue purposes. There are also a few service shafts dotting the mountainside, but they're overgrown. You'd have to know exactly where they are to find them. Either of these will be the best bet." He pointed to the entrance on the south side, closest to town, and the east side at the base of the mountain.

Seb pinched the bridge of his nose and squeezed his eyes shut, a headache pounding through his temples. He dropped his hand and looked over the group.

"This is a long shot, but I don't know where else to look. If anyone else has an idea, speak up."

Thoughtful frowns turned down everyone's face, but no one had any other suggestions.

Gentry entered the room carrying a rolled map. He handed it to Seb, who spread it over the other one and tacked it up. There were a few shafts off the main that were marked as unpassable, but there were several, including some they had explored as teens, that were possibilities.

He stepped back. "All right. Let's get busy. Declan, I want you to lead a team through the east entrance. Take Gentry with you as the police lead. I'll take the south. Reeves, coordinate with state officials and set up road blocks for a fifty-mile radius from the mine entrances, and send out a description of both Marsters and London."

The room broke into a hive of activity as they began to plan their routes through the mine. Seb sectioned off the deputies and volunteers into two groups, and soon they had a plan.

Hope lit in his chest for the first time since they found the hardware store closed. If Ryan was in that mine with London, they would find him.

Commotion in the bullpen caught his attention, and he looked out to see the top of a strawberry-blonde head over the cubicles. Heart in his throat, he stopped talking to his deputy mid-sentence and flew out the door.

"London!"

He rounded the edge of the office dividers and came to a halt. Abigail stood there, tear tracks on her face and her chin wobbling.

"Uncle Seb, is it true?"

He sighed and walked forward, taking her into his arms. "Yeah, honey. I'm sorry."

She broke into sobs against his chest. "No. You can't let her die."

Seb tipped her head up to look in her eyes. "Sweetie, I have no intention of losing your aunt. I love her and am doing everything I can to find her."

"What can I do? I want to help."

"You can help by staying at the ranch where I know you're safe."

"But—"

He laid a finger over her lips. "No buts, young lady. I don't know that the killer won't snatch you up if he sees you in a bid to get me or London to cooperate. The best thing you can do is keep my mom and dad company."

She frowned, but her tears cleared. "Jenny was pretty upset when Maggie came in and told us the news."

Seb nodded. "You go back to the ranch and distract her. It'll be good for both of you."

She huffed and wiped her face. "Fine. But I want to know the minute you find her."

He drew a cross over his heart. "You will be the first person I call."

She stepped back. Alaina Wilder came forward to wrap her hands around the girl's arms. "Come on, Abigail." She looked up at Seb. "I'll make sure she gets back to the ranch safely."

"Thank you." He dropped a kiss to the top of Abigail's head. "I'll talk to you soon."

"You better. Find her. I can't lose her too."

The first press of tears formed behind his eyes and he blinked hard.

No. They couldn't lose her.

The scuff of shoes on the dirt floor alerted London to Ryan's return. He'd left her alone for about two hours, and she'd made good use of that time. After she pulled herself together, she changed into jeans and a long-sleeve shirt, because it was chilly in the mine. She also wanted to be prepared to stay out in the wilderness all night just in case she managed to escape.

She wasn't leaving that to chance, either. She'd made a few modifications to the room. There wasn't much she could use as a weapon, but there were some things, and she had stashed them in some strategic locations. He wasn't going to do anything to her without one hell of a fight first.

She sat down on the couch, a book stuffed next to her between the cushions with a plastic knife stuck into it. She'd used the hot light bulb to melt the plastic and mold it into a point. She'd made several of them and hidden them around the room, including under the pillows on the bed.

His lean form entered the cavern, a box tucked under one arm. London fought to control her heart rate. She needed steady hands and even emotions if she was going to get out of here.

He walked to the cage and smiled at her.

"Hello, my dear. I hope you've settled in. I see you found the clothes. Those came from some other ladies I thought were you. They disappointed me, though, and turned out to just look like you. But I know I found you this time."

Horrified, she realized she was wearing clothes from his previous victims.

He unlocked the padlock and stepped inside. He closed the door behind him, but didn't relock it.

Her adrenaline surged, and she made a conscious effort not to stare at it.

"You didn't put on the dress, though." He set the box on the table and frowned at her.

She shook her head. "I was cold and wanted something warmer. Maybe next time."

He nodded and offered her a smile. "That sounds good."

An awkward silence fell as he stared at her, his eyes roving over every inch of her body, making her skin crawl.

She looked past him to the box. "So, what did you bring?"

"Ah, yes." He turned and opened the flaps and motioned her over. "I've had this stuff stored in a safe location out here in the wilderness. I knew one day I'd need it when I found you again. Come see."

Wary, but not willing to piss him off, she stood and walked over to the table. He took a stuffed rabbit from the box and handed it to her.

"That was your favorite as a child. Daddy gave it to you, do you remember? You'd hug it tight, and cry into it anytime you were upset."

She could imagine why she'd need to cry into it. She took the toy, her fingers sinking into its plush fur.

"I also brought some music. I thought we could dance. You like to dance." He lifted a portable CD player and a stack of CDs from the box.

Her skin crawled again, but she held back the shiver of disgust at the thought of being in his arms.

"I also brought some wine. You're old enough for that now."

"How old am I?"

He looked at her like she was a bit loony, but smiled. "You're twenty-one, remember? You just had your birthday last month. I've been waiting until you were old enough. Daddy said I had to wait, so I did. He said it wouldn't do for me to have a child-bride. Even after he died and you kept trying to leave, I waited."

London couldn't stop her eyes from widening, but she masked it by stepping closer and looking into the box. "Is there anything else in there?" A scrap of white chiffon on the bottom made her tremble.

He reached in and pulled it out, holding it up by the skinny straps. She stared at the lacy, sheer gown and swallowed hard, all her muscles going rigid.

"I wanted you to look pretty for our first night together. I've been saving this for our honeymoon, but with the sheriff looking for us, it might be a while before we can have one of those. Mama always wore pretty things like this for Daddy before she died. Then you did, so you'd look more like her. Daddy always said you looked real pretty."

London pressed her trembling lips together as she got a better picture of the sick family Ryan had been raised in. That poor girl!

Deciding it was best to play along for now, she took the scrap of chiffon and wrapped her hands in it, holding it against her chest. "I'll be happy to wear it for you later. How about we sit down and talk? It's been so long, I'd like to catch up before we go to bed."

His smile was bright, even if his eyes looked a little crazed, and he nodded. She led him over to the couch and sat back down next to the book stuffed in the cushions. She draped the nightie over the arm of the couch and tucked her hands under her legs. Her fingers nudged the book, and she curled her pinky and ring finger over the edges until they touched the knife.

He sat down next to her, and she prayed he wouldn't notice the book between them in the couch. His thigh touched hers. Even though it made her want to hurl, she didn't flinch away. She needed to keep him calm.

"So, what have you been up to since I've been away?"

"Well, I bought the hardware store about four years ago as you know. I couldn't believe it when you walked in. I wanted to say something, but I didn't want to spook you. I knew I looked different because it's been so long. But you. You still look the same." He touched her cheek. "So beautiful."

She bit her tongue and held his gaze. "That's nice. I'm glad you're doing well. Do you have any children?"

He shook his head. "No. Not yet. I was waiting to find you. Our babies will be beautiful. They'll have your red hair and pretty blue eyes. Daddy was smart when he married your mama. He got a pretty wife and an adorable baby. I was skeptical. There was a squalling infant in my house suddenly, after all. But as you got older, I realized you weren't so bad."

She frowned. "Wait, so I'm not really your sister?"

Ryan laughed. "Of course not. Incest is bad. I would never marry my real sister."

Well, at least he drew the line somewhere.

"I didn't know that. I guess I always thought he was my dad. I never knew any other one."

He rested his hand on her thigh. London was thankful she'd put on a pair of jeans so she didn't have to feel his touch against her bare skin.

"No. Your daddy died in a mining accident right after you were born. Your mama was dirt poor, so Daddy took pity on her. I needed a mother. I was only four. My mama had cancer."

"I know. I'm sorry." She didn't, and she wasn't, but she didn't want to break him out of his delusion just yet.

He frowned and looked down at his hand on her leg before returning his eyes to hers. "Why did you run away, Cora? We took good care of you."

Oh, boy. London took a deep breath and lied her ass off. "I needed to spread my wings. See more of the world than our tiny town. I'm sorry if I hurt you."

"You did, but we're together now."

"Tell me about those other women you thought were me. I know they weren't, but why didn't you move on with one of them?"

"Because I only ever wanted you. None of them were good enough. You were always so *good*. The woman I found around New Year's—she came close. I really thought she was you. She was good like you. She had a friend she refused to leave behind. The other woman fell and hurt her head when I went to surprise you—well, who I thought was you—and she insisted I bring her. I thought it might help make her transition to her new home a little easier if she had her friend, so I agreed." He paused and shook his head. "The friend, though —Rebecca—was nothing but trouble. I had to tie her up anytime I wanted to have time with that woman. She even tried to hit me over the head once, but I was too quick for her. The only reason I didn't kill her then was because I still thought the other woman was you and she begged me not to. I kept her chained after that."

London listened with rapt attention, amazed at Amy and Rebecca's bravery. It was too bad they hadn't been able to stop him.

"She still managed to convince her friend to run away, though, even though she'd stopped fighting me. I chased them all the way up the mountain before I caught up." His eyes took on a faraway look. "She had a beautiful end, though, there on the edge of the water. She looked so pretty and peaceful in that gown. They all did in the end, even though they weren't you."

Her stomach rebelled, and she did her best not to react to the story of Amy and Rebecca's last days. She drew in a breath and let it out slowly to calm her emotions, and looked around the cell. "So, is this where they stayed too?"

He nodded. "All the women did." His mouth turned down. "Except the last one. I was mad when I saw you with the sheriff, and when she smiled at me when I saw her in town that night, I thought maybe I was wrong about you and she was really my Coraline. She had a tattoo, though. You don't have any tattoos."

"How do you know I don't? We've been apart a long time."

"Because you would never defile your body like that." He ran a finger along her jaw line. "You're perfect. Pristine. I had to get rid of her. She was just in the way. I can't believe she survived. I blame the sheriff. He's too persistent. That's why I put Adelaide's necklace in Declan Briggs's SUV, and smeared some paint on Rebecca's hair. I remembered seeing him in Aspen when I took her and the other woman. It seemed like it was meant to be."

He leaned forward and traced her lips with his finger. "Enough about them, though. I've missed you so. Can I kiss you?" He pressed closer, his weight making her sink into the couch.

She swallowed her disgust and nodded. If her plan was to work, she needed him close and off balance.

She put a hand on his chest and made sure both her arms were inside his, so she didn't get tangled when she tried to run, then leaned into him. The first touch of his mouth on hers was a shock, and she had to clench her fist to control herself. The urge to push him away was strong.

Instead, she let him kiss her and touch her. He was never going to see this coming.

His mouth opened against hers and she let him in. He swept a hand over her hip and up her waist to grasp her breast through her long-sleeved shirt. London slid the hand on his chest down to his lap, hesitating only a moment before she let it settle in his lap. Disgust sent bile up her esophagus as she clasped his hard length through his pants. He moaned and increased the pressure on her mouth.

It was now or never.

She slid her freehand down into the cushions to curl her fingers around the sharpened knife inside the book. In one smooth motion, she brought it up and stuck it in his chest, then shoved him as hard as she could.

He bellowed and fell back.

London didn't look to see if he followed her. She launched herself off the couch. Scooping up the sweatshirt at her feet that hid a flashlight, she fled, banging through the door. She ran as fast as she could through the tunnel, using the light from the cavern to guide her. She hoped she could find her way out of here. It had been a long time since she'd been in the mine.

His voice echoed off the walls as he called Coraline's name, closer than she'd like. Heart pounding and breath coming in quick pants, she ran faster.

She came to a junction and skidded to a halt. She couldn't remember which one they'd come through.

The scuff of shoes in the tunnel behind her sent her running forward. She went left and prayed.

TWENTY

The slam of car doors echoed around him as Seb exited his cruiser at the mine. A lone car sat near the entrance. It was Ryan Marsters SUV.

He got on the radio and called Declan.

"He came in the south. His car is here."

"Okay. We'll still go in this way. We can sandwich them between us."

"Copy." He hooked the radio back on his shoulder and motioned everyone in.

"You all know which shafts you're exploring, right?"

Nods greeted his question. "Good. Watch yourselves and be careful where you shoot. We don't want to accidentally hit London. And keep an eye on the tunnels. The whole place is crumbling. I don't need anyone trapped. If it looks unsafe, turn around. Let's go."

As a whole, they moved toward the entrance. Twenty feet away, Seb heard a faint shout and came to an abrupt halt. He looked at Jace.

"Did you hear that?"

Jace nodded. They all stood motionless, listening.

The sound of a male voice, yelling, came from their right. It was faint, but there.

Wide-eyed, Seb looked at the others, then pointed at two of his deputies. "Stay here and guard the entrance. Radio if you see any movement. The rest of you come with me."

Seb didn't wait to see if they followed his orders. He led his contingent of twelve men and women up the side of the mountain toward the noise.

Legs pumping and muscles burning, it didn't take him long to crest the ridge. In the distance, he saw two figures running.

London.

She ran ahead of Marsters by a couple hundred yards, leaping and scurrying over the rocky ground, but he gained on her, his longer legs and stronger muscles eating up the ground.

Seb took off, pushing himself to run faster than he ever had. The others would have to catch up. Thankful for his six-five height, he used every inch to his advantage as he dashed through the trees and over the rocks toward her. He scanned the area ahead of them and realized they were heading for a cliff. He ran the angles in his head. He'd never be able to get in front of them before they reached it.

"Shit." He ran faster.

As he gained ground, Ryan saw him coming.

"No! She's mine."

London looked back at Ryan's shout, which made her stumble, and she fell. Ryan was on her in an instant.

"No!" Seb shouted. He skidded to a halt, now only twenty yards away, and drew his gun. "Let her go, Ryan."

Ryan hauled London against him and held a bloody piece of plastic to her neck, the point digging into her skin. "Stay back. You can't have her. I finally found her again. She came back to me and she's mine!"

"No, Ryan. She's not."

Tears streamed down London's face, but she was calm. She waved a hand at him, halting him.

"Ryan. You don't want to do this. I'm sorry I stabbed you. I got scared because we were moving so fast. How about you put the knife down and I'll go back to the mine with you, okay? Seb will let us go. Won't you?" Her eyes implored him to agree.

He glanced between her and Ryan, who now had some indecision on his face. Slowly, Seb straightened and lowered his weapon a fraction. He could hear the others scrambling to catch up, and he turned to wave them to a stop. They all halted a few yards back.

He turned back to Marsters and London. "I guess we can talk about this," he said, his tone beseeching. "If London wants to go with you, I can't stop her. I'd really like it, though, if we could all go back to town and talk about this."

Marsters shook his head. "No. You're going to move out of the way and let us pass. She's my bride. Daddy said so." He buried his face in London's hair. "You can't say no. Daddy said you're mine."

Jesus Christ. He was off his fucking rocker. "Okay. That's fine," Seb said. "How about we all go down to the courthouse then? I'm sure Judge Brandt would be willing to marry you."

Ryan straightened at that. London took advantage of his lapse and elbowed him in the stomach as hard as she could. He let go of her, and she dove to the side. Marsters made a grab for her, and Seb fired his weapon, striking him in the shoulder. It spun him around, but the shot wasn't quick enough. Ryan's grab for London knocked her off balance, and she stumbled backward. Her feet slid at the edge of the cliff and she went over.

"No!" Seb's shout was loud enough to bring down the trees. He flew forward.

Ryan turned toward Seb and lunged. "You took her! You took her away from me!"

Seb didn't let him get close. He fired again, this time hitting the other man square in the middle of his forehead. Marsters dropped like a sack of stones.

"No, please," Seb's pleas came out broken as a lump formed in his throat. He ran to the edge of the cliff and skidded to a stop. He looked over, expecting to see the only woman he ever loved lying at the bottom, broken and bleeding. Instead, he was shocked to find her dangling one-handed from a tree root.

"Oh my God! London!" He laid down on his belly and reached down. "Give me your hand, baby."

She swung her free hand up, but missed his fingers by over a foot. "I can't reach you!"

"Shit! Okay, hang on. Put your other hand on the root and hold tight." He scooted back from the edge to look up at his brothers and Jace, who had run forward.

"Hold on to my legs and lower me over the side."

They sprang into action. Brady grabbed his left leg and Thomas his right, while Tara, Maggie and two of his deputies formed a chain and grabbed onto Brady and Thomas to keep them from slipping over the side. Jace stood near the cliff edge ready to grab ahold of London when Seb lifted her up.

He eased himself over the edge, just the strength in his brothers' arms keeping him from falling head first to a certain death.

"Reach up here, honey." Seb stretched as far as he could.

She lifted her hand and their fingers touched. The root gave a bit, and she shrieked, grabbing hold of it again with both hands. "Sebastian, please! I'm slipping."

Seb's heart leaped into his throat. He took a slow breath to steady himself, then looked up. "I need a few more inches."

His brothers grunted and stepped forward. Seb's knees cleared the clifftop.

He stretched again. "Come on, baby. Reach!"

She tightened her arms and pulled herself up, swinging her left hand toward his. Seb snagged her fingers and held on. "Grab on with your other hand." His hold was precarious at best.

She stilled, then let go, snagging his hand and holding tight. Seb reached with his other hand and grabbed her wrist, sighing in relief as he got a solid grip.

"Pull us up!"

Scrambling at the top of the cliff sent rocks and dirt skittering down the side to pelt them as Brady and Thomas backed up. Seb felt them inching up the cliff face. Once his knees touched the ground, he started helping them back up. Jace reached over to grab London's arm and lift her over the side. She braced a hand in the dirt and pushed herself over the edge on her belly. Seb scrabbled back and pulled her up and into his arms.

She fell into him, sobbing. He clutched her to his chest and buried his face in her hair. Tears of his own trickled out of his eyes.

"Oh, baby. I'm so glad you're safe. I love you so much."

"I love you too." She raised her head to look at him.

He brushed dirt and tears and hair away from her face. "Are you okay?"

She nodded, sniffing. "I'm fine. Is Ryan—?"

"He's dead."

Her shoulders sagged, and she nodded. "It's over."

He kissed her gently. "Yes."

"Can we go home?"

He stood and helped her stand on shaky legs. "Definitely."

TWENTY-ONE

Despite saying they could go home, they spent another three hours on the mountain, waiting for Dr. Randall to arrive and then bringing Ryan's body down. When Seb pulled into the B&B, London was beyond exhausted.

As she climbed out of the cruiser, the front door opened and Abigail ran out. She was down the steps and wrapping London in a hug in an instant.

Tears welled in London's eyes all over again as she hugged her niece. "I'm okay."

"I was so scared," Abigail whispered.

"I know. I'm sorry, honey."

Abigail pulled back. "It's over, though, right? He was the killer, and he's dead."

She nodded. "Yes. It's over. Ryan Marsters will never hurt anyone ever again."

"Good." She hugged London again.

London stroked the girl's hair, thankful to be alive and holding this beautiful young woman again. It pained her to think she nearly lost another parental figure in an act of violence.

Seb's hand on her shoulder had her straightening.

"Let's go inside."

She nodded and stepped back, draping an arm around Abigail's shoulders and leading her into the house. Seb followed, a hand on London's back. His parents stood in the doorway. Jenny moved forward and enveloped London in a tight embrace before letting her pass.

Inside, London was surprised to see Doug Brown. He rose from his seat on the couch when she entered.

"Ms. Scott. I'm so glad you're all right."

While she still didn't trust him and questioned his motives for being in the area, he seemed sincere.

She offered him a tired smile. "Thank you, Mr. Brown."

He nodded. "I just wanted to tell you that. I'll leave you to your family now. And don't worry about breakfast the next few days. I need to take a trip out of town, but I'll be back this weekend."

"Oh. Do you want me to cancel your reservation until then?"

He shook his head. "No. I don't want to take all my things with me, so I'd like to keep my room, if that's okay? I'm also not sure which day I'll be back."

London nodded. "That's fine. Have a safe trip."

"Thank you." He nodded to both her and Sebastian and retreated upstairs.

She looked up at Seb. "That was weird."

His eyes were on the stairs. "Yeah. I need to find out why he's really here. What it is he's investigating."

He looked back down at her. "But that's for another day. How about we get you upstairs and into a nice hot bath?"

London smiled. "That sounds wonderful."

Abigail stepped in front of her, an unabashed grin on her face. "After Lee—" she stopped and looked at the man standing off to the side, "I mean, Grandpa Lee—fixed the faucet, I helped Grandma Jenny make dinner for you guys. Lasagna. It's in the warmer." She hooked a thumb toward the kitchen. "The rest of us already ate, and I'm going home with them, so you can get some rest and have some alone time."

A blush stole over London's face at the implication, and she glanced at Jenny, who beamed at her.

"Thanks, Mom. We appreciate it," Seb said.

Jenny leaned in and kissed her son on the cheek, then London. "You're welcome, my dears." She looked at her husband and Abigail. "Okay, you two. Let's get going. London looks like she's ready to fall down."

She did feel rather tired. The adrenaline crash was hitting her hard.

Lee patted Seb's shoulder and filed past them out the door after his wife. Abigail gave them a wicked grin and waggled her eyebrows before disappearing after them. The door closed with a bang and silence filled the house.

Seb looked down at her, his eyes hooded. London felt her body respond even through her fatigue.

"Come on, woman. Let's go find that bath."

She grinned and turned, running for the stairs. "First one there gets the hot water!"

Laughing, she ran up the stairs, Seb on her heels, growling about her cheating.

∼

Keep reading for an excerpt of *Wildfire*, book 2 in *The Broken Bow* series.

Thank you for reading A Beautiful End! I hope you enjoyed it.

Want to read an EXCLUSIVE and FREE book? Sign up for my mailing list. You can find the sign-up form on my website, ashleyaquinn.com. My list also receives sneak peeks of my latest work and access to exclusive giveaways. Also, please consider leaving a rating or review on Amazon and or Goodreads. It would be greatly appreciated!

Thanks again for reading!
- Ashley

~

Keep reading for a sneak peek at Book 2, Wildfire in the Broken Bow series.

WILDFIRE

BROKEN BOW
BOOK 2

ONE

The hot late-June sun beat down on Tara Miller's neck as she worked on her ancient truck. She knew she should just drive the fancy SUV parked in her garage, but there was something about driving the old Ford that calmed her soul. Life was busy, and the truck made her think of simpler times. When life wasn't so complicated. Or painful.

Her hand slipped off the wrench she used to tighten the bolt on the air filter, and she banged her knuckles on the engine mount.

"Fuck!"

She snatched her hand back and cradled it between her breasts. Straightening, she turned away from the vehicle and looked out over her family's ranch, The Broken Bow. Golden prairie grass waved in the light breeze, birds chirped, and cows mooed. Nestled against the mountain, the ranch had been in her family since the eighteen-sixties. She and all her siblings still lived on it. Some of them—like herself—had left and come back, but they always found their way home again.

She shook her aching hand, then swiped at the sweat rolling down her face with the blue bandana tucked in her shorts pocket. It was hot. Summer had come early this year and hadn't let up.

A red truck with a motorcycle strapped into the bed rolled up the drive, catching her attention. She narrowed her eyes and watched as it made its way to her brother Seb's house.

Great. Jace is here.

The truck pulled up to the house and stopped. The driver's door opened and long, denim-clad legs emerged to drop to the ground, followed by a narrow waist, broad chest, thick arms, a face to die for, and a head of golden hair that begged her to run her fingers through it.

Heat rushed south to flood Tara's core. Why did Jace Travers have to be so damn sexy? And why did her brother think it was a good idea to let the man stay in his house until he found a place of his own?

Shaking her hand again, she turned back to her truck, determined to ignore him and his sexiness. She would just pretend he wasn't a hundred yards away.

She glanced up. Muscles bulged as he lowered the tailgate and hopped up into the truck bed to undo the straps holding the motorcycle in place. He bent over with his back to her and she dropped her wrench at the sight of that tight butt encased in even tighter denim. It clanged through the engine to drop to the stones below.

He looked up at the racket. She ducked her head and prayed he wouldn't come over to see if she needed help.

Tara counted to thirty and chanced another glimpse across the grass. He had mounted the bike and was walking it backward down a metal ramp. Relieved, she crouched down to retrieve the tool she dropped. It had fallen farther back than she thought. Lying down, she scooted on her belly under the vehicle and stretched. Her fingers closed around the cool metal, and she shimmied her way back out.

As she cleared the bumper, she rolled to sit up and found

herself looking at a pair of long, jean-covered legs. She followed them up over strong thighs, a very intriguing bulge, a flat stomach and a well-built chest to a face so handsome it should only be seen on a movie screen.

He arched one perfect golden eyebrow at her and a corner of his mouth quirked. The breeze ruffled his honeyed hair, and those deep blue eyes carried a spark of humor as he stared down at her.

"You need some help?"

And that voice...

It rolled over her like fine wine. So smooth and rich, but with a bite.

She cleared her throat and stood, waving away the hand he offered. "No. I just dropped my wrench." She held up the offending tool.

He gave a slow nod, then looked at the teal Ford. "Car trouble?"

She shook her head and blew a piece of hair out of her eyes that had come loose from her ponytail. "Just routine maintenance."

"Like an oil change?"

She nodded. "Among other things."

"You know how to do all that? I thought you were a chef."

"I grew up on a ranch. I can take apart the tractor and rebuild the engine in the middle of the pasture if I have to."

"With just dental floss and a hairpin?" He flashed a teasing grin.

She rolled her eyes and crossed her arms, tapping her foot and ignoring the MacGyver reference, no matter how accurate or funny it was. "Did you have a reason for coming over here, or did you just feel like bugging me?"

His smile faded, and she thought she saw a flash of hurt in his eyes. Her conscience niggled at her, but she shoved it back into its box. He was dangerous to her sanity and needed to leave.

He held up his hands. "Just thought you might need a hand. My mistake." He backed away. "See you around, Tara." With a brief wave, he turned and jogged back to Seb's house.

Tara turned back to her truck and tried not to watch that perfect ass of his flex as he ran. Focusing on the air filter, she tightened the cover and lowered the hood. It closed with a bang and she tossed her wrench into the toolbox on the ground.

Scooping it up, she walked into her garage and deposited it on the workbench before going inside, stripping off her clothes and stuffing them straight into the washer. Naked, she walked to her bathroom and turned on the shower. She might be a grease monkey, but that didn't mean she wanted to smell or look like one.

After a brief shower, she dressed in a pair of mint green capris, a sleeveless white blouse, and brown leather sandals, then headed outside to her truck. She had time for a quick trip into town before she had to be at the restaurant to prepare for dinner. She needed a latte and a dose of Macy's craziness to banish the image of Jace Travers from her brain.

Windows rolled down, she savored the breeze as she drove the ten miles to town, letting it wash away some of the tension. She needed to find a way to cope with his presence since he would be her next-door neighbor for a few weeks at least.

It wasn't that she didn't like him—she liked him too much. The man was sex on a stick. And he was nice. Any single woman in her right mind would love to have him hanging around. But she had sworn off adrenaline junkies and men who looked like they could break her heart. She'd had enough heartache.

That old, familiar pang stabbed her in the chest as she

remembered her husband, and she took a steadying breath. No, she never wanted another man like that again. She couldn't handle it.

She cruised into Silver Gap and headed straight for Peppy Brewster, Macy's coffee shop. She tucked her vintage truck between two SUVs and shut off the engine.

"Yikes." A peek in the mirror revealed the wind did a number on her hair. At least it was dry now. She scraped it up into a messy bun and stepped out of the vehicle.

Inside the shop, the scent of fresh coffee assailed her. She took a deep breath of the heavenly smell.

"Hey, girl. What brings you to town?"

Tara smiled at Macy and walked up to the counter. "I needed a latte before work and to clear my head. Jace arrived."

Macy's grin was wicked. "Ooo, yum! That man is so hot." She grabbed the filter for the espresso machine and packed it full of coffee grounds, then affixed it to the machine. "You want your usual?"

"Yeah, but iced. And hot or not, he still irritates me."

Macy giggled and scooped some ice into a plastic cup and poured milk over it. "Yeah, because he gets you all hot and bothered. Would it hurt to give into that? It might lighten you up a bit and get you to relax."

"I don't have time to relax." Her phone dinged, and she opened her purse. It better not be her old editor again. He kept calling, but she'd yet to listen to his messages, read his texts, or call him back. She wasn't interested in that life anymore.

Finding her phone, she turned on the screen to see a message from her assistant manager, Cassie, groaning as she read it. Her produce shipment was late.

"Case in point." She sighed and showed the message to Macy. "I have to go straighten out this mess now and hope I have enough stuff to come up with *something* for the menu."

"Go talk to Rayna. See what she's got that might tide you over for today." She dumped the two shots of espresso into the milk and gave it a stir.

Tara's face brightened. "Hey, that's a good idea."

Macy smiled and stuck a lid on the drink, then handed it to Tara. "Duh." She flipped her hair and batted her eyes.

Tara laughed. "Thank you. I can always count on you to turn my mood around." She passed her friend her credit card and took a sip. "And this." She moaned in delight. "I can always count on this too. I don't know how you do it. Mine never turn out this good." She had an espresso machine at the restaurant, but her lattes never tasted as good as Macy's.

Macy shrugged and handed her back her card and a receipt. "Magic."

"Sure." She narrowed her eyes at her friend. "One day, you're going to tell me where you get your coffee beans."

"Trade secret." She leaned on the counter and grinned.

Tara tipped her cup toward Macy as she backed away. "One day."

Macy laughed.

Tara grinned. "Thanks for the tip about Rayna. I'll drive out there now."

"Sure. I hope she has some things left for you to use. Her farm market's been going gangbusters lately. That greenhouse she put up has already paid for itself."

No kidding. Rayna was one of the few locals who grew vegetables year-round, and she was the only one who grew on such a large scale.

Tara waved and left the café. Hopping back into her truck, she backed out of her space and headed toward the ranch. Rayna's family owned the property that bordered The Broken Bow to the east. They ran cattle, but Rayna had also turned a section of the ranch into a profitable vegetable and herb farm. Tara just wished it was bigger. She would buy all her fresh produce from the Nyderts if she could. But Rayna ran that part of the ranch alone, and what she cultivated was as much as she could handle.

The breeze blew through the cab, and she sang along to the radio in a much better mindset than when she left her house. She knew it wouldn't take much. She just needed a good laugh. And coffee.

She picked up her cup and took another drink. No more golden boy clogging up her mind. Thanks to Macy's magic latte and the frantic text from her assistant, she could focus now and switch gears to plan a new menu for tonight. Thankfully, her meat delivery had arrived. She just had to worry about sides. Rayna's greenhouse grew food all year, so if she had any produce left after today's market, she would have some decent choices.

She passed the entrance for the Broken Bow and continued down the highway another three miles before she reached the turnoff to the Nydert's ranch, the Double Moon.

Bumping down the dirt road, she headed for the greenhouse where Rayna's SUV sat outside. As she pulled to a stop, Rayna came out to greet her.

"Hey. Macy called and said you needed a hand."

Tara stepped out of her truck and shut the door. "Yeah. I ran into a minor snag. My produce delivery didn't arrive. I need whatever you've got."

Rayna blew out a breath and swept a hand over her hair and down her ponytail. "That's not much. But come on in and take a look."

Tara followed her inside to a set of tables laden with crates. She peered over the edge of the first few, then looked up at her friend.

"Wow. I'm both happy and sad. Happy for you, but sad that I'm going to run out of side dishes tonight."

Rayna laughed. "I do have some other things I haven't

harvested. They're on the edge of ripe, so I was going to pick them for tomorrow's market. Don't worry, we'll get you enough to hold you. Grab a crate." She pointed to a stack of empties on the floor.

They walked down the aisles of plants, and soon, Tara had enough produce to last the night.

She loaded the last crate into her truck and shut the tailgate.

"Thank you so much. I will cut you a check once I get back to the restaurant."

Rayna shrugged. "I know you're good for it. And you've saved me from hauling all this to market tomorrow. I don't mind a slow day." She leaned against the side of the truck and sent a coy smile at Tara. "So. Macy also said you had a run in with a certain hunky detective."

Tara rolled her eyes and groaned. "It was nothing. He moved into Seb's house today. We said hello."

She waggled her eyebrows. "Really? Is that all that happened?"

The image of his butt in those jeans popped into her head. "Yes."

Rayna pushed her tongue into her cheek. "Uh-huh. Okay."

"What? What do you want me to say? He came over and said hello, then he left. As far as I'm concerned, he can stay away."

An eye roll was Rayna's response. "Oh, come on. You know you find the man attractive."

"Of course I do. Have you seen him? But I'm not ready for a relationship, especially not with a man who rides a motorcycle and looks like the sun god himself."

"Those are the best kind of men. And Tara, it's been three years since Sean died."

"There's no timeline on grief, Rayna."

Rayna straightened and moved closer to lay a hand on Tara's arm. "I know that, sweetie, but you aren't grieving. You aren't even really living."

Tara glanced away, her mouth set in a firm line. "What are you talking about? Of course I'm living. I opened my restaurant."

Rayna shook her head. "No, that's a distraction, and it keeps you from thinking about things. From feeling."

Tara shifted, uncomfortable with the turn in the conversation. She wanted to say Rayna was wrong, but deep down she knew her friend was right. But it was easier to stay busy and stuff her feelings down where they would never see the light of day than to deal with them.

She shrugged and opened the truck door. "Yeah, well, it's how I deal. Look, I need to get going. Thanks for helping me out."

Rayna sighed and nodded. "Anytime. Remember what I said, though. Think about it at least?"

Tara nodded and climbed inside. The door closed with a creak. She had no intention of doing any such thing. That particular can of worms could stay right where it was. But she offered Rayna a genuine smile. "Have I told you lately how much I appreciate you? Thank you for looking out for me."

The other woman beamed. "You're welcome. Now go. Make something delicious."

Tara pulled away with a wave.

Dammit. She picked up the now tepid latte and took a sip. Its magic was gone, though. But it wasn't thoughts of Jace that wouldn't leave her mind now. It was thoughts of another man who was never coming back.

ABOUT THE AUTHOR

Ashley started writing in her teens and never stopped. Her first novel, Smoky Mountain Murder, came out in 2016, and she has since published two more series and has plans for more. When not writing, you can find her with her nose stuck in a book or watching some terrible disaster movie on SyFy. An avid baseball fan, she also enjoys crafting and cooking. She lives in Ohio with her husband, two kids, three cats, and one very wild shepherd mix.

Website: https://ashleyaquinn.com

[g] goodreads.com/ashleyaquinn

[a] amazon.com/Ashley-A-Quinn/e/B07HCT4QST

ALSO BY ASHLEY A QUINN

Printed in Great Britain
by Amazon

27672458R00182